THE BURNING

THE BURNING

Frank Norwood

THE DIAL PRESS

Published by
The Dial Press
Bantam Doubleday Dell Publishing Group, Inc.
1540 Broadway
New York, New York 10036

Library of Congress Cataloging-in-Publication Data
Norwood, Frank.
    The burning / Frank Norwood.
        p.   cm.
    ISBN 0-385-31380-2 : $21.95 ($28.95 Can.)
    I. Title.
PS3564.O78887   1995
813'.54—dc20   94-40987
                                           CIP

Manufactured in the United States of America
Published simultaneously in Canada

June 1995

BVG   10 9 8 7 6 5 4 3 2 1

For Susan, Joni and Bob,
and for my family,
especially Diane,
for her love and support.

But ain't that America

—JOHN MELLENCAMP

THE BURNING

CHAPTER ONE

An eleven year old was the first to see him. The kid was bopping along when he saw the guy up so high, balanced by his nerves and a spindly old umbrella. A finger dragging on his lower lip, the kid stood there taking it all in. Then he went and found a few friends and brought them back. Pretty soon some other folks came along. Got to be a fair sized crowd. The mood was good. Ripple and Colt Malt passed from mouth to mouth, all eyes lifted to where the cat was doing his thing. Going back and forth across the wire in a pigeon-toed walk under the noon sun. Doing it with style, braving the wobbles and the sweat growing across his floppy red shirt and baggy gray pants. Keeping one arm out for balance, the other arm holding the umbrella out like a handshake. Somebody knew the cat. Said his name was Lester. Used to do this shit in a circus. Strutting it, the way he was now, putting on a show. Somebody said, "Ol' Lester, he must think it gonna rain." Somebody else said, "Yeah man, it gonna rain shit." Then a big voice boomed out, "No babe, it gonna be raining bullets when the cops get wind," and they all had a good laugh over that.

1

. . .

Larry and Karl were low-gearing down south Clayton, putting in their time. They drove by a new car wash and clean service stations and small but presentable black businesses. This isn't bad, Larry thought, not bad at all.

They crossed some railroad tracks, iron riding up through the Chevy Caprice's shocks, the stations and businesses opening onto a stretch of factories and warehouses and scrap metal yards, and then they were on a street of barred stores of dubious convenience. Music reached them from somewhere, a black woman's voice fine stitching sounds; sweet, anxious prayers.

"I'd sooner burn in hell than have to listen to that shit."

They left the song behind as Larry absently acknowledged his partner of less than a week.

"Hmm?"

"That shit they call music."

"Some of it isn't that bad."

"Yeah, right," Karl snorted.

Shrugging, Larry gazed out his open window, taking in the sun's warmth. Karl stopped for an old woman crossing the street with a toddler. Light skinned, the color of coffee stirred with cream, the child stared wide-eyed at Larry. He smiled at the girl, who continued to stare as the old woman yanked her along. After they were clear, Karl eased up to twenty, keeping his speed steady.

Larry's attention wandered to cheap wood-frame residences and to a corner church of modest dimensions. Out front, the message for the day was *Jesus is the Reason for the Season.* Since it was after Easter and well before Christmas, Larry didn't know which season was being flattered.

"You have a listening problem, don't you?"

Larry turned to Karl as they left the church behind. "What?" he asked cautiously.

"I've noticed," Karl explained, "half the time, you aren't there."

Larry felt his face flush.

"I'm sorry."

"More than half."

"I hadn't realized it."

"One thing you gotta do on this job is listen. You hearing this?"

Larry nodded.

"Good," Karl said. He removed his right hand from the steering and patted Larry on the shoulder. "Good. That's what you gotta do. Listen."

Larry gave Karl what he hoped would be perceived as a smile of respect. He tried not to look away too quickly, but he wasn't comfortable with the older man's face. Karl was only forty two, but he had ruined skin and rheumy eyes and fast shifting moods.

"You graduate?" Karl asked abruptly.

"The Academy?"

Karl's laugh stung.

"Shit, man, I know you graduated the Academy, else you wouldn't be sitting here now, would you? College. Remember? You told me you went."

"Two and a half years." Lifting his face to the sun, Larry thought how nice it would be to be lying on a quiet beach somewhere.

"What'd you take?" Karl asked.

"General courses."

"Like it?"

"Yes. I plan on going back."

"Waste of fucking time." Karl glanced at Larry. "No offense."

Larry kept his voice neutral. "None taken." He wondered if Karl meant going to college was a waste, or if Larry going was. The distinction was troubling him when Karl's laugh strafed him again.

"None taken. Yeah, you went to college alright." Karl shook his head. "College. Jeez but the force is hiring them these days."

Karl said this with wonder and disdain, then his eyes clamped

3

onto a black kid on roller skates looping in front of their car. The boy was far enough away, Karl barely had to touch the brakes, but the kid swerved in an exaggerated manner and gave them the finger. The boy's skates flashed sunlight and he was gone. Karl jerked his head in disgust.

"You see that?"

"I saw."

"Little shit," Karl swore. "I should bust open his fucking head, but these days, who knows who's got a fucking camera, right?"

"Right," Larry said without conviction.

They drove for two blocks with Karl grousing and Larry avoiding his face. When they reached the next block, Karl told him to roll up his window. Larry stared at him.

"Too hot?"

"Roll it up."

Larry pressed a button, watched the glass shut out the heat. He reached down and turned on the air. There were only a few people on the street, but the neighborhood they were driving into gave off more heat than the weather; something that snaked up from the sidewalks and the dirty writing on the walls, graffiti with the boldness of cynical art.

"Eight Trey turf," Karl said, pulling a face. "Vicious bastards, worst in the city. I tell you about Tim Rogan?"

"I heard."

"See that intersection?"

Larry looked up ahead to where Karl was pointing.

"Southwest corner. Tim was stopped for the light. Carload of them drove up alongside ballsy as can be and emptied a full clip into him. Seats, windows, steering, Jesus the blood."

"You saw the car?"

Eyes glazing over, Karl nodded.

"You better fucking believe it, I saw the car."

Larry tried to visualize the carnage, but the only image he could get seemed posed, unreal.

They stopped for the light. No one pulled alongside. After the light changed, they drove in silence for a few blocks while the neighborhood got progressively worse. Larry didn't have to visualize its images: A ripped billboard advertising mild cigarettes, a swaybacked church with bullet holes grouped in a flank, a crushed beer can and chipped crack vials on a bus bench, vacant lots spliced by weeds, kids loitering, every face black. One of them yelled something Larry couldn't make out when Karl hung a left.

"Out of the war zone."

"That bad?" Larry wanted to give the impression of nonchalance. Karl stared at him as though he were crazy.

"Didn't you hear what I was saying?"

Another billboard swept by their cruiser, a sleek, handsome man filling a sexy girl's glass with Seagram's Extra Dry. The man was wearing a flashy suit and smile, and the girl's low-cut dress displayed wonderful cleavage. Their black faces promised sex that danced between sheets.

"Niggers," Karl muttered. Larry waited for him to say more, but he didn't.

Their radio crackled to life and the dispatcher's seductive voice slipped into the car:

"You in or out, Karl?"

"Out and smiling."

"Lower those lips."

"Say it ain't so, darling. Which direction?"

"East Ninety-fourth."

"Thank God for large favors. Have I told you you're a sweetheart?"

"You proposing, Karl?"

"Wife's gone, the kids, God knows, so why not?"

"Spoil a girl."

"Trying."

Larry had heard this before too, the sex play. At least it improved Karl's disposition.

"So what've you got?" Karl said.

"Monkey on a wire."

"How high?"

"No, for real," the dispatcher said. "One of them's up on a line. You know, like for clothes, stretched between buildings?"

"There a reason?" Karl asked.

"That's your job. Mine is just to grease your balls."

"You're right. I'm proposing."

"Spoil a girl so."

The dispatcher signed off. Karl's smile was close to adolescent glee. He looked at Larry and his grin faded.

"So what's your problem?"

"I'm spoiled," Larry said. He hoped Karl would take it as a joke.

"You got no idea," Karl growled, and he accelerated until they reached East 94th, a street of seedy apartment buildings and even seedier stores. People were massed on a sidewalk down the block, looking up, some shielding their eyes from the sun with their arms. When Karl got close, Larry could see that the crowd stretched into the easement between two tall tenements. His stomach felt tight. He turned to Karl for reassurance. Karl gave him a wink and parked across the street from the action.

Jesus, what a sight, Larry thought as he stared past Karl. There had to be at least a hundred blacks crammed between the two buildings. There seemed to be a lot of drinking, but Larry still couldn't understand why they were having a good time; when he looked up, all he could see was risk.

"Christ," Larry swore.

"I'm counting on it."

Before Larry could ask what he meant, Karl got out of the car. Larry had no choice but to join him. Heads turned their way from across the street, where a scrawny girl in a cotton dress was re-marking on the entertainment: "Toss the muthafucker a bottle, sure do look like the muthafucker be needing a drink." A friend tugged on her sleeve and she turned; anger and a hint of fear flashed in her vivid violet eyes and her laughter died.

"They don't look happy to see us," Larry said.

"So let's go spread some joy." Karl's hand was by his holster as he started to walk.

"Maybe we should wait for backup." Larry could feel his heart-beat quicken with his steps.

"That what they're teaching at the Academy? Or was that out of college?"

"I was just thinking that—"

"Don't think. Just walk. And don't sweat it. East Ninety-fourth is Pastor Manley's turf. The natives cause any trouble, they know he'll sling their fucking asses in hell."

Larry glanced at the pale blue sky. The man looked like he'd be small even if he wasn't some fifty feet up. The wire he was walking on was stretched between the roofs of the two tenements. His oversized clothes were comical and he was holding an umbrella out like a weapon.

"Eyes front."

Larry obeyed and kept on walking, half a stride behind his part-ner. The faces lost shape and definition as they drew near, became something set and solid and waiting. Silhouetted against the sun, the little man on the line was also waiting.

Stumbling over a spot where the street was broken, Larry dropped to one knee. Laughter passed through the crowd.

"See, they like you." Karl grinned down at him. "Hat's crooked."

Larry straightened his hat, got to his feet and brushed off his pants leg. From deep in the crowd a bass voice boomed, "C'mon, white boy, we're waiting."

Larry took a deep breath. His senses drifted to objects, stayed away from people; doorways without doors, bruised tenement stucco, warped window frames, a pigeon shitting off a roof, shards of glass and the acrid stench of spilled gas pooled in pale rainbow colors on the pavement.

"Waiting on you," the big bass voice called.

A smaller voice threw in, "The Man's coming."

Another voice said, "Put your hands together."

"Karl?" Larry said nervously.

"C'mon, they're waiting," Karl told him.

"Waiting," the big voice echoed.

Karl and Larry went into the crowd, which parted. Larry could smell the alcohol on their breaths as they took shape again, as they became different sizes and features that he passed by. A small child held out a can of Colt Malt, which Larry declined. A rangy Muslim in a suit and blue block shades smiled and greeted Larry in a strange language.

"See? A walk in the park." Karl was smiling, showing teeth. Larry tried to smile too, but he couldn't seem to lift the corners of his mouth. The tightness in his stomach had been replaced by a mild queasiness and a fluttery feeling in his chest. He didn't realize that Karl had stopped walking until he bumped into his back.

"You proposing?" Karl grinned, and there were guffaws from the crowd.

"Sorry." Larry coughed and stared down at the ground, where he caught his reflection in a pool of iridescence before a whim of the sun broke the mirror into pieces.

"Okay, give us some room. I got elbows I need to stretch." Karl rolled his shoulders and shook his arms lightly and the crowd laughed and stepped back.

"A little more," Karl suggested.

The crowd moved back a few more feet, forming a casual circle around Larry and Karl. Larry glanced at his partner. "Watch my back," Karl whispered, looking up. He was almost directly under the high wire artist, with only that fifty feet of fast drop separating them. Karl covered the distance with his voice:

"Hey you!"

The little man didn't respond. Larry shielded his eyes with a hand and squinted as he attempted to get a better sense of the damn fool; he had an impression of high cheekbones, salt-and-pepper hair and skin so black, blue burned through. Larry brought his gaze back to the crowd. There weren't as many people at the back end of the tenements. Almost without realizing it, Larry edged a foot or so in that direction. Beyond the tenements he could see open ground, then a cluster of two-storey apartment buildings; he remembered something Karl had said about an abandoned project. His eyes returned to the crowd. He appreciated the way they'd given him some room. He found that he could smile at them. People smiled back.

"You coming or going?"

Karl's loud voice was cheerful, but the little man didn't appear to find Karl funny; Larry watched his body tremble slightly, watched him spit into his hand.

"Okay, pal," Karl yelled. "I ain't got all day. C'mon down."

"Maybe he don't want to," someone said.

"Yes he does. Don't you, pal?"

A woman in a bathrobe and curlers leaned out a third-storey window.

"His name ain't pal."

"Don't you, pal?" Karl repeated.

The little man twirled his rickety umbrella and rubbed the wire with the toe of his grungy shoe. The clothesline was holding his weight easily, barely sagged. He lifted his face to the sky and his skin glistened, shone like a newly minted coin. Taking in the sun's brilliance, the little man slowly shook his head.

"What was that? I can't hear you," Karl said, cupping a hand to his ear.

"He said he don't want to." The same voice from the crowd again.

"Fuck yes he does," Karl insisted. "Only a crazy bastard would wanta stay up on a fucking clothesline. You ain't a crazy bastard, are you, Jack?"

"Show the man some respect," an older voice said.

A younger voice said, "His name ain't Jack."

"I don't give a fuck if it's Amos n Andy," Karl sneered.

The woman in the bathrobe swore and slammed down her window. Larry's eyes went to his partner but, his hands planted on his hips, Karl was steady on the motionless figure above him.

"Move it, man. I'm not waiting for a fucking net."

There weren't any more guffaws from the spectators. Larry heard glass breaking; a bottle tight in a huge black hand flashed across his imagination, the bottle's jagged neck so close, he could feel the sharpness against his throat.

"You watching?" Karl whispered.

"What?"

"You watching?"

Larry blinked. "Yeah." He was more concerned about his own back now. Suddenly, he thought how nice it would be to shoot his partner.

"Good," Karl said, "good," and then his voice turned hard. "Move it, Jack."

"His name's Lester, motherfucker," the Muslim shouted.

"Or maybe you'd like it if I shoot you the fuck off of there?"

"Sheeit," a heavily muscled young black near Larry swore. "Sheeit." Other expressions of anger tumbled from the crowd. Flung beer and a live cigarette landed near Karl's boots.

"What the fuck are you saying, why're you talking like this, are you crazy?" Larry whispered hoarsely, the words spilling out.

"I'm sick and fucking tired of playing around," Karl hissed back.

Sweat crowded Larry's eyes; the crowd merged with the sun and sky and in that instant, he felt secure, as though he were only in a dream, and then he heard an eruption of anger and his vision cleared to people pushing against those in front, so that the circle tightened.

"What're you doing, what's going on?" he whispered frantically to Karl, and Karl told him, "Eyes front," and out of the corner of his eye he saw Karl lifting his service revolver toward the man on the wire.

"What the . . . ?" Larry exclaimed, fumbling his gun out of its holster. The people stopped moving but the crowd looked huge and his gun felt small and he smiled involuntarily, a tic, while Karl's voice was reaching for an authority equal to the mob's—"That what you want, Jack?"—but their anger drowned him out. Larry's eyes went everywhere, but there were too many directions to look. The shouts assailed him with a force that left him dizzy and from somewhere he heard Karl ask his question again and suddenly the shouts stopped.

Chest heaving, Larry looked up to where everyone's eyes had gone. The little man seemed to have grown, filling all the space above him. Twirling his umbrella, he smiled down at his audience. Larry prayed that the smile was for him.

"This what you want?" Karl's revolver was still raised but his voice was faltering. Lester twirled the umbrella once more and grinned and cupped a hand to his ear.

"I can't hear you, Jack."

Laughter went through the crowd. Lester held his arms high over his head, playing his triumph for all it was worth before he lowered his arms and said, "Coming down."

The crowd laughed some more and applauded and whistled appreciatively and eased back while Larry released his breath and lowered his gun, certain that his world had returned to normal.

Lester fell so suddenly, most of them missed it. For a moment Lester's hands groped the hot air, then he plummeted silently, the umbrella twisting behind him, his baggy pants billowing, his body blotting out the sun. He landed with the thud of heavy groceries.

Same effect too. Spillage. Blood spritzed the pavement and flowed evenly from his head. The umbrella bounced and did a half turn balanced on its rim.

"What the fuck?" Karl said. There was a hint of pleasure in his amazement. What the fuck.

A strong pair of hands gripped Larry and flung him to the ground. He looked up and saw the pigeon take flight and Karl go under, a desperate hand and a black boot among the reckless bodies. Blood spurted where the fierce shoes and fists swung down. The rage shoved and dug, turned back on itself. Somehow, Larry got his Smith & Wesson up before the fierceness could reach him. Whimpering, he fired wildly into the air, but he was shaking so much, the gun slipped from his hand. Down on his knees, he lunged for the gun just before the mob was on him. Crablike, he scrambled backward, scraping skin, falling on his butt, firing aimlessly twice more, pissing himself. Those close to him fell back and the air was charged with heat and screams and mayhem.

They were still pounding on Karl. Larry got a glimpse of him through their legs. His uniform was in tatters and dappled with his blood and one boot was off and his big toe was sticking through his sock and his face was all lumps and silly putty, and then a fat lady was flailing Karl's face with his boot, splaying more blood, and Karl's hair and the fat lady's huge breasts rocked with the rhythm of her effort and Karl's blood mixed with little Lester's, puddles that people splashed through, and a freak in gang blue tripped over the umbrella and swept it away swearing, and everyone was swearing, Kill The Motherfuckers, Shit, No Please, Fuck, Oh God, Burn The Cocksucker, Line 'Em Nine 'Em, God, Fuck, No, and they were rocking the cruiser to the deranged beat until it was on its side, and someone threw gas and someone threw a match and danced clear and flames shot up through the window and blistered the paint and erased To Protect and Serve and there was joyous laughter, only a kid was sitting on the curb crying with his face in his hands, and then someone flung a trash lid, slamming it into Larry's shoulder, spinning him, waking him, and he maimed the wounded air with another shot, his only protection, and the noise and the bodies and the faces spun around him and through it all, through the flames and high heat, the dispatcher was asking again for Karl in her cool, sexy voice, and Larry laughed as he soiled himself thinking, Oh yeah, spoil me sweetheart. And then he was up on his feet and running with too much breathing and too many footsteps hard behind him and he ran lurching, trying to keep his balance, praying he wouldn't fall, and then he was chased only by mocking laughter, but the fear kept him running across open ground until he staggered into an abandoned building and then his foot blazed with pain and he was falling so far he knew he'd never stop.

CHAPTER TWO

Arletha Mae Jones was on the move. There was her baby to feed, prettifying up to do, a few songs to sing. God knows Jesus in his sweet mercy had given her the voice. Didn't her auntie say, and these were her very words, standing there smiling with her hands on her hips, 'Girl, Janet and Whitney, they be right proud have a voice like yours.' And Arletha Mae, when her auntie would get to bragging on her like that, she had to work real hard at keeping from swelling up with pride. Easiest way was to remind herself her auntie had this habit of saying some things that was pretty suspect, like that one 'bout dancing on your enemy's grave 'fore he dances on yours. Now no way was that good Christian thinking. Maybe it was that hoofing her auntie always be doing in Fat Jack's, that mean and evil ol' juke joint down on DeJaynes, kinda place turn anybody from the righteous path.

Arletha Mae heard Jason wheezing and snuffling in the bassinet behind her. She went and gathered up her child, opened her jamy, smiled down at him as he took in her nipple. He was such a wondrous mix of smooth and rough, new and old, flesh wrinkled yet unformed. He was her blessing, her Glory, praise Jesus.

The television was on in the only other real room in the apartment. Humming to herself, Arletha Mae took Jason from one small tidy space to another. Her granny was asleep in the wide chair, her housecoat and bulk flowing out over the armrests. Sunlight came through the kitchen window and reached the screen, where the colors never seemed right and where the sound was on low. Arletha Mae eased down with Jason and sat cross-legged in front of the TV.

A handsome white man and a beautiful white woman were talking in earnest of love and vows broken. The more they spoke, the madder they got. Finally, the beautiful lady slapped the handsome man's face and pivoted and tried to walk away but he grabbed her arm and twisted her to him and they yelled some more, even louder than before, then suddenly for no reason they started in kissing and clawing off each other's clothes. Arletha Mae guessed maybe they been spending some time in Fat Jack's.

The phone in the kitchen rang. Arletha Mae turned to the wide chair. The old woman's eyes opened but the rest of her didn't move. Her eyes followed Arletha Mae to the phone and closed when her granddaughter picked up the receiver.

The call was from a chum kiss sister, Wanda Lee, saying there was something on TV Arletha Mae ought to see.

Ben Stouder and his son stared through the news. Some trouble in a foreign part of the city. A cop was dead, another was missing. Their car had been torched and a building was burning. Newly arrived officers in Plexiglas face plates and body shields had formed a skirmish line. Batons across their chests, they were marching toward some fifty blacks of both genders and all ages. Everyone on the scene seemed conscious of the camera, as though their presence could be fixed in time.

Ordinarily, Ben liked to watch the news, which was always trying to take flight but was always grounded; the news gave you a sense of the dilemma of the world. Today, Ben wasn't much into sense. He gazed at the screen for a moment longer before he got up and went into the kitchen for a cigarette. It was his ninth or tenth in the last hour. Inhaling, he could feel the smoke burrowing deep within him, seeking his soft places, his scarred lungs. An image of his insides, his loopy mortality, flashed before him. Black on gray. Those were his colors. He was sorry it was Saturday. He'd rather be at the unemployment office. He didn't smoke as much there.

Ben turned on the tap and drowned his cigarette, then glanced guiltily back at David. The child was still on the living-room sofa, that dead uncomprehending gaze locked on the TV or somewhere beyond it. Ben wondered what lived in his damaged son's head. Did dragons appear out of mists or was ennui the product of his days? Did he dream of soft velvet or shocks wired to the nerves? Ben knew that all too often his own thoughts screamed bad intentions, but hell, he had cause.

Firing up another Winston, Ben shook out the match and looked out the window. Mirror of the world, his anyway. He and David lived in a nice enough neighborhood. Residential. Patios and passive dogs behind gates, things edged and pruned. There were even a few trees with shade.

Ben exhaled some smoke and stifled a cough. There was a yard sale across the street. The owner of the house, a prick named Schultz, was slouched bare-chested in a lawn chair, his hands idle over his crotch. Schultz's appearance repulsed Ben. His neighbor had a profusion of black hair, on his arms, his torso, even his hands. Looked like an ape, Ben thought. All Schultz needed was a banana, a peel for a pratfall. Ben closed his eyes and pictured a brutal spill. Opening his eyes he saw that a blowsy woman in cutoffs and halter had stopped to browse. Schultz ran his eyes over her body. The woman fingered a stained bathrobe and left.

Laughing, Ben savored Schultz's frown. Last week he had been walking by with David when Schultz had started up his power mower. The sudden detonation had reduced the kid to blubbering terror. After Ben had gotten David calmed down, he'd looked up and seen his neighbor laughing.

Ben heard the high urgency of a siren from the next room. Either someone was hurt or the cavalry was arriving. Going to the doorway he faced the TV. The police line was faltering under a barrage of bottles and paving, while a squad car raced down the street. A bottle from nowhere smashed into its windshield. The car swerved then straightened into a direct route for anywhere else. Ben didn't know why but he felt like cheering. Then he noticed that David was gone. Just before panic and a vague sense of relief kicked in, Ben thought, hell, his son had cause.

CHAPTER THREE

J. D. Lawson rolled the bullet between his fingers, digging its grooves, trying to figure, a damned hard thing, how something so small could spread so much fucking grief. Seemed like anything that could leave a hole big as your fist should be that size. Well, that was the fine mystery of it, now wasn't it, the attraction.

The gun was on the orange crate J.D. used for a nightstand, along with his portable radio, his General Relief bus tokens, his hot plate, his rumpled Army camouflage cap, his other five bullets and his works. He picked up the .38, admired its shiny blued steel, its walnut grip, its lethal function. There was a drop of blood on the barrel. J.D. spit into his hand and tried to rub out the spot with his palm, but the blood had been there too long. He smiled faintly, accepting the fact that there were just some things you couldn't understand, some things you couldn't erase. The smile stayed on his face as he opened the cylinder and slid the bullet into a chamber.

J.D. turned on his radio and lay back on the Murphy bed in the small drab room. He had moved into the midcity hotel ten days ago on a welfare voucher good for two weeks. The fleabag was called The

Paradise. J.D. liked to tell strangers he'd been in Nam and Paradise was worse.

The radio was on low to KGIL, a soul station with an attitude. A deep, wracked voice was crooning threats to the white world, the new gospel. J.D. turned up the sounds just enough to provoke the cat in the room next door, did cadence in time to the music, one, two, three-fucking-four, here it comes; the pounding arrived right on cue, rattling the thin wall. J.D. turned down the radio to make himself heard.

"You're supposed to say, Knock It The Fuck Off," he told Bobby. On impulse, J.D. imitated the singer's raw voice. There was a long silence so J.D. turned up the volume again. The pounding was even louder this time, shaking a sliver of plaster free from the ceiling.

"This game got rules," J.D. said with a bitter laugh over the music and the thuds.

"Fuck you," Bobby said firmly through the wall.

"That's the first," J.D. agreed. "Number one."

"Fuck you."

"Yeah, fuck me," J.D. said wearily. He snapped the cylinder shut. Lock and load. He turned off the radio and rested the gun on his chest. He was wearing jockey shorts and a tank top spattered with a substance he couldn't define. His legs and hands were smooth. Only the veins in his left arm showed the abuse. He flexed the arm, lifted his hand to his chin and scratched his stubble, which was becoming a beard, which was becoming an itch. Bobby shaved and showered several times a day. J.D. hadn't showered since Wednesday, hadn't shaved in a week.

Two stories down, traffic tried to make itself understood.

"You there?" Bobby asked tentatively.

"No, man. I'm in Phoenix."

"Phoenix?"

"Phoenix, Biloxi, Peoria, Davenport, Lansing, pick one you fucking like."

Bobby tapped on the wall again, possibly with his head, no doubt mulling over his options, maybe counting his change for bus fare. J.D. listened to his own breathing and stared at a blotch on the cracked ceiling and waited.

"J.D.?" Bobby said finally.

J.D. yawned. Lately, he had been finding himself in a state of exhaustion. Idly, he picked up the baggie that contained his works; syringe, bottle cap, cotton ball, coke and horse. Maybe he'd do a one-and-one, get that mule kicking in his stall.

"J.D.?"

"I'm here." Stretching out his legs, J.D. put his works aside. The mood wasn't right.

"I still like you." When he wasn't busy being deranged, Bobby sounded like a little kid.

"Just like? Not love?"

"Yeah, well, fuck, you know. It's gotta be like. I mean, I'm not a fucking homo."

"You coulda fooled me," J.D. said, mostly to himself.

Bobby's voice went up a notch.

"What?"

"Never said you were. You high?"

"Not 'til my wakeup."

The plaster was so cracked, J.D. wondered if the blotch might drip. He cupped his hands to catch the drops, then became aware of movement; he lowered his eyes to a cockroach migrating across the dirty hardwood floor.

"Which is?" J.D. asked Bobby.

"You know."

"No. I don't." J.D. watched the cockroach detour around the rucksack that contained his basics, including the old snapshots he no longer looked at. J.D. used a forefinger to trace the names of past griefs on his belly. "I don't," he said, scratching an itch.

"Six, no, five o'clock," Bobby told him.

"Babe, you're looking at a long four fucking hours."

Bobby giggled and J.D. smiled with satisfaction. Bobby was an ofay cat from Davenport, Iowa, hooked on fuck all. He'd been getting General Relief tokens and vouchers even longer than J.D., and J.D. had been using the system on and off for many years.

"Three and a half," Bobby said.

"Come again?"

"I'm looking at the time and it's closer to three and one half hours."

"Whatever," J.D. said.

"They taught us at the compound that time was the essence of God."

"Whatever."

"We prayed three times a day."

"You told me."

"Facing the sun."

"Great for the tan," J.D. remarked.

Before he'd come to The Paradise, Bobby had belonged to a cult that stockpiled rocket launchers for Jesus. He was what the workers at Social Services called a blue folder, their way of saying he wasn't playing with a full deck; in Bobby's case around fifty cards short. Bobby blamed the drugs but J.D. knew that was just a sad, desperate excuse. Truth was, Bobby would've been fucking nuts even if he'd never touched a needle.

First night J.D. was here, they'd done a gallery. It wasn't an experience to repeat. Bobby had shot into the neck to facilitate the rush to his brain. The kid had started drooling and speaking in astonishing tongues, not to mention making unspeakable love to the floor. J.D. had had to do him some slight violence.

"What about you?" Bobby said coyly. "You high?"

"No."

"You sure?"

"I can usually tell."

The cockroach stopped near J.D.'s bare feet. The bug was a dusty gray. Adapted to its environment, J.D. supposed. Its antennae weaved in his direction. J.D. guessed it was checking him out for signs of rot. He spun the .38's cylinder sharply.

"What was that noise?"

"Traffic."

"No it wasn't."

"It was nothing, Bobby."

J.D. pointed his gun at the cockroach. What passed for its eyes seemed to clock his intent, but it didn't move. J.D. pulled the trigger. There was a loud snick as the hammer struck an empty chamber.

"I suppose that was nothing too," Bobby whined.

"Depends how you see things." J.D. lifted his foot over the cockroach, covering the bug with shadow.

"You want I should come over?"

"No, that's alright, Bobby."

"I mean, maybe you're lonely?"

"No. I'm not."

Twisting his foot slowly, to complete the act of self-degradation, J.D. squashed the cockroach with the calloused padding near his toes. The antennae swayed then lowered. A gesture of surrender.

"What're you doing in there?" Bobby wanted to know.

"Sick and stupid things," J.D. told him.

"Yeah?" Bobby said hopefully.

"Actually, I'm thinking about shooting myself," J.D. admitted. This had been coming for a while. Today seemed right.

"That's not funny," Bobby said.

"No, it ain't, but it's God's hard truth."

J.D. listened to Bobby shuffle away from the wall in the new shoes he'd jacket-stashed at Kinney's. J.D. gazed at his own sneakers and his boots at the foot of the bed. The sneakers were old, the boots even older, the leather cracked. "Need saddle soap," he said to no one as he put the gun to his head. He held the gun there steady. Sunlight through the room's only window mingled with shadows, patterning the floor. Traffic murmured outside; songs of nostalgia seemed imprisoned in the sound.

J.D. sighed, wondered if his fatigue had led to a confusion of his senses even without a drug high. He lowered the gun to the crate and looked up at the blotch. If he waited long enough, the songs would become shadows that fell from the ceiling. He sighed again and closed his eyes. Maybe he'd go to sleep, kill the rest of the afternoon, only someone outside was leaning on a horn. He tried to ignore it but the horn wouldn't quit.

Swearing softly, J.D. scraped the cockroach off the bottom of his foot and onto the hardwood. Putting on his cap, he went to the window and looked down at the street, where a clunker was blocking a lane. A blade-thin black was leaning in through the driver's window, talking to three other young blacks inside. An old Hispanic was staying steady on his horn behind the clunker, but the brothers were paying him no mind.

J.D. pushed up the window and rested his elbows on the sill. "What's shaking, bro?" he called out, affecting a jive accent. Startled, the Mex, or whatever he was, let up on the noise. Four pairs of black eyes looked up at J.D., measuring his forty plus years and the dubious sincerity of his argot.

"What the fuck's it to you, old man?" the pedestrian said. Cars maneuvered around the two that were stopped.

"J.D.?" Bobby called anxiously from the next room. J.D. ignored him, gave the punk below his best grin. "For a cat ain't got no wheels, you awful loud," he said.

The brothers and sister in the car broke up. Their laughter drove their friend away. He flipped off J.D. and strode angrily down the street. The Mex cut around the clunker and fell in behind the kid, who made no move for the sidewalk. J.D. had the impression that the Mex was suppressing an urge to run the kid down.

"J.D.?"

The Mex gunned his engine. Watching him swerve around the punk, J.D. experienced a profound disappointment.

"J.D.?"

"Chill out, Bobby."

He heard Bobby swear to himself and begin pacing. J.D. listened to the new shoes squeak. He could picture the frail body, the skin drug-bleached and waxen, could see Bobby picking at his zits and running a hand through his wild, clean hair as he worried over everything J.D. had told him. Bobby had a lot of pain and it kept him busy.

"Hey, man?" It was the fat-ass squeezed behind the wheel of the clunker.

"Yeah?" J.D. replied.

"Who you talking to up there?"

"The roaches," J.D. told him.

Fat ass laughed shrilly, his falsetto climbing.

"You a pretty funny cat for old."

"Comes from seeing the young die, from seeing a lotta people get fucked over."

The laughter was weak from the car. J.D. knew he should've skipped the embellishment, should have remembered he was dealing with dropouts who couldn't cope with more than one-liners. He guessed Bobby was taking this all in with an impulse to shoot up.

Fat ass stuck his head out the window of his car and glared at J.D.

"Run that by me again, nigger?"

J.D. smiled pleasantly down. His .38 was another option.

"I said what's shaking, bro?"

The sister, who had a wide scar across her throat and dead eyes, leaned past fat ass and pointed a long finger at J.D. "You like to see people get fucked over, home?" she said without rancor.

"Beats shooting holes in the walls," J.D. answered.

Smiling, the sister lowered her finger and happiness split fat ass's face again. "Then check it out on East Ninety-fourth," he said as he floored it. J.D. watched the clunker snake dance down the cruddy asphalt, inviting mayhem and leaving behind a screen of black exhaust.

"J.D.?"

"Yeah?"

"What the fuck was *that* all about?"

"About time," J.D. told Bobby. "About sweet fucking time."

Larry was walking on a wire. He was a thousand feet up, looking down on snarled white clouds. A strung out angel in grungy shoes and nothing else was in his ear, giving him advice in a Satchmo growl. Fall, motherfucker, fall. Larry scoped the angel with malice, spat on his ragged wings and growled back, I already have, fool, I already have.

Rubbing his eyes, Larry shook his head, trying to focus on what had happened. He recalled running from the crowd, across open ground and into the abandoned project, remembered glancing back in his panic as he ran through a doorway looking for a place to hide, and then he'd gone down hard. Hit something in full stride just past the door and whatever he'd stumbled over had tossed him. He hurt where he'd landed, hurt so damned much. Skin was scraped off the heel of his left hand, his ankle was at an angle and his knee was throbbing to a point past pain.

Shifting his body, Larry surveyed what had once been a living room. No furniture, no personal effects. The plasterboard walls were streaked and pale where wallpaper had been peeled away, strangely charred where the rose-patterned wallpaper remained. The floor had been removed, leaving only the concrete foundation, which was littered with plaster and dust. Tentacles of insulation tubing hung from the broken ceiling. A toilet that had once been white was visible through another doorway. Everything in the apartment was fetid, except for a shiny upright shopping cart that was in the living room for no imaginable reason.

The room blurred. For a moment Larry was back trying to keep his balance above the clouds, but the shabby angel was goosing him and his knees were Charlestoned out and shaking and he was starting to drop and Christ but his knee hurt and so did his ankle, and then he was twelve and down on his football-jersey butt where his old man had dumped him and his father was in his face yelling, "Get up, sissy, whasamatter, you a fag?" Larry rubbed his eyes and shook his head again and the ugly images faded.

A mangy gray cat wandered through sunlight that flowed through the doorway and sat a safe distance from Larry, ignoring him. It stuck a leg in the air and started to wash. Larry glared at the animal while the thick pink tongue kept stroking the damp fur. The licking had the sound of soft, deep sex. Larry wanted to scream, wanted to scare the cat from his sight, but he was afraid someone outside would hear him. He bit deep into his thumb to keep from crying out, bit until he felt the sour taste of blood slide into his mouth. Just because it was quiet, just because they'd laughed, that didn't mean they weren't looking for him.

Placing a hand over his eyes, Larry imagined Karl's killers stealing barefoot and in loincloths between the ruined buildings, saw them materialize through shimmering heat waves, carrying spears level and umbrellas held high to hide their darkness from the white sun. Their leader left one bold footprint in the dust; he was wearing Karl's boot, which sloshed as he walked. The sloshing grew louder, the prints deepened into red rivers until finally the leader stopped, pulled off the boot and shook it fiercely. Blood flooded out and spread with astonishing speed across the ground, washing over Larry, drowning him.

Larry squeezed his eyes to make the blood vanish. Once again he saw his partner sucked under by the crowd. Poor Karl. They probably had his head up on a stick by now. Why the fuck hadn't he let him call for backup? Because the asshole was putting on a show, the same as the fool on the wire. Karl. His partner. Bastard brought him to this, hunkered down hurt in a shitty room with sounds and visions he couldn't shake free of in his head.

The licking stopped. Larry opened his eyes. The cat, its leg still in the air, was staring at him. Caught by the sunlight, the cat's cold eyes were flecked with fragmented colors.

"Get the fuck away from me," Larry whispered. "What's the matter with you? Leave me the fuck alone."

The animal eased off its haunches and walked to a wall. Facing Larry, watching him with those cold eyes, the cat lifted its tail and sprayed. The creature's rear quivered and the plasterboard darkened.

A fierce hatred rising through him, Larry got up to kill the cat, but after two steps his leg buckled and he screamed in pain and dropped. The cat finished spraying and left the room as casually as it had entered. Larry wished to God he still had his gun.

Breathing heavily, his body pulsing, Larry lay with his cheek pressed to the concrete. He wondered if he was going into shock. Reaching down, he fingered his bad knee. The flesh felt hard, rubbery. Gradually, he leaned forward and drew back the bottom of his pants leg, exposing his ankle, swollen and purple and bringing back another memory of dad, who worked in construction and was violently intolerant of most things, especially the weakness of his son.

Once, when things got ugly, his father had hit him so hard, he had broken his arm. He tried to remember how his arm had looked that day. Worse than his ankle, he hoped. He touched the old break near his elbow. Sometimes, late at night, it would ache and he would remember the fury in his father's face. Both of them had cried afterwards, but Larry recalled his father's fleeting look of satisfaction when he realized what he had done.

The memory was replaced by a siren skirling somewhere, too far away to help but close enough for hope. I have friends out there, Larry told himself. They'll find me and won't judge me by my failures.

Please God.

Ben **felt lost.** Always have been, he laughed ruefully to himself, but then that was just an existential joke.

He had been driving for over an hour, canvassing blocks removed from the riot, residential and then city. He had first gone to David's school for the mentally challenged to check out the bank of swings David loved so well. A custodian had even taken Ben through the empty facility, a slow moving, arthritic man offering sympathetic clichés. In the dayroom, some of David's artwork was on the walls. Ben had been relieved to see that most of the sketches were benign.

The stoplight Ben was approaching turned yellow. There wasn't any traffic, so he pressed down on the accelerator to beat the red. The neighborhood was getting worse, deteriorating brownstones replacing steel and brick silhouettes. Gaps between buildings got his heart going. The implications of shadowy alleys frightened him. If he couldn't find his son before dark, if something happened to him . . .

He flicked on the radio to escape his feelings of guilt. The news was the same as what was on TV. Escalating was a word he heard for the first time. He tried to calculate distance and determination. East 89th through East 94th. He and David lived at least eight miles from East 89th. David didn't have bus fare and wasn't likely to hitch a ride. Eight miles had to be too far for David to walk.

Static kicked in on the station. Ben adjusted the dial. The newscaster was spending media coinage; urban rage and police response. The one term Ben didn't hear was containment.

Ben turned onto another avenue, Monroe. David might manage the few miles that Monroe was from home. Aromas of potent sauces drifted from open windows whose sills were lined with drab potted plants; a radio next to a geranium sang of amour with acute distress. Parked cars had flames painted on their sides and steering wheels wrapped in chains or striped fur. Posters clustered on a wall adver-

tised films Ben had never heard of. A muscular Latino was buying a
chili dog from a sidewalk vendor for his girl. Children were playing
hopscotch nearby. One had David's languor, but the kid was Hispanic.

East 88th the newscaster said solemnly.

Luck was in Ben's pocket. There was a police station several
blocks down. What he should have done in the first place. Parking, he
paid his quarter and went into the precinct house's small, empty
lobby. A large American flag hung by the entrance, next to photo-
graphs of officers killed in the line of duty. Flanking the lobby, two
long hallways disappeared into shadow. Ben went to a dark Formica
counter that was backdropped by the squad room, row upon row of
desks. Uniformed cops, most white, were milling about, seemed to be
impatiently waiting for blood to wear.

The dumpy sergeant seated behind the counter was deep in paperwork. Ben stood in front of him and cleared his throat. The sergeant
looked up and took Ben in under heavy lids.

"Yeah?"

"I've got a problem," Ben said.

A phone rang on a desk directly behind the sergeant. A balding
cop pacing near the desk swore loudly, walked over and snatched up
the receiver.

"So do we," the sergeant told Ben.

"My son is missing."

"How long?"

"About two hours."

The sergeant made a sour face, coughed once, picked up a pen
and positioned a small notepad on the counter.

"How old is he?" the sergeant asked wearily.

"Ten."

"What's his name?"

"David."

"Last name?"

"Stouder." Ben spelled it for him.

"Maybe he's with friends," the sergeant suggested.

"He doesn't have any."

"No friends," the sergeant said, writing this down too.

Ben shook his head.

"Not really."

"No mother either?"

"Of course he has a mother," Ben said tensely.

"Where is she?" the sergeant asked. He'd stopped writing.

"In another state."

"Divorced?"

"That's right."

The cop who was losing his hair came over and whispered something to the sergeant without ever looking at Ben. The sergeant nodded.

"Look," Ben told the sergeant, after the other cop was gone, "I'm not here to give you my personal history. I want you to find my son."

"Relax, the kid's only been gone a couple hours. He'll come home." The sergeant's expansive gesture took in the room. "Like I said, we've got our own problem. Don't you know what the hell's going on?"

"I want you to find my son," Ben repeated.

The sergeant sighed and began rummaging under the counter. White wrinkled flesh popped out of his pants at the waistline as he bent over.

"You'll have to fill out a form."

"A form?"

"That's right."

"Goddamn it, listen to me," Ben said.

"Watch your language," the sergeant warned him.

"I'm sorry, but someone has to take this seriously. My son, he's . . ."

"He's what?" The sergeant's face seemed all hooded eyes.

"Retarded." It pained Ben to say the word. The sergeant gazed at him vacantly for a moment, then returned to looking under the counter.

"I'm sorry," the sergeant said in a tone that could marginally pass for sympathy.

"So am I." Ben looked away. "So am I." From deep in the corridor to his left, a disembodied voice said something rapidly and angrily in a language Ben couldn't place.

The sergeant sighed once more and tucked his shirt in as he straightened up.

"Looks like we're all out. I'll have to get one in the back."

Flab shifted under the sergeant's loose uniform as he trudged toward the rear of the station.

"Isn't there someone I can talk to?" Ben said to his back.

"You just did."

Ben watched the sergeant disappear through a door that he took care to close behind him. Ben swore to himself, wished he'd lied about David. The sergeant's sympathy had been more like a negative assessment, as though Ben had somehow been at fault for David's condition. He felt like shouting that this wasn't true, this wasn't fair, that nature had simply tricked his son, deceived them both.

The sergeant's silhouette passed across the frosted pane of the door. Ben dug out a cigarette and lit up, forced his attention to wander. Three handcuffed cholos in flared white chinos had just been ushered into the hallway on Ben's right. The side of one's face was scraped raw. The cop with the cholos was examining a long and lethal razor with tender fascination.

A tall black woman and a white man of medium height brushed past the cholos and came out of the hallway. The woman was wearing a tight sweater, a miniskirt and red boots that rode nearly up to her knees. The man was wearing a frayed suit and platform shoes. Hugging herself, the woman walked quickly from the station with a puzzled look on her face. The man had trouble keeping up. Ben watched them leave before he turned back to the squad room.

Phones were ringing, many were ignored. A woman with short blond hair was adding a name to a list on a wall. Other uniformed cops were gathered around a colleague who had his shirtsleeves rolled up and a map spread out over a desk. Conversations were low, incomplete. A sunburned officer stood at a water cooler, filling a paper cup. Ben looked away. Cartoons were under the glass top of a desk near the counter. He couldn't make out the captions, but one of the cartoons featured a caricature of a black man that would have made him the beau at a Klan ball.

Laughter turned Ben to two plainclothesmen who had wandered into the lobby. He thought they might be laughing at him, but they were busy with each other. One was mousey with a stunted moustache. The other, big enough to have played a muscle sport, had the sly grin of a man who kept small sins in his pockets.

"This is gospel," the mousey one said, touching the other man's arm. "You know Sam's old lady, right?"

"Right." The big man smiled with closed lips and folded his large arms across his chest.

"Right. Anyway, last night Sam goes home beat, dead as a dog, and he drops on down on the couch and looks up at the cunt and says, 'I work so hard I don't even have time to die,' and you know what the fucking bitch says?"

"Tell me." The big man's face looked like it was about to burst, that it took all his willpower to keep his hilarity down.

"She says, Make time."

The two cops howled until they noticed Ben through their tears. Their laughter faded. Glaring at Ben, the jokester segued into a less abrasive story.

There was still no sign of the sergeant, only empty light through frosted glass. "Fuck it," Ben said. The plainclothesmen glanced at him with hostility. Ben could feel their eyes drilling his back as he left.

Out on the street more squad cars were arriving at the station. Ben had to maneuver his car with care to avoid the congestion. Home seemed the best option. After all, where else *would* David go? Gearing down to second, he swung a right. A siren abruptly splintered the hot air then was gone. Ben switched on the radio.

East 86th the newscaster was saying.

CHAPTER FOUR

Arletha Mae watched the riot spread from a foot away, her guide a blue and white helicopter hugging the madness from not so high up. The people below clearly liked the chopper's presence. They would stop running every which way to stare up and point. The helicopter kept a steady nose on the action, following it like dinner.

"Ain't that something," Arletha Mae said softly. Several hours had passed since Wanda Lee had called urging her to watch the news, but her granny had taken up most that time with stoop and sweep chores; now Arletha Mae was getting a fair idea of what she'd been missing.

"Lawd, lawd, lawd," Arletha Mae's granny said from the wide chair behind her. "Ain't fit for no child to watch."

Arletha Mae yawned. Sitting on the floor with her baby in her lap, she was deep in afternoon shadow; the sunlight through the kitchen window was fading.

"Ain't fit t'all."

"He ain't but six months," Arletha Mae said, rocking Jason gently.

"Wasn't talking 'bout him."

"I'll be sixteen in two weeks."

"Lawd, lawd, lawd." Her granny grunted as she shifted in the chair. "You gonna watch, do something 'bout that there color."

Arletha Mae adjusted the color, but the screen stayed wavy with too much red and green no matter how much she turned that funny little knob. The action had gone to ground level. An earnest, prettified black lady with a mike was talking to the camera, saying things were getting worse, though to Arletha Mae things looked the same.

"I like her hair," Arletha Mae commented. "Ain't it pretty?"

"Your hair jus' fine way it is."

"Wasn't what I was saying."

"Next you be looking to get it conked."

"Wasn't t'all."

"Or getting yourself a curling iron."

"Wasn't," Arletha Mae said sullenly.

Her granny grunted again. "What's the time?"

Arletha Mae shrugged and faced the screen. The lady was still talking. Rioters or jus' kids—who could tell the dif'rence—grinned behind her. Several gave gang signs. One held up and jiggled his arms, showing off the many watches he was wearing. Another had a bandana tied round his head with CALL 911 written on it. Another stretched his mouth with his fingers and thrust his ugly-ugly face in front of the camera. All of them seemed to piss off the reporter, whose expression showed an undisguised dislike.

"Got to be near four," Arletha Mae's granny said, rubbing her deep ditch eyes.

"She don't look happy," Arletha Mae remarked.

"Who?"

Arletha Mae gestured to the screen.

"Why should she?" her granny snorted.

Arletha Mae laughed gleefully, did a half spin and would have clapped her hands together too, except for her baby.

"Look. One of 'em's white."

"No, he ain't. He's jus' high yaller." Her granny's words were a heavy presence behind her, but Arletha Mae felt light, free of the world's burdens.

On the TV, the lady looked ready to kill.

"Look like she sure could use herself a shoofly," Arletha Mae said. "Like you had back home in 'Bama."

"Better she have a gun."

Arletha Mae's laughter pealed. Even her granny smiled. Jason remained limp and silent.

"You best change channels now."

"Why?" Arletha Mae asked, with laughter still in her voice.

" 'Cause I can't find the remote."

"No, I mean why?"

" 'Cause my show is coming on and 'cause you got things to do."

Arletha Mae reached for the dial, but two scatbacks scooting on out of a convenience store stayed her hand.

"That ain't looking good," her granny said.

The flat roof of the store seemed to bubble up before their very eyes.

"Huh huh," Arletha Mae's granny said, shaking her head.

Flames appeared through the walls and roof. The helicopter veered away from the smoke.

"Told you. No good t'all."

"Gonna be the onliest one. 'Sides, even if there be more, they put out the fires," Arletha Mae said with conviction.

"Best you be changing now," her granny said tenderly.

"Have to?"

"Yes you do."

Arletha Mae turned the dial to the familiar channel. Bold music heralded another tawdry drama. Arletha Mae said, "There, there, there," to her sleeping baby, then she said, "What things I gotta do?"

"I need some things from the store," her granny said. She waved a hand in the general direction of the kitchen. "There's a list and money on the table."

"Seem like there jus' ain't never 'nough," Arletha Mae complained.

"Girl, you don't know poor. You growed up in the South, you'd know poor. Now don't you be forgetting my medicine this time."

Arletha Mae cut her eyes to her granny.

"You want I should go out in all that crazy assed trouble?"

"Keep your faith in Jesus. He'll protect you. 'Sides, trouble is six blocks away, less'n you planning on goin' on by Fat Jack's, see your sinning aunt?"

Arletha Mae shook her head emphatically.

"No ma'am."

"Then you get yourself goin' now. You can leave Jason here with me."

"Don't like to leave him when he sleeping. When he wake, he got so much misery he don't see me there."

"Jus' don't dawdle."

"I won't."

But Arletha Mae did, long enough to watch more fine-looking people on the TV. They were fighting. So was the whole world, seemed at times.

J.D. knew the world was haywire long before today, but now he was riding with absolute and irrefutable evidence of the fact.

The bus was going down a midcity street rife with neglect at thirty mph and J.D. was feeling the bumps all the way up his spine. After hearing the sweet news from fat ass, he'd napped for a couple of hours before trudging downstairs to the bus stop that was just outside The Paradise. Bobby had heard him leave and followed him. J.D. had to shoo Bobby away like a stray dog, almost caused him to miss the bus; the driver had stopped only after J.D. loudly questioned his ancestry, a pretty fair indication that the driver was as batshit as a blue folder from Davenport, Iowa.

"Run that by me again?"

"I said, and this is God's honest truth, son, I jest doan know."

The driver was an old cracker with frizzy white hair, bottleneck glasses, a deep bucket drawl and the red face of a lush. He and J.D. were the only people on the bus, whose seats were scored with psychotic slashes, tagger insignias and used gum. The only other passenger, a normal looking lady of the Jewish persuasion, had gotten off at the first discreet opportunity, eight blocks back.

"I jest doan," the driver said again, shaking his head.

J.D. had Johnnie Walker squirreled. He took the pint out of its brown paper bag and held up the bottle like a small road kill for the driver to see in the rearview mirror.

"Shit, man, this has gotta be the best damn offer you had in a month of Sundays."

"My day off."

"Name your day, comes to the same good thing. Forty proof and free." He waggled the bottle, but the driver's attention had returned to the road.

"I ain't arguing that," the driver said, "but I have to firmly believe this ain't a direction I should be going."

J.D. tucked the booze back in his coat, a tactic the driver failed to notice. "It's your route, ain't it?" J.D. asked gruffly.

"I ain't arguing that neither," the driver said, scratching the back of his red, flaky neck, "but it doan make no kinda sense, and this you gotta admit. . . ."

"God's honest truth?"

"God's honest truth, it doan make no kinda sense for a white man to be going down there."

"All I'm asking," J.D. said, "you get me close."

"How close?"

"Easy walking. Say a mile?"

The driver had no views on what J.D. felt was a reasonable distance. J.D. took the bottle out of his coat, unscrewed the cap, and took no more than a sip before graffiti carved into the seat beside him drew his attention; JESUS LOV GOD. J.D. considered this a risky assumption, although a worthy subject for debate. He scratched LONG ODDS into the seat; the letters left by his fingernail vanished as soon as he completed them.

Stopping for a red light, the driver turned—his eyes no more than glints of reflected light behind his thick lenses—and faced J.D.

"Mind if I ask you a personal question?"

"I'm here," J.D. said absently, his mind still locked in debate; if the assumption was correct, Jesus was a chump, considering the time He'd done on the cross.

"Ain't none of my business, but why do *you* want to go on down there?"

J.D. dropped his arms over the back of his seat, the bottle loose in his hand. "Needs and desires." He tilted his head toward his shoulder. "Needs and desires."

Leaving the driver to mull this over, J.D. took a few hits and scanned the ads that lined the sides of the bus. There were radio stations, the March of Dimes, and a camel in a tux smoking his name. For J.D., these were familiar appeals from years of travel.

"I can live with needs and desires," the driver told him. "But the main problem is, I seriously doubt you got enough left in that there sack to make it worth my while."

J.D. peeked inside the bag.

"Close to half."

"Half won't cut it, son."

"And here I was thinking you were a moderate man," J.D. said.

"O.K., listen up. Here's what we'll do." He gestured with the bottle. "You see that liquor store up there on the left? You let me run on in and buy you a full load."

The driver nodded. "This might be something else I can live with."

The driver pulled up in front of the store, easing into the red on the wrong side of the street. J.D. left the bottle on the floor, got out in the middle of the bus, past the hiss of compressed air, and went inside the store.

Several rows of overpriced paper goods and snacks lined the aisles. Beer and soft drinks were behind glass. The hard stuff was behind the counter with the young clerk, who came from one of those distant countries where attitudes were formed by suspicion and lethal moves.

J.D. gave him a Tom grin but the clerk stared back hard, even though J.D. was wearing his best; camouflage fatigues and cap and a long brown Army Surplus jacket neatly sewn in four places; he'd left his rucksack at The Paradise; the appearance of migratory tendencies usually didn't play too well in most neighborhoods. Waving at the security camera, he affected a carefree swagger, tried unsuccessfully to think of a tune to hum. The attraction of ridiculous items made him pause. He picked up a defense spray whose label claimed a 97 percent success rate at fighting off panhandlers, psychopaths, and the homeless. Returning the can to the shelf, he continued to browse, selecting some animal crackers, a tube of Sta'-Put glue, and a container of Johnson & Johnson bandages for when he found himself hungry and damaged in some other life. J.D. carried these treasures to the register and placed them down for the clerk to ring up.

"And a quart of Johnnie Walker black label," he said, resting his elbows on the counter. The clerk jabbed out the price.

"Thirty six forty eight."

J.D. glanced lazily out the window. The bus driver was hunched over the steering, his glasses low on his nose as he read a paper. J.D. smiled faintly.

"Thirty six forty eight."

"Yeah, I heard you." Leaning in a little closer to the clerk, who flinched from the intimacy, J.D. lowered his voice to a depth worthy of desires and needs.

"See here, thing is, I'm flat broke—"

"Get out."

"—but you loan me that pen you got there in your shirt, I'll write you an IOU good as my—"

"Get out."

Keeping the eye contact constant, J.D. sighed and tapped the counter. "Yeah, well, in a minute," he said agreeably. "But you mind if I ask you a personal question first?"

"You leave now," the clerk said. Parts of him had to be clenching but his voice was steady.

"You come from Vietnam or someplace pretty damn close, am I right?"

The clerk was starting to tremble.

"Anyway, they got this snake there. Little, about yay long." J.D. spread his hands a few inches apart.

"We used to call it Two Step. Reason was, it bit you, you were dead before you finished your second stride. Now I found this to be such an interesting creature, what with its strange and amazing power, I brought one back home. Tamed it by feeding it crickets and telling it sweet lies."

J.D. could see the fear in his eyes.

"Matter of fact, he's right here in my pocket, and I'm willing to bet my life I can throw him on you before you can reach that gun you just gotta be keeping under the counter."

The clerk reached but J.D. smashed him across the face, breaking the bottle and spraying glass and booze and blood and dropping the clerk like discarded laundry.

Catching his breath, J.D. glanced out the window again. The driver still had his nose in the paper. This was good. He liked the old man and didn't want to have to hurt him.

Walking quickly around the counter, J.D. stepped over the clerk, who was out cold on his back, blood solid over most of his face. The gun, a snub-nosed, H&R Ruger .32 with a silver finish, was near his outstretched hand.

"This is what comes from not believing in the power of the imagination," J.D. said, gazing down at him. Squatting, he picked up the .32 and checked its action; sharp and clean, pleasing to the hand. There were six shells in the six chambers. He stuffed the revolver into one of the deep pockets of his coat, down with his own gun. After he'd jammed the crackers and Band-Aids and glue into his other coat pocket, he took another quart of Johnnie Walker from the shelf and a book of matches from the counter. He left the store without rifling the register.

"Glad to see you didn't get a ticket," J.D. said when he was back in the bus.

"What took you?" the driver asked, putting the newspaper aside.

"The clerk, he was slow with the language," J.D. replied, handing him the bottle.

The driver adjusted his glasses, scratched his neck and looked at the store.

"Where is he?"

"Fuck if I know. Maybe checking the stock. We saddling up, or what?"

The driver picked carefully at the black seal on the Johnnie Walker.

"Jest as soon as I git this sucker open, son. You wanna ride up front, keep an old man company?"

"Thanks, but I prefer the back. Allows me to catch the whole fucking panorama."

The driver nodded. "A wise man's thought."

About the time the driver went mouth to mouth with the booze, J.D. settled into his old seat, where Jesus still loved God. The bus started to roll and J.D. kicked back, enjoying the rough synergy of gears and tires. He looked out the window, felt a tingly pleasure as he watched the low rent scenery pass by. He had chow and healing and more than one kind of heat in his pockets. A man could travel a good many miles with such blessings.

David hadn't come home. He wasn't waiting on the doorstep or in any of the six rooms of their house. Ben had even checked the closets and shower.

Nerves were making his skin prickly; he needed a cigarette. More than one. David hid his packs sometimes, a game, a ritual. He'd stash them in the strangest places, in coffee cups, pillow cases, scotch-taped under the sinks. Once, Ben had discovered a pack in a black widow's sticky web, in a deep recess of the garage. Desperate that day too for a smoke, he had delicately disengaged the pack. When he shook out a cigarette, the spider had crawled out and perched on the cellophane wrapper, arched and looking for trouble. Before squashing it under his shoe Ben had smiled and thought that maybe the widow also had a habit.

Usually though he would find his smokes in David's room, so he went there and searched. The bedroom had the trappings of a five year old. The wallpaper had sunflowers and cartoon character pinups, Bart Simpson, Big Bird, Tigger and goggled turtles. Toy cars and planes, small enough to be easily held in Ben's palm, were on the dresser, along with some of David's crayon drawings. David favored pastures and trees and good-natured animals. Occasionally, he would include a stick man or woman, hastily sketched figures with fierce expressions and distance from the inviting landscape.

Ben reached for a recent sketch but stayed his hand; the primitive artwork brought back too much of his son and his feeling of culpability in David's disappearance. So many things could happen to him out there. Good as well as bad. A compassionate stranger or the police could pick him up, see his condition and keep him safe. Ben saw himself opening a door to a room, a station of comfort, where David would be waiting, tried to keep that picture in his head as he glanced about the bedroom for his smokes. He found a pack in a Lionel freight car on the floor, a snug, clever fit. Ben shook out a cigarette. The curtains for the only window were drawn, edging the room toward darkness. Lighting up, Ben watched the smoke blend in, gray on gray. He knew he would have to go out again soon, fill out a form and prowl for his lost boy, have to ask questions of people who saw David as a source of pity or sport, but at the moment all he wanted to do was sleep. He couldn't, of course, but he could lie down for five minutes. His search would be more focused if he wasn't exhausted.

Stretching out on David's short bed, legs dangling, he tracked the plumes from his cigarette up to the ceiling. David's bloody and lifeless body flashed before his mind's eye. The image was too vivid and he forced his thoughts to other things, back to when he wasn't much older than David. He remembered how his own father used to lie on their sofa and smoke after a long day at the office. Sometimes he'd invite Ben to sit with him. His father had a confiding manner and these talks were among Ben's best memories. Most of the time they discussed Ben's future and its promise. He saw himself growing up to be strong and serene like his dad, a provider of good advice and reassurance for his own son. Having a family was a balm for his every need, but first he needed a wife.

Maggie was a pistol. Black Irish with a temper to match. At first Ben saw her flare-ups as passion. They'd met at a party where drinking clouded judgment; Ben often thought the strata had lingered for years. She had long, dark hair and great legs and Ben, just out of college and flush with a damned decent job, resembled a catch. They were a pair. Glitter yuppies, a friend had called them.

Ben wasn't an innocent but he hadn't exactly packed the aisles. Maggie was the fifth or sixth girl he'd slept with, depending on whether or not you counted the head he'd deliciously received from an engineering groupie in his sophomore year. Maggie, on the other hand, had really been around. The fact excited Ben rather than scared him; AIDS wasn't part of the vocabulary yet. Their lovemaking was varied. Maggie taught him positions that had scope.

She miscarried before they were married. David was her second pregnancy, born four years after the wedding. They named him after Ben's father. He weighed eight pounds six ounces and had spacious, gold flecked eyes and crying was a condition he seemed to have avoided. Ben did designs for a company in aerospace. Maggie did Parris Island aerobics and somersaults in bed. Everything was perfect. Their friends wanted to kill them.

The signs first appeared when David was a year and a half. Little response, no effect. Their pediatrician was a cold joker. Took Ben aside and said at least the kid wouldn't have his mother's temper. Everyone had noticed by now. Their friends no longer contemplated mayhem.

Ben and Maggie took David to other doctors. Phrases of the profession bounced off each other. Learning disorder. Sensory deficient. Hypokinetic. Severely language delayed. Aphasia. Autism. A few of the doctors were encouraging. Said his behavior could be deliberate, something he might outgrow like baby teeth. He didn't. David stayed the same. Always would. All the directed activity, attention arousal, commands, intervention, and touch couldn't change that simple fact.

Ben took a long drag on his cigarette, let out the smoke and tracked the plumes as they rose to the ceiling.

Patience. That was the trick, only how much could you keep pulling out of your hat and which one did you wear? Maggie's had been red. That fierce Irish temper. If David had been hyper, she could have managed, even related; for Maggie, going ballistic was empathetic. She needed a child who would run and scream. Instead, she got a kid inhabiting moon space.

She took out her frustration on Ben. After a while he didn't even bother replacing what she broke. Got so bad, he started behaving like David. Kept his back turned even when she flayed it.

Maggie walked when David was seven, seven days after his birthday, as though the number carried some sort of inverse luck. He tried to get her back out of habit, but she had changed her number then moved to another state. A year ago she married a lawyer, which seemed apt. His friends were sympathetic, gave him all kinds of advice. Ben wanted to kill them; eventually he simply lost them. He was on his third job and no longer a comer and his father was dead.

In the three years since she left, he and David had managed, but never easily. Ben took him to more doctors, hoping to draw out a little language, but David remained mute. They cultivated routine in place of communication. Ben ran their lives by the clock. Breakfast at seven, day care at eight, home from looking for work at five, dinner then kill the evenings with TV. David would lose himself in the images, the shifting points of light, the bland repetition. Ben told himself things could be worse, but he couldn't bring himself to say this with any conviction.

His cigarette was down to burning his fingers and he put it out on the undercarriage of the bed. Getting up, he went to the window and opened the curtains. The fading afternoon light hit his eyes, tossing his vision.

Hello sunshine.

CHAPTER FIVE

Arletha Mae was walking along North Burton, a skip in her step
even with Jason in her arms. There was smoke rising three blocks up
on East 86th, brothers and sisters and sirens high booting toward the
trouble, lawd, lawd, lawd. Walking down the quiet street, she looked
up at the darkening late-afternoon sky, got her thoughts hooked on
chasing the sun, the game she'd played since she was little, 'fore there
was singing, 'fore there was boys.

Way the game went had to do with her thoughts on heaven and
earth and music. Way she saw it, God had sweet fine rhythm with
backup to beat all. You start seeing things like this, ain't hard to
figure the sun was nothing more'n an old high hat cymbal. You could
follow it all day long, but you could never catch up to hear the glory
of its wondrous ring. Wasn't 'til you died and went to heaven God let
you get close to be blessed. That didn't mean you stopped trying
down here on earth. All Arletha Mae was hoping was to get near
'nough to get a tingle in her ears.

The siren slowed her then the big voice spun her. A loudspeaker
was tossing words like punches, ordering her to Stop Right There.

Pressing Jason to her chest, she waited by the curb for the black and white to pull up. A window went down and an elbow rested where the glass had been. The two young white cops were as fine looking as the heroes on the soaps. "Nits make lice," she thought she heard the driver snicker.

"What're you doing out here?" his partner said. Without the loudspeaker the man's voice was near normal.

"Doing my granny's bidding," Arletha Mae told him. She was glad Jason was still asleep.

The officers stared at her in amazement. The one behind the wheel had a deep tan. His partner was pale with red hair. "Fuck," the driver said, pinching the bridge of his nose and looking away from Arletha Mae in disgust.

"What did you say?" Red's jaw was hanging and his eyes looked huge.

"My granny give me a list."

"For what?" The man's mouth stayed open. A little wider and Arletha Mae felt he would devour her.

"Shopping," she answered.

"For what you can steal?" Although this wasn't funny, it got the driver laughing. His club was on the dash. Arletha Mae couldn't quite see far enough down, but she knew there were leg clamps on the floorboard behind him. She shifted Jason up higher and patted her imitation leather purse.

"I got money right here."

Red's mouth twisted into a sneer. "I'll bet. I'll just fucking bet you do."

"Leave the girl alone, motherfuckers!" a man shouted from across the street. The officers stiffened and veins bulged in their necks but they didn't turn to the anger. Arletha Mae guessed they'd stopped her because she was safe.

"I'm goin' to the market."

"With a baby?" Red's eyes were getting even bigger. His partner revved the engine.

"It's not unheard of, Jeff. C'mon, let's go."

Keeping his eyes on Arletha Mae, Red put up a hand.

"Let her answer my question. Why didn't you leave her with your granny?"

" 'Cause *he* don't like it," Arletha Mae answered sharply.

Red was staring at her hard. The sun through the window was in his eyes, but there was no music here, no blessings of the mind, and this wasn't no game. For a moment Arletha Mae felt fear snake through her. She was afraid he might draw and use his gun. Afraid for Jason, not for herself.

"And why the fuck would you go shopping with this shit going on?" Red gestured to the trouble. There was smoke now from East 85th and shouts Arletha Mae could distinctly hear. A cop car came tearing down Burton and swung a vicious left onto 85th, strobes dancing through the smoke and the five o'clock light.

"Nothing to do with me," Arletha Mae said.

The officer behind the wheel revved the engine again.

"C'mon, Jeff."

"I'm just trying to find the sense," Jeff said to his partner.

"I done told you." Arletha Mae pressed her baby tighter against her. Jason stirred but didn't wake.

"Jeff," the driver said wearily, but the green eyes stayed on Arletha Mae. She took in his face, the pale skin, the red hair, the uncompromising smirk. The sun made him look older than he was or deserved to be.

"Tell me something I can believe," he said.

In the distance, another cop car seemed to burst out of the low sun.

"I gotta be goin'," Arletha Mae said.

"That I can't believe."

"Please, I gotta."

51

"Not unless I let you."

"That's enough, Jeff."

The mean cop pointed a finger at Arletha Mae.

"Get the fuck back on home."

Arletha Mae watched them leave her. They went a block and turned, away from the trouble. She figured she'd handled it 'bout as good as she could manage. Her granny always be telling her, police get in your face, crouch on down and get your arms covering your head for when they start swinging them sticks. But that was Selma in '65, and you did things a little dif'rent here and now.

Arletha Mae kept herself going down the sidewalk, past worn-out shops, liquor stores with bars, a check-cashing establishment, and a gas station with shiny pumps. She had Burton to herself. People were either staying inside or hanging with the smoke. From the look of things only three buildings were burning down the block and round the corner, but there was more smoke beyond East 85th, spreading, becoming thicker, turning everything blind in front of her. She was still far enough away, the fires didn't seem real, just a few gray wisps reaching her to let her know that the burning was up ahead. Sounds knifed out of the pall, more angry shouts and shrieks of panic. A fire engine screamed past her. Clamped to its sides, the firefighters looked fearful and intense. She watched the smoke swallow the hook-and-ladder and the polished redness, then shapes began coming out of the smoke. A high-backed Pontiac with a dented fin and caved-in door blew by in a straight path to a happier ending; the eyes of the Mexs inside were fixed on that destination. Arletha Mae wished them luck and then she followed their example, angling away from the madness, making good time through an alley in her sneakers until she was to the market, which was bright and clean and untouched.

Once she was inside, she breathed a sigh of relief. The familiar aisles stocked with nourishment made everything outside seem like a scary show she'd turned off. The air, cold and direct, helped too. Arletha Mae took a deep breath and got the rest of the market in focus. The only person she could see was the store manager, Mister Emmett, a tall, bony tight ass who'd played in the old Negro leagues, a slap hitter who still liked to slap, jus' ask any of the kids who had their hands stung when they tried to stuff their pockets.

"We're closing," Mister Emmett said rudely from behind a register.

Arletha Mae said, "Only need a few things."

"Make it quick." Mister Emmett moved to another register, yanking open the drawer and stuffing the bills in his apron pockets as Arletha Mae went through a turnstile and put Jason in a cart. A tabloid on a rack near the turnstile said that Magic had run off with Rock Hudson's ghost. Arletha Mae wasn't so sure 'bout this.

"You hearing me?" Mister Emmett called to her.

"Sure am." Arletha Mae saw Mister Emmett heading for the store's entrance as she got herself going toward an aisle.

"Keep your pockets empty and take her the fuck with you," Mister Emmett yelled, jerking a crooked thumb at Produce. Arletha Mae turned and saw the Sad Witch there.

The Sad Witch didn't appear to hear the manager. She never seemed to hear where, what or how. She was even older than Mister Emmett but that didn't have nothing to do with it. She'd been this way long as people could remember, and that was a long time. Rumor was tragedy had fuzzed her mind when she was young. One thing certain, they'd named her right, pointy chin and all that hair poking out and never cracking a smile. She always wore that falling apart coat that drooped to her floppy slippers and she lived out of the shopping cart she was pushing, filled with more rags than food. Where the money came from, that was a mystery deeper'n Sherlock. Arletha Mae sighed and went about her business, pushing the cart middling fast and grabbing what she needed.

Mister Emmett came back inside. "You almost done?" He'd been out putting up a sign, Black Owned, on one of the automatic doors.

"Just 'bout," Arletha Mae answered. She had the milk, the bread, the DulcoLax, the Pepto, the canned goods and Jason loose in a basket. All she lacked was his diapers. From the crunched look on Jason's face, he needed them.

"Hurry it up." Mister Emmett was addressing Arletha Mae but he had gone over to Produce. She could see him off to her left, hauling the Sad Witch's cart toward the front of the store. Head down, the ol' lady stayed attached to the cart's handle like it was part of her, shuffling them floppy slippers 'long a little faster to keep up.

"I don't see the Huggies," Arletha Mae called out.

Mister Emmett shot back, "I ain't waiting."

She found them then, two rows of pink boxes. Arletha Mae was looking for the blue when she heard Mister Emmett.

"Shit!"

She looked out the front window and saw them coming, ten to twelve in the lead, bangers joy-bopping along in their sneakers and tight jeans and colors, gold jewelry and navy blue bandanas in their pockets and on their heads. They came in confident and quick, owning the store, maybe thirty altogether, fanning out, taking whatever they fancied.

"Pick and save," their boss man said. He had a comb in his short Afro, one glass eye and tree trunks for arms. Arletha Mae knew him like she knew old griefs. She cut her eyes from the bangers to Mister Emmett's warning:

"I got a gun."

"We got more," the boss man laughed as he slammed a register open and shut and scanned the aisles for opportunity. His name was Roy but everyone called him Slope. A friend of Michael's; back when Michael believed in sinning, they'd boosted four wheel drives together.

Mister Emmett was awful quiet, which jus' wasn't natural. Fearing his demise Arletha Mae got herself back to where she could see him. He was trembling with rage, jaw working silently while the bangers went round him like he wasn't there. Only the Sad Witch paid him mind, pushing her cart against his scrawny butt. When he didn't move, she stayed planted.

"Hey Arletha, hey little girl, over here sweet honey baby." Three joy boy studs had spotted her and were talking their nasty nasty talk, "Get you somethin' real soft for yore knees," making loud and filthy noises all the while.

Slope sauntered over. His muscles had their own life. "What's shaking, Arletha Mae?" That familiar, cool fuck you voice.

Arletha Mae aimed her head at Mister Emmett. "Him," she said tensely. Slope laughed. One thing you could say for ol' Roy, he could take a hostile joke. Quick large hands with their manicured nails began to load her basket.

"You ain't got much. Take more."

"Don't want more." She put the items back as fast as he put them in.

"Same ol' Arletha," Slope chuckled. His gray glass eye glinted in the low overhead light. The eye looked like a marble. A shooter.

Slope clearly felt like playing. He dug into his pocket and came out with keys that he wiggled in front of Jason's face. Jason smiled and reached, but his stubby fingers fell short. Arletha Mae slapped the keys aside. The keys had sharp edges that stung. She pressed her fingers against the damp comfort of her mouth.

"He ain't no kitten."

Slope smirked. "How's Michael?"

"Out in six months, behavior and jail reduced." She pushed her cart toward the registers, hoped Slope wouldn't tag along.

"My my how time flies," Slope said close to her ear. "Seem like jus' yesterday they throwed away the keys." He had his own keys over her shoulder, tempting Jason again. Shoving Slope's hand away, she got the cart's wheels turning.

"Something you might be doing too," she told Slope, "giving the wages of sin some thought."

Slope laughed, twirled the keys and jammed them back in his gray jeans. He followed her close, close enough for her to feel the sway of his long heavy gold necklace brushing against her back. She could sense his eyes stroking her rear, sense the hardness of his cock.

She got clear of the aisle, but two joy boys batting a tennis ball with cereal boxes got in her way. Arletha Mae cussed them politely, veered left and headed fast for register number one, but Slope stayed right with her.

"How long it been, baby?" he crooned.

"Little over a year." It could have been worse. Night Michael found out she was pregnant, he'd gone out and got drunker'n drunk and wrapped a tire iron round some poor fool's skull. Michael'd copped a plea and the judge had given him a deuce and an ace.

"We goin' get married. When he get out."

"Married. Well, now, ain't that jus' fine. Boy needs a father."

Arletha Mae hated how he was laughing at her, hated even more the way her juices were stirring, the fact she wanted to fuck him. Trying to escape her sinful thoughts, she got her mind fixed on the letter from Michael she had in her purse, tried not to think about the other letter that was also there.

Parking her cart at the register, she looked around for the Sad Witch. 9-T, a skinny cat with more bones than sense, was tugging easy on her cart, doing his damndest to spook her, tossing her rags, draping them over his head, scatting in her face. The old lady was grim and fierce and tugging back. This gave 9-T so much pleasure, he appeared to be building to a howl you could hear in the bleachers. Mister Emmett looked ready to cry.

"My, my, my, ain't we having fun," Slope said, pitching his voice high. Swatting away the hand he placed on her ass, she removed her items one by one, examining each price, adding up the total in her head as she set her groceries down at checkout. Slope's eyes got big.

"Girl, *what* are you doing?"

"I am paying," she told him, no ifs, ands or buts about it. Drawing open her purse, she picked out her bills and change, mouthing the amount as she carefully counted. Arms folded across his gut, Slope was laughing near as hard as 9-T.

Suddenly, sirens were arriving fast. "My, my, my," Slope said with a curious wonder, then brakes were squealing and the homeboys were fading out back and the cops were coming in the front and Mister Emmett was screaming, KILL THE MOTHERFUCKERS, as Arletha Mae placed her money on the counter. I AM PAYING.

"This is looking to be an interesting evening, you gotta admit."

The bus driver's remark barely registered; J.D. had fallen deeply in love with a soiled paper he'd found under the seat. The news was six days old but he didn't give a shit. The light he was reading by came from the sun, a shopworn glow on the horizon.

"I most definitely agree," he said, "but it ain't evening yet."

"This is a matter of a differing opinion, son."

Distracted, J.D. put the newspaper aside, pulled off his left boot and used the glue from the liquor store to moor his loose sole before he studied the driver from the distance of the long aisle. The old man had killed over half the Johnnie Walker but didn't seem drunk; his voice was as steady as his steering. The terrain they were passing was well west of the inner city, unpopulated miles of sloping landfills, rust-coated railroad tracks and desolate space.

J.D. said, "Nothing personal . . ."

"I take things as they come," the driver interrupted.

". . . but this does not look in the least like what I fucking paid for."

The driver took a heavy swig and returned the bottle to between his legs. "This is what you might call the scenic route."

Gazing at the dirt and gravel, which stretched into fields of flowering weeds, J.D. realized the driver had taken him as close to the action as he was going to. J.D. sighed in exasperation and slapped the folded newspaper against his window. The frizzy white head tipped toward him.

"Something the matter?"

"A bug," J.D. said, lacing his boot back up over the sultry rankness of his sock. The old man shook his head and they rode in near silence, the only sound the drone of the bus's engine. Sunlight glanced off the window where J.D.'s reflection was a ghost in the glass. A vague disappointment worked his body, other aches as well, and he ran a thumb and forefinger over his eyelids, kneaded his shoulder, swore silently over the tyranny of his tendons and joints. His neck was stiff and he twisted it hard to snap out the crick. The driver jumped in his seat.

"Jesus!"

"Just my neck."

"Damned if I didn't think I'd been shot."

"Not even close." Gunshots were nothing like that. Gunshots echoed, stayed in your mind.

They traveled a little more, the bus rattling loosely with the whims of the deserted street. J.D. watched the sun drop another slow inch before he reached for the cord over the window.

"You know I met Merle Haggard once."

He could just make out the old man's eyes, obscured by his thick glasses, in the rearview mirror. The eyes had taken on the glow of happy memory. J.D. let his hand fall.

"Don't say."

"Yes I do. It was nineteen and fifty eight, before you was even born."

"A little after." J.D. rubbed one red eye and opened the paper to an article on the decline of family values.

"It was in Amarillo. You ever been there, son?"

"Austin once."

"I was barely growed, well, maybe twenty five, but working my first serious job, wildcatting. Man, you think it's hot in this here damn city, you shoulda been out there in them fucking fields. Ten hour days under a killing sun. Sweat, it'd be pouring off you 'til you'd think you're gonna drown in yore own damn juice."

"Uh huh." The experts quoted in the article were discouraged by recent trends.

"Anyway, one night I git off work jest dog beat, so I go on into town to git myself some refreshment, if you git my drift."

"Uh huh."

"I find myself in this miserable juke joint, poor ridiculous people but hell, I was one of 'em, right?"

"If you say so." The experts didn't have any answers. J.D. put the paper down and took a hit from his own bottle.

"Right," the driver said, "and they got this band, guitar and piano, drums and vocalist, and man, they was even worse, I mean, drunk goddamn sailors sound better. So there I am, ready to puke the brew when all a sudden, the door swings open and who should walk in?"

J.D. tasted a cracker shaped like a hippo. "Elvis?"

The driver laughed. "No, shit, that woulda been like meeting the Almighty hisself. But ol' Merle Haggard, he was close enough. Turns out the drummer was a cousin, so ol' Merle does 'em this favor and sits on in. And let me tell you, he was dressed like a man, natural jeans, shirt and boots, not one of 'em queer dazzle outfits with them flashing butterflies on the back. A real gentleman too. Took off his hat."

"His hat?"

"Nine saddle bronc Stetson. There was ladies present."

"Uh huh."

"And I don't haveta tell you, what a voice. Break your heart. He only did this one song then he left, but it was this experience I never forgot. Never will."

J.D. placed his bottle between his legs just like the driver's, so that it looked like an eager cock.

"Thought you said you met him."

"He smiled at me once or twice."

"Maybe he was thinking butterflies," J.D. said.

"What?"

"He still have his own natural teeth?"

"Huh?"

"Nothing."

With a catch in his throat the old man started to sing to himself, the song Merle Haggard might have sung. Drunk sailors sang better, but from what J.D. could tell, it was about this cowboy who killed himself after first his wife then his horse left him. J.D. tolerated it briefly, then he once more regarded the filial affection scratched into the seat: JESUS LOV GOD. He was willing to accept this sentiment of simple faith, but the greater question was did God love Jesus? There was evidence to the contrary and if God couldn't love his own kid, what chance did man have? Residence in The Paradise was probably part of His divine scheme; rushes to the brain and a Murphy bed.

J.D.'s attention returned to the front of the bus, where the liquor was finally kicking in; the driver's voice abruptly got louder, the lyrics more slurred, as he described how the cowboy deliberately impaled himself on a cactus which shed tears. J.D. lunged for the cord. The driver tossed him a startled glance and braked hard enough to twist the bus, which thudded to a stop, throwing J.D. forward.

Slumped over the steering, his glasses gone, the driver asked sorrowfully, "Why'd you do that?"

"I'm getting off," J.D. told him.

"And here you'd been saying you wanted to go where the action is."

"Changed my mind."

Straightening up, the old man picked his glasses up off his lap and returned them to his nose. "What can I say?" he said, turning the engine back on.

J.D. paused by the steps. "Not much."

"That'll do."

Glassy-eyed and swaying slightly, the driver toasted J.D. with the nearly empty bottle as he got off the bus. With the doors hissing shut in his face, J.D. gave the old man a farewell salute. The bus swung around sloppily and headed toward the sanctuary of familiar routes, the old man's head settling on the steering again for a moment before he snapped to.

J.D. surveyed the terrain. A fuck all no man's land. Maybe two klicks to the inner city, where a few tall buildings were silhouetted against the darkening sky, and where he could see remnants of smoke. This didn't suit him; maybe he'd missed the party. Nevertheless, he set out toward the skyline, following the railroad tracks. J.D. liked trains, hated planes. Planes took you fast to places you didn't want to go. Trains were music and motion without designs on the future. He listened to his heavy combat boots tromp over the rails, a brittle sound. He had worn the boots as a practical consideration, in case he needed to kick someone in the teeth. A warm breeze flirted with his face. Rice paddy weather. He felt like he was walking on point. Cadence, he told himself. He scatted the beat to the bus driver's song, thinking only a lame geek cowboy would off himself over a woman or an animal.

Life itself was what gave you cause.

"**W**elcome back," the sergeant said smugly. "I take it you didn't find him?"

Ben frowned. "No." His glance followed the sergeant's to a clock on the wall. 6:42.

"Getting late," the sergeant said.

"I know. I need a form."

"Saved it for you." The sergeant reached under the counter. "You should've stuck around," he said, handing the paperwork to Ben. "Saved yourself some time and a trip."

"I know."

Ben took in the room. The station was comparatively quiet. No more milling cops, although the two plainclothesmen were still around, cracking wise over Styrofoam coffee.

The form, mimeographed with a carbon copy, was in English, Spanish, Farsi and Korean. Ben filled it out quickly on the counter, jotting down dates, names and times while trying to ignore the sudden jangle of phones and the oblique laughter from the plainclothesmen.

"I brought a picture," Ben said, after he was finished.

The sergeant took the form from Ben and studied it at some length, as if for errors. "I was going to ask," he said.

Actually, Ben had brought two photos. He dug the one with the sharper focus out of his wallet and gave it to the sergeant, who compared the snap to the information on the mimeographed sheet.

"Nice looking kid. This recent? He doesn't look ten."

"It's two years old." David at eight looking somewhere other than the camera, the sunshine behind him more animated than his soft brown eyes. "I haven't taken any pictures for a while."

The sergeant stared at Ben from under those heavy lids, as though he'd committed a parent's sin, then looked away.

"Go home, get some rest. We'll find him."

Ben doubted it. "I will."

Back in his car he fired up a Winston and tried to map out a strategy. Maybe he'd start with the mall near his home, something else he should have done before. David liked motion. The only other time he'd wandered off was last year on the Fourth. Ben had celebrated the holiday by obliterating his senses with a bottle of wine. When he woke, the front door was standing open. David had managed less than a mile; Ben had found him riding an escalator in the center. Up and down, up and down.

Ben turned on an all-news station while he drove. There was some banter between two newscasters, and a spot about an AIDS benefit Liz Taylor was giving at Michael Jackson's estate. There would be food and celebrities and Michael performing, along with a few of his trained animals. There wouldn't be any children.

What he was listening for came on next. According to the police and a telecopter, the rioting was, with the exception of a few flash points, under control. There had been some looting. Four buildings had been set on fire; only one couldn't be saved. Twenty-six people had been arrested. The rumor that a cop had been killed was now confirmed. His name was Karl Ceric. He was forty two and survived by his parents, an ex-wife and two daughters. His partner was still missing. The partner's name was Larry Spencer. He was twenty four and had been on the force less than a week. Two rioters had also been killed. Their names weren't given.

The mall was a dead end. A security guard remembered David with fond irritation. Up and down, up and down.

The car's needle was trembling in the red. Ben went to a 76 station and filled up. Bought a fresh pack of Winstons from a machine and showed the snap he'd kept to the attendant, a glum kid with a ponytail and pants that showed off his endowments. The kid hadn't seen David but did tell Ben he needed brake fluid.

The sky was getting dark, the color of a bruise. Leaving the station, Ben turned on his lights. What was left of the day kept his headlights faint. He had no idea where he was going, just going. He switched the news back on. A cordial voice told him the Dow Jones was down; the same voice said a gala was planned to celebrate the marriage of two notoriously promiscuous stars. Ben shifted into third, ready to let tabloid religion carry him through the night.

The singing lifted Arletha Mae before she reached it, the gospel according to North Springer Street Baptist. Turning a corner, she could see the big ol' V-roof church rising out of the spreading darkness and surrounded by empty lots and beat down block walls; her shortcut home, through the Lincoln Heights project, was just beyond. Springer Baptist was low on funds; the clapboards were peeling and fading, daisyweed was ruling the lawn, and nobody had done nothing yet 'bout the bullet holes in the south wall, but praise Jesus the spirit was there.

Arletha Mae carried Jason and her sack of store boughts toward the beckoning lights in the high windows. She'd been damn lucky to get out of the market. The officers had given her a hard time, though not as hard as the two in the car, who'd given her a diff'rent view of the soaps. Still, for awhile there in the store, things had got pretty bent. Mister Emmett wouldn't stop yelling, 'Kill the Motherfuckers' even after the motherfuckers were long gone, and the cops at first thought Mister Emmett was meaning shoot *them* and they'd near to close shot him 'til they'd sorted things out. And nobody knew what to make of the Sad Witch who wouldn't give up her cart or her frown. Finally, the officers had gotten the Sad Witch to smile and Mister Emmett quieted down with only a couple quick-strike baton blows while Arletha Mae convinced them she had in fact paid, spell out the letters please sir, PAID, see the green and silver on the counter?

The wide double oak doors to Springer Baptist were open. Arletha Mae wiped her Nikes on the Welcome and went inside. She paused in the entrance, caught breathless as always by the beauty of the place; the windows of stainless saints, the long polished altar and aisles, the familiar faces of the congregation. Half the benches were full, a fair average, and Pastor Manley was leading the choir of which Arletha Mae was a shining member.

Dressed in their gold-and-green silk gowns, they were rendering *River Jordan* with joy, swaying and snap-clapping to the thumping offered up by Mrs. Cornelia Farbane on the pipe organ. Wanda Lee spotted Arletha Mae in the doorway and waved her on up to join them. Wanda Lee had a special place in Arletha Mae's heart—the sister had brought her to Jesus when Arletha Mae was thirteen and already lost—but she was here to humbly repent for her wayward thoughts regarding Slope. So she smiled and shook her head and sat in the back near Miss Lanny Blair, who went over three hundred pounds and had breasts that could cover a table.

Arletha Mae clasped her hands under Jason, closed her eyes and breathed in the glory that swelled around her: "Roll, Jordan, roll, Jordan, ride me on your waters deep and wide, to the other side, roll, Jordan, roll, Jordan, keep me moving with that Heavenly tide . . ."

Got to be the truest words man ever conceived, Arletha Mae thought. The choir juiced the lyrics, Wanda Lee's reckless voice rising above the rest, "Take me, Take me," the sweat of exultation bright on their faces under the hot lights while the brethren jammed with them. "Amen, Tell it, Amen, Yes, Huh huh." Feeling the Majesty and the Power, Jason smiled and jiggled and tried to clap his doll-like hands. Then, 'bout the time the tears were coming and every sin was begging on the floor, the singers stopped and let Wanda Lee bring it all the way home:

"Take me to the land of Glory, there won't be no dying there, take me, take me, I know the other side of Jordan is better than this, there ain't nothing on this side that I'm gonna miss, when you see me leave to go to that other side, ain't no need to cry, you know faith is the boat going to keep me afloat, row, row, row, row . . ."

Wanda Lee built and built and built the feeling, pulled higher and higher by the brothers and sisters, whose arms were working those invisible oars, carrying Wanda Lee across that river we all must cross, 'til she lifted a fist and hauled on in one last note from deep inside that stretched to the hidden sky.

"Amennnn," Preacher Manley intoned, removing his glasses and wiping the sweat from his face with his handkerchief. He went to the shiny pulpit and clutched its sides, as though he might be swept away by all the strong feeling if he didn't hold on tight. "Amennn," he repeated, laughing, and his congregation laughed with him. He had a big voice for such a small man. Seemed like black preachers were either all flesh or the size of a hungry child. Arletha Mae guessed God was sending a message with that.

"It is a fine, fine, *fine* evening to have the spirit," Pastor Manley said in a near shout, then he closed his eyes and raised a hand, surrendering himself to the spell that filled the church. "Oh yes, we should all be glad the hurt and the evil Satan cast over us today has been washed, and you all, every man, woman and child out there, you all know what I mean, Huh huh, yes, has been washed away, yes, we should all rejoice God chose to cleanse our streets with so little pain, glory be to Him, raise your arms, testify to His truth, brothers and sisters, Huh huh, rejoice even as we bow our heads, bow your heads, do it now with me, and pray for the souls of those so recently departed, no matter how much they may have strayed, yes, put your heads down low so they may be lifted for Thomas Carver and Reginald Boyd, knowing they are in the bosom of the Almighty and absolute Lord, redeemed by His grace and mercy, oh yes, as we all, all of us sinners, one day will be."

Pastor Manley went on like this for a considerable time, as only a man infused with the spirit could. The brethren punctuated his sermon with shouts of encouragement, jus' as they'd done with the song, and 'fore too long everyone was clapping their hands and singing, raising the dead and the blind and washing away the corruptions of the day with the blessings of the approaching night.

CHAPTER SIX

Larry was hurting. He didn't know which was worse, his leg or what was in his head. Inside, he was still on that wire, a thousand feet up with the wasted angel growling soul sounds and threats in his bloodied ear. The bastard's wings were made up of hundreds of fluttering moths and his pores were sprouting nails and his eyes were moons to howl by.

Larry opened his eyes and checked himself out to keep from going fucking nuts. He was an assortment of dim colors and sharp odors: The purplish swelling where he'd scraped the heel of his hand; the flour-like plaster on his pants; the shadowy stain where he'd pissed himself in his terror. The animal stench of his sweat and his urine and his blood revolting him.

A breeze crept through the hot, moist air outside. Larry listened for other sinister sounds. He hadn't heard anything for a while. No traffic, no sirens, no voices, no help. He was dead meat in a dead room.

He gazed out a window devoid of glass. The sky was placid, deepening; he could almost see the disappearing light change shades.

Shadows covered most of the cracked concrete floor and climbed the scaly walls.

He was drooling. He wiped the wetness off his chin with the back of his hand, was relieved to see it was saliva, not blood. Drooling like a baby. His old man would've slapped him to tears. Self pity worked him. He needed comforting, his mother's arms. His colleagues weren't even trying to find him. They knew what he was, a sissy who'd cry if you knocked him on his ass. They disguised their contempt with amiable slurs, rookie, kid, wet behind the ears. In the locker room their eyes and their jokes went dead when he walked in. They were Karl, they were his father.

His left side ached. Shifting onto his elbows, he felt the pressure in his bowels. He was determined not to take a dump in his shorts or on the floor; he wouldn't lie in or near his own excrement. He stared at the dirty toilet. It was maybe fifteen feet. He could crawl that far.

Turning over onto his stomach, he heaved himself forward but the pain was too great in his bum knee and the ankle that was undoubtedly broken. Stifling a cry he gingerly moved his weight to his right side. It was a ridiculous position but he found he could drag himself along by thrusting with his forearm and hip. His efforts caused the plaster dust to dig deep into his nostrils and eyes and the grain of the rough floor tore through his sleeve and pants leg, but it was pain he could bear. Dad, if you could only see me now, he thought with a laugh—a fucked up rookie in a fucked up tenement trying to avoid crapping in his already fucked up pants—but the bravado brought back too many bad memories. He groped for anything pleasant to concentrate on. He wasn't dead, he hadn't shit himself yet. These observations were worth a few more feet.

His hand reached up and gripped the toilet and came away with grime and rust and maybe something worse. Still, he'd made it. This gave him as much satisfaction as anything he had experienced in his short life. Pressing his right forearm down on the bowl's rim, he pushed up to his knees. His breathing was labored and he paused to rest. By degrees he twisted his body until he was sitting on the cold porcelain. There was no seat or water or paper, but he was doing what was proper. Pushing down his pants, he waited for his bowels to release, then he heard footsteps outside and everything in him tightened.

By the time J.D. neared the inner city, the sun had said goodbye and the moon was a ghost under foreboding clouds, conditions compatible with his mood.

The railroad tracks had brought him to a block of low slung warehouses fronted by forklifts, pallets, tarps, tiers of iron, scrap lumber and a guard dog on its belly behind tall chain-link and concertina wire. The aromas of grease and pollutants strung out the damp air.

J.D. stopped and used his cap to wipe the sweat from his forehead. Taking a hit of Johnnie Walker, he scoped the area. The unpaved street he was on was free of traffic; he wondered if a curfew was in effect. Dark buildings loomed half a mile beyond the industrial grunge. Another mile or so along, the spotlights of two helicopters were probing what was probably the focal point of the extinguished riot; the evening was so quiet, he could hear their engines. He scowled and took another pull, killing the Johnnie Walker. Winding up, he threw the bottle as far as he could over the chain-link. The dog, a mush-faced brute, watched the bottle break then charged, barking hoarsely and salivating. J.D. casually took out his .38 and poked the barrel through the chain-link, sighting on the animal. "You are in an unenviable position, friend," he said. The dog was chained to a stake but kept trying to get at him, twisting and choking against the restraint. This was worthy of J.D.'s respect as well as his pity. He dug out what remained of his crackers and lobbed them over the fence, calming the beast. "Short rations," he sighed.

J.D. resumed walking—past amputated cars braced by two-by-

fours—gravitating toward the glow of neons a couple of blocks up
and over to his left. He twirled his .38, imagined bringing down one
of the choppers, passing the time until he reached the street,
DeJaynes, a stretch of rundown bars and other idle pleasures. The riot
hadn't reached this far—no debris, nothing burned out—but the citizens on the sidewalks were scattered and moving with ill defined
purpose, while a cruising squad car with straight up shotguns visible
offered evidence of unease.

Tucking the revolver in his coat pocket, J.D. looked around. A
joint whose logo read TOTAL NUDE and featured a sample blowing
the L was close, but he wasn't into futile hard-ons and five dollar
beaver tucks tonight. Down the street a drunk staggered out of something called FAT JACK'S and threw up on a stripped Chevy Nova.
J.D. believed this might be the sort of place where a man could sit in
vicious contemplation without running the risk of being flung out on
his ear.

The drunk was facedown, drooling on the dusty hood of the
Chevy. After checking for a pulse J.D. patted him on the arm then
sauntered into Fat Jack's, nodding at the few heads that turned. The
compact bar was somewhere between a club and a dive; a sense of
violence given a week off. Ten patrons were enjoying the slack. The
bartender, young and like everyone else, black, had on a pressed
white shirt and a pinned tie and appeared to be disciplined in other
ways as well; the floor and the small round tables were clean. A juke
with deep, lovely illumination was playing the Pointer sisters' *Yes We
Can Can*, a sexy beat selling brotherhood and love. Photos of third
string black notables crowded the wall to J.D.'s left, while the back
wall featured deadlight shutters and an anchor over a tank of exotic
fish, decor that seemed to belong to another establishment; nothing
else in the bar was nautical.

The bottles lined up behind the shiny mahogany counter gave off
dark, inviting colors. J.D. eased onto a stool and ordered a Bud,
spreading his money out while he waited for the bartender to return.

He had twenty three dollars and change left from last month's General Relief check. Short rations.

The bartender brought him his drink. Up close, the brother had tolerant eyes and the musculature to discourage the sporting and the rash. In the spirit of bonhomie, J.D. asked who Fat Jack was. The bartender said he didn't know. In the spirit of the bartender's response, J.D. gave him a nickel tip, adding that he'd almost shot a dog ten minutes ago. The bartender snickered and offered J.D. his back. When J.D. put away his money, he noticed there was a spot of the Asian clerk's blood on his pocket.

Sipping his beer, J.D. checked out the other customers. Down the counter two twitchy cats were jiving a pair of wide-eyed girls in halters and shorts. The girls had to be underage, and judging by their apparel and style, the cats were either bangers or wannabes wearing their cocks in their mouths. At the far end of the counter an old geek with a cigarette burning between his fingers was mumbling shit to the cleavage of a high-yaller redhead who was without question a pro. J.D. faced the rest of the room. A girl was dancing by herself in the spaces between the tables. Two studs in matching tight jeans and teeshirts were playing languid pool. A guy wearing frayed, beltless polyester pants, a lavender silk shirt and shades big as lakes was loudly setting pieces on a checkerboard at a back table.

J.D.'s gaze returned to the dancer. She was actually a woman, not a girl. Good looking, on the long side of thirty. Smooth black hair that fell to her shoulders, dark brown skin that held a certain splendor, snug green dress cut high and low, displaying her fine figure. Hugging herself, dreamy-eyed, she was swaying to the insistent beat of the music. Her head was nearly resting on her shoulder, but she didn't seem crazy or drunk, just going with the sweet sounds. On another night he might have tried his luck.

"Hey, you, with the hat."

J.D. turned to the velvety command. The guy in the shades had shifted his chair, so that he was facing him.

"That's right, man, I'm talking to you. You a player?"

The challenge was friendly and teasing. J.D. felt like he was being wooed. Smiling, he lifted his brows and his Bud to the man. "One never knows."

The bartender was the only one paying any attention to the exchange. "Go on, play him," he urged, getting close to J.D.'s ear. "Maybe you'll get your nickel back."

"Don't be bitter, babe," J.D. said. "I found it in the street. Bring you luck."

"Go on," the bartender insisted.

J.D. rolled his neck then took his drink to the back table and sat down. The man pushed his shades up onto his forehead and grinned, revealing several gold teeth. He had a short torso and stubby arms and he was losing his hair and his gray-brown face was lumpy and he had bags; pockets for kinky greed, if you went by the gleam in his amber eyes. Reaching across the board he offered J.D. a childlike hand.

"Name's Harold."

J.D. shook Harold's hand, which was soft and clammy and easily lost in the palm.

"J.D. We doing this for money or each other's fine company?"

"Take your pick."

"I can spare a nickel."

"So can I."

They each placed a coin by the side of the board. Harold pushed his shades down onto his nose and they began to play.

"Why'd you almost shoot the dog?" Harold asked.

"You heard?"

"I got good ears."

"A passing impulse," J.D. told him.

"I had a dog once."

J.D. waited for Harold to elaborate, but he didn't.

"Way you're dressed, looks to me like you're going to war. What kind of piece you packing?"

"Your move," J.D. said.

"What you're wearing, could be a howitzer."

"Your move."

"Like I said, you look like you're going to war."

"I was hoping."

J.D. turned his head to the dancer. She was selecting another song on the juke, bent down in a way that offered her rear, a perfect roundness.

"That's worth staring," Harold said angrily, "but it's your move."

J.D. reluctantly faced the board. The Stones' *Jumping Jack Flash* filled the void between himself and the dancer, punctuated by the crack of billiard balls and giggles from the counter. He and Harold were evenly matched. It was obvious the game was going to be a draw, but they kept on maneuvering anyway.

"What were you hoping?" Harold asked.

"That things wouldn't quiet down," J.D. said, "but they did."

"They'll start up again."

"When?"

"When it gets good and dark."

"How do you know?"

Harold smiled slyly. He had an odd mouth, the upper lip thin, the lower fat, like a fish that had been hooked often. The eyes, the mouth, the body; a character out of a cartoon. Harold's gaze lingered on J.D., as though aware of the appraisal, before he said smugly, "Harold knows everything."

Harold made a move that seemed designed to confuse matters. J.D. looked absently around the room. The pool studs were comparing tattoos. The dancer was rocking lightly to the Stones, making no attempt to flaunt her sex. Her arms were folded over her stomach, as if she were trying to prevent an ache of serious intent from climbing to her heart. His gaze reached the counter, where the hustlers were telling sweet lies to the jailbait, leaning in lower and closer to the girls. The hooker and her trick were gone. The geek's cigarette was disintegrating in his unfinished drink.

J.D. realized that his opponent was touching his arm. "Besides, it's the word on the streets," Harold said confidentially.

This lifted J.D.'s spirits. He started to play as though it were possible to win.

"Like your clothes," Harold told him in that smooth voice.

"Do you now."

"I was in the war."

"Which one?" J.D. asked, as he removed two of Harold's checkers from the board.

Harold laughed. "The only one either of us could've been in. I mean, we're around the same age, right?"

J.D. looked up. He was forty six. Harold had to be at least ten years older.

"Right," J.D. said. "I take it you're talking Southeast Asia?" His eyes were back on the board. There was the laughter of approaching copulation from the bar.

"That's the one," Harold said.

"What year?"

"Late sixties."

"Where?"

"Where it was heavy, man, where it was heavy." Harold laughed dryly. "I could tell you stories."

"I imagine you could."

J.D. knew the man had never seen combat.

"Things I seen done to my buddies. Ugly memories you never can shake loose."

"Must be hard."

The man had never even crossed the ocean.

"Shit, you can say that again," Harold said. "You in the war?"

"Naw, but I had friends," J.D. answered.

"So you heard."

"Often."

"Looks like a draw, don't it."

"Looks like it."

"You want to play another?"

"I have to piss."

"Come back."

"I will."

J.D. got up and went to the john to shoot up. The Stones followed him down a short, dark hallway that smelled of wax and ammonia. He heard sobs from inside the restroom before he could open the door, the sounds spaced by a staggered emotion. He started to go back to Harold then curiosity took him inside.

There was a sink, a mirror, a urinal, a stall and the whore and the geek. The whore was standing with her dress down to her waist, the geek was on his knees and forearms at her feet, with his pants around his ankles. His cock was flaccid, the wiry hair on his balls was gray and white. So was the stringy hair on his head. His forehead was pressed to the floor and his fists were clenched and he couldn't seem to stop crying.

J.D. and the whore stared at each other. She had never been good looking but she must have looked better at one time. She had false lashes, too much makeup, and glossy red hair that had to be dyed or a wig. Her breasts were large and sloping; the pale pink of her nipples was in sharp contrast to her blackness. She had track marks on both arms but her legs were long and unblemished.

The Stones were remote but still working the room. The whore shrugged and smiled at J.D., her teeth pink with her lipstick. Something about the whole scene excited him and he stepped around the geek and eased her into a corner, where she began stroking his balls and dick through his pants.

When he was as hard as he'd ever been, she pulled his pants and shorts down to his ankles and started to blow him, but J.D. positioned her on her hands and knees. She reached back and squeezed his balls while he fucked her like a dog. He was surprised at how wet she was; she seemed to be getting off as much as he was. They caught each other's rhythm, their breathing harsh and reaching, the sweat light on their bodies. Looking up, J.D. could see parts of himself shifting hazily in the streaked and tarnished mirror. He frowned at his reflection then pressed his body to the hooker's back, his rough face and cap brushing against her smooth red hair. Her wig slipped and she straightened it with one hand and finished what they'd started without once uttering a word. The geek never lifted his head from the floor or stopped crying.

The whore checked her wig and fixed her lipstick in the mirror while J.D. pulled up his shorts and pants. Slipping into his coat he left his works in his pocket; the whore had been, for the moment, enough of a high. She was down comforting her trick by the time he left, saying, "There, there, baby, it's alright, everythang gon' be O.K.," more sweet lies.

Harold was finishing J.D.'s beer out front. The juke was silent. The lady in green was leaning on the counter, talking earnestly to the bartender.

That perfect roundness.

Harold looked up, his eyes hidden behind his shades, where J.D. could once again see his own distorted image. "What'd it cost you?" Harold asked. Foam was on his mouth.

"Less than what's on the table," J.D. told him.

"I'll buy you another."

"Not what I meant," J.D. replied.

Harold wiped the residue of beer from his mismatched lips.

"Have a seat."

Placing a red checker on a black square, J.D. sat. "Something I'm asking for the sake of asking . . ." He could smell the whore's perfume on his body. Harold seemed to catch the scent too. Wrinkling his nose in disgust he folded his short arms across his chest and leaned back.

"Such as?"

"Who would a man see if he was looking to cause some righteous trouble tonight?"

Harold shook his head. "Not me. I seen all the trouble I'm seeing in Nam." His eyes were lost behind his shades.

"I was just saying."

"For the sake. Serious trouble?"

"Major league."

Harold sighed, took off his glasses and cleaned the lenses with the hem of his silk shirt. "This looks like another draw, don't it," he said.

"Nature of the game."

Placing his glasses on the table, Harold fished an ink stained pen out of his pants pocket. "You got something to write on?" he asked, tapping the pen on the side of the table.

"No."

Harold sighed again then went to the bar and returned with a cocktail napkin. Sitting, he put his shades back on and jotted something down.

"I got light-sensitive eyes. It's a curse." He handed the napkin to J.D. The address was on East 92nd.

"How far is this?"

"One block west, six blocks north," Harold told him. "Eight Trey Rangers would be closer and better, but they'd probably shoot you before you could even knock."

"Thanks." J.D. folded the napkin and tucked it in the left pocket of his coat, where his works were. Pushing away from the table, he started to leave.

"You weren't in the war, why do you wear those pants and boots and that cap?" Harold's question was almost a challenge. J.D. stared stonily at him then manufactured a harmless smile.

"Helps get coins in the cup," he said, a hustler's response that made Harold happy. J.D. gave him a snappy farewell salute, flat hand to the sagging bill of his cap, and walked. Before he got to the door, there were sounds of heavy violence from the john, thumps and the whore's fierce shrieks.

J.D. pulled down his cap and kept on walking.

Ben was passing a street he'd never seen. He pulled over and spread his Thomas Guide out on the passenger seat. East 67th. Streets that were numbers instead of names bothered him. Names suggested cozy communities, numbers suggested the inner city. The area ahead looked the same as what surrounded him, rows of neat tract homes. There was security in their conformity and he drove on, his headlights gradually getting brighter in the growing darkness. He glanced at himself in the rearview mirror. Last week he'd noticed gray in his hair. He stole another look but didn't linger. It was getting to where he hated his own face.

He felt dazed by life. He needed the distraction of the radio, something familiar to anchor him, all the news, all the time. According to police sources the ghetto was going to explode again soon, possibly tonight. He tried to visualize the cops working the streets. They would be young blacks with the moves of third basemen. Hot corner. Dive for that bullet down the line, throw the runner out from your knees. When Ben was a kid they had put him in the outfield, where he'd shied away from flies and pitches that crowded him. Maggie had lettered in three sports and fierce cello.

Down the block, ringed by the pale, skewed glow from a streetlamp, a kid was sitting on his hands on a bus bench. Around fifteen. White, like the faces in the cars passing by. White like Ben's car. A Buick Skylark. Eight years old. Lasted longer than his marriage. Ben stopped and showed the kid David's picture. The kid hadn't seen him. Ben got back behind the wheel and drove on.

More tract homes eased by, neutral, reassuring colors. Fragments of a John Mellencamp song came to him. Little pink houses. Vacationing in the Gulf of Mexico. Little pink houses for you and me. But ain't that America.

When he and Maggie were first married, before David, they'd bought a fixer-upper. On the weekends they would roll up their sleeves and jeans and work dawn to dusk, caulking, plastering, railing, restoring. In the evenings they would make love on the stairs, in the kitchen, on paint spattered sheets. Little pink houses. For you and me.

A light went on in a bay window. Ben could see parents and kids. Everyone looked happy. A sprinkler was tossing lazy arcs of water on their lawn, and something of the freshness, the perfection of mown grass filtered through the vents of his financed, unwashed vehicle. Ain't that America. He saw this as a question. Mellencamp had vocal splits that stressed the disparity between dreams and reality.

Ben approached an intersection. The light turned red and he stopped, hitting the pedal harder than he intended, enduring a brief skid. Explode. That was what they'd said on the radio, wasn't it? He could see the whole city disappearing in a shock of white light and mushrooming flame. He had grown up when the bomb was still a cataclysmic threat, when words that now had only local significance promised Armageddon.

The light changed and he drove on, the engine coughing then calming. He needed a tune-up. When he had time. A flight pattern of birds crossed over the low pale moon. Going south. There was moisture on his windshield and he turned his wipers on. The blades snicked and the glass smeared. He turned the wipers off.

It had been raining on their first date. The windows of his car had been blind with water. Back then bad weather had seemed romantic, an adventure. She had sat close to him. Caught briefly by passing headlights, the beauty of her young face had taken away his breath, a moment of movie magic.

East 69th changed to East 70th. Streets should have names.

Homes should have families. Cities should stay whole. He couldn't get his thoughts to connect. He pulled over to the curb.

He had to stop to keep from breaking down.

J.D. liked the looks of the street. East 92nd. Lampposts casting long shadows on the sidewalks in the calm light. Steam issuing from a grate in the pavement. Broken bottles. Crumpled old papers. Two cats of the smaller species fucking in an alley. The promise of refuse, quick sex and blood and, in the brick tenements, of intrigue, of cats of the larger species waiting for the right moment to howl.

He walked to a streetlamp, where he could read Harold's napkin. The number on it was 753. J.D. checked the progression. 753 was half way down the block. He watched his shadow lengthen until he was out of the light. The cats had quieted down. His bootsteps, soft from the aging of the leather, were the only sounds. He realized he was walking solo. Another no man's land.

753 was a two storied, concrete building made decrepit by neglect. The letters over the entrance said Youth Opportunity Center. Orange rinds and a week of newspapers were piled up at the padlocked door and the many windows were dark.

Harold's careful directions took him to an alley on the far side, where he saw garbage spilling out of a dumpster and graffiti marking turf on a wall; Nine Deuce Crips. Sketched blood dripped from a three foot knife under the large letters, which were illuminated by the moon.

An arrow on the napkin led up fire-escape stairs. J.D.'s gaze followed the steps to a door where light seeped out from under the crack.

When he was just past the dumpster, he heard quick movement behind it. He felt the muzzle of a gun pressed against his head before he could turn.

"Where you goin', motherfucker?" The voice behind the gun was adolescent. J.D. felt his face heat up. Surprised by a kid. He was getting old, out of practise. His embarrassment made him bold.

"You live there or you just breeding, baby?"

The kid cocked the gun. The click of the hammer was sharp in J.D.'s ear.

"What you say, nigger?"

"That I'm glad to make your acquaintance." J.D. felt the sweat gathering on his skin. He held his arms away from his body as the kid's free hand groped inside his pocket. The kid yanked out J.D.'s .38 then the clerk's .32.

"You looking to fuck with someone?" The voice had bass breaks; J.D. could hear the boy becoming a man on the spot.

"Not with you, son."

The kid's gun dropped to J.D.'s back and shoved him forward.

"Up the stairs, nigger."

The gun walked him up. His footsteps and the kid's were tinny on the corrugated risers. When they reached the top of the stairs, J.D. felt the gun's barrel shift to his side as the kid eased around him and knocked in code on a corroded door. The kid offered some dubious solace while they waited.

"Don't be real hard on yourself, mijo. I'm a genius of sneak."

"Most of what passes for genius nowadays," J.D. said, "is brag and bullshit."

The gun's muzzle dug into his side.

"You pushing it, man."

"I know. Habit." He could probably take the kid if he moved fast.

Footsteps lazed across a floor and the door creaked open on loose hinges and the gun prodded J.D. into a large room designed for recreation. The lighting was conspiratorial, fanning out from a bare ceiling bulb flickering with the certainty of a short life. Long gray coats not unlike J.D.'s were parked in a corner, next to weapons of repeating prowess. The graffiti on the sallow walls celebrated the joys of fellatio with strangers. The pinups were ecumenical in flavor.

A dozen bangers were scattered around the room, occupied in various desultory pursuits: Directly under the bulb, seeming to collect all the glare on his exceptionally black skin, a stone stud J.D. pegged as their leader was straddling a collapsible chair at a foldout table and cleaning his nails with a penknife. Near the door a fat geek with a blue bandana tied sloppily around his head was reading a comic book whose cover showed good and evil on steroids. Off in a corner a cold-eyed cat sitting on his heels was sorting through a large pile of groceries. Two of the bangers were playing ping pong; the net and the walls were winning. Three husky gumps seemed to be searching the stale air for their minds while others were freebasing, carefully measuring portions of liquid and powder onto a spoon and feeling their arms for whatever veins hadn't collapsed before striking a match. J.D. found this distasteful. He was old fashioned, preferred shooting straight in without the preliminaries.

"Look what the cat dragged in," his captor said proudly. No one else seemed to particularly care. Looking at the kid for the first time, J.D. saw a rickets-skinny, curly haired boy a little under five feet and dressed like the others; dirty expensive sneakers, and a blue teeshirt cut off at the shoulders and tucked into bleached out jeans. He had a tagger's marking pen sticking out of a pocket, thyroid eyes and hints of mixed blood and lunacy. J.D. figured he was around twelve, give or take a year.

"My humiliations are coming younger all the time," J.D. said. He realized he'd said it out loud.

The kid's eyes bulged grotesquely. "You really pushing it, mijo." The gun was roaming in his hand. J.D.'s back throbbed in anticipation of a bullet, the shearing of his insides. Despite his habits, that wasn't what he wanted, not yet. As a diversion he gestured to the players. "Sorry. Hey, man, look at that." He sensed the kid's eyes drifting to the ball's flight. One of the bangers was using a sponge paddle, the other bare wood; the sounds went kiss and smack, kiss and smack. A slam ticked the white border of the table. "Sweet shot," J.D. whistled.

"Me, I'd call it rare luck."

J.D. faced the speaker. The stud had large link gold around his neck, a gold ring on a little finger, a comb in his short Afro, flat features almost native American, muscles on muscles and a smoky glass eye. 92 CRIPS was tattooed on his left arm, a cock shaped like a dagger was tattooed on his right arm, and Porsche sun glasses were at his elbow. J.D. hadn't misread him; a true leader of men, even in the offhand way he gestured:

"Who the fuck is he?"

"Don't know," the kid answered, "but he had this g'd-up shit on him."

The twelve year old displayed the .38 and the .32. The stud closed the penknife, leaned back and folded his arms across his broad chest. He and the kid were looking at J.D. with curiosity. They were a three-way. None of the others gave fuck all.

The stud lifted his deep voice, revealing a range. "You coming here like my enemy, old man?"

That age thing again. J.D. could live with it. "Who's your enemy?" he said, smiling with peace in his heart.

The cat smiled back, Cheshire grin sparkling in the twitchy bright light. Good teeth. Probably capped. " 'Bout anyone you can name," he said, his smile spreading.

J.D. could like this man. One of the players chasing the bouncing ball paused to hand J.D. a foldout chair which he took to the small table. He sat opposite the grin.

"Let me guess. You're the boss man here, right?"

The grin grew wider, the penknife tapped a tooth. "Boss man? You jus' off the plantation, dad?"

Fathers and sons. J.D. was being called a lot of things tonight. Clasping his smooth hands on the table, he smiled.

"Lansing, Michigan, actually, but I'm an observer of the habits of people."

This kept the stud amused. "Yeah?" he said, as though J.D.'s remark offered an opportunity. There was a sharp, cool intelligence in his good eye, although his glass eye, gleaming in the overhead light, seemed to take on a malevolent life of its own. "Name's Slope." He put up his hand and J.D. gave him a tepid soul shake and introduced himself.

"J.D.?"

"James Donald."

"Any chance you O.G.B., James Donald?" Slope asked. "Green derbies, starched peggers?"

"O.G.B.?"

Both of Slope's eyes gleamed. "No, guess you ain't. Original Gang Blood," he explained.

"Doesn't suit my nature," J.D. said, "though I have to admit I was tempted to pick your lock out front, but then that would've demonstrated skills offensive to the race."

"Not in this neighborhood." Slope shifted his big body to the kid. "Let me see the weapons, Nine."

"Nine?" J.D. said, lifting his brows. "That's his name?"

"Half of it," Slope replied.

The kid gave him J.D.'s guns then left to shag balls for the players, whose shadows jerked on a wall. Setting the .32 down on the table, Slope turned the .38 over in his palm. J.D. heard a loud pop behind him. Turning, he saw the twelve-year-old scraping bubble gum off his teeth.

"Cavities, kid," J.D. said. "A few years of that and you'll be chewing with your roots."

The kid looked at him insolently, blew and popped another giant bubble. "Ain't no thing."

J.D. heard a click. Sounds were choosing his direction. He turned again; Slope had snapped open the cylinder of his .38. Seeing that the chambers were primed, he looked up at J.D. with mild surprise.

"Why you come into my home like some damn gump on fucking dust?"

"Because I'm a victim of needs and desires?"

Slope stared at him in a way that could level the soul and J.D. decided that it was prudent to avert his eyes. The heat from the overhead bulb penetrated his skin, but the light in the rest of room seemed cool, shade for the freebasers, who were nodding off. The ping pong ball slapped into the net and died on the sporting table. Shadows twitched and the gum went pop.

"You dissing me?"

Slope's voice had assumed an edge. J.D. glanced at him with what he hoped would pass for field hand humility. He could see Slope wasn't buying that shit.

"I'm just explaining the reason for my behavior," J.D. said carefully. "Needs and desires."

Slope pulled a face and looked away. "My, my, my. You ain't 'xactly a fuck all example for my generation." He almost sounded disappointed.

"No," J.D. said. "I'm a fuck all example of what went wrong."

Slope snickered then opened his knife and went back to cleaning his nails. "Let's cut the gaming," he snarled. "What you want, man? Who the fuck pointed you here?"

"Harold."

"From Fat Jack's?"

"I take it you know him."

"Like I know every other damn gump on the block. He blow you?"

"We played checkers."

Slope's laugh shrilled. "That's the start," he said. J.D. realized that not all of the pinups were women. Slope fingered his dark glasses.

"Know what Harold's other trouble is?"

J.D. shook his head.

"His shades," Slope told him. "They from K-Mart."

"Thought we were done gaming."

Slope took in J.D. and laughed again then hunched forward, knees pressing against the bottom of the table, the size of him blotting out the rest of the room. "Okay, let's walk it back," he said softly. "What you want? 'Sides love."

"Blood on the streets," J.D. replied.

Slope looked at him for a long moment, then leaned back and returned to his nails.

"That's coming."

"When?"

"Soon."

"Look outside," J.D. said. "It's dark."

Slope's good eye briefly took in J.D. "You been watching TV. TV don't set my watch."

J.D. realized that Slope had no more intention of bringing blood to the streets than the bus driver had of taking him all the way. At a loss for words he looked around the room. One of the dopers had gone to sleep, his head resting on the shoulder of a neighbor who was about to join him. The twelve year old was chasing the ball; he pinned it against the floor like a slow, small bird.

"We'll be making plans," Slope was saying, even softer than before under the flickering light. "Come round later maybe." The knife scraped under his nail. When he glanced at J.D., he looked embarrassed.

"I'll do that," J.D. said. "Can I have my guns?"

"They hot?"

"The .32."

Slope ran his thumb lovingly over the barrel of the .38.

"This blood?"

"Afraid so."

"Fresh?"

J.D. shook his head.

"Old, just like me."

Slope tucked the .38 deep into his own waistband. "The price of admission, nigger." He handed J.D. the .32. "Like I said, come back later."

"Like I said, I will."

J.D. stuck the gun in his coat pocket as he got up and walked. The ball bounced off his leg but he ignored it. He went down the stairs, bitterly humming the bus driver's tune. I am constantly being disappointed by people, he told himself. God's fucking will.

Ben tried to make out the street sign as he drove by. An 8 and a 2. East. East was declining at an alarming rate. No more pink houses with neat lawns. Vacant lots of dirt and weeds instead, black faces replacing white, in the passing cars, on the billboards pushing smokes and liquor; the landscape was definitely changing. A family in a clunker cut around him. Riding in the back, a young girl whose hair was in a pageboy craned her neck toward Ben, staring at him with a blend of hostility and yearning.

Ben went past a market whose windows were smashed in and his stomach jumped and his spine tingled. He turned up the radio. Fears had been scaled down. The mayor and the police were confident that the rioting was over. The news gave Ben the courage to go on.

His tank was over half full but he hadn't flashed the snap of David in a while. There was a Mobil station up ahead. Ben pulled into Full Serve. An old black man burdened with greasy overalls was closing up, shutting down the service bay. He waved Ben off. Ben shrugged helplessly. The old man frowned and trundled to Ben's window with a hitch in his heavy stride. He put the nozzle in the tank and used a squeegee on the windows, struck Ben as a conscientious person, since it was obvious he'd rather have left Ben on empty and blind.

Ben showed the old man David's picture, expecting nothing. The man gave Ben the picture and his change and said the boy had been here. Wandered in dusty and lost about an hour ago. The old man had given him a soda and gentled him about where he belonged, but the boy never said a word. Just stared at him with big, faraway eyes, then walked off. Ben weakly asked which way he'd gone. The old man pointed south. Ben thanked him in a whisper and drove out of the station. His heart pounding, he looked up. The sky had deepened to a blue black and dark clouds were set in wild explosions.

Arletha Mae glanced at the sky while she walked. The black clouds and damp air were a comfort, promising rain. She hitched Jason up on her left side, her groceries up on her right, keeping their weight balanced as she hurried on through the project where there hadn't been no folk for months. The dark empty windows round her were like eyes watching her every step, but she wasn't scared, no way; the fine feeling at Springer Baptist had done chased her sin and her fears. Smiling, she breathed in the night and the natural God given smell of the dirt under her feet. The light from the low fat moon guided her through the shadows 'til she reached a breaking down building where she heard something moving 'bout inside. Nothing but a mean ol' rat, she told herself, but won't do no harm to look. Taking another kind of deep breath, she started through the doorway, laughed without realizing she had when she saw the cop on the toilet, then she dropped her groceries and her hand shot up to her mouth in fright. Way he was reaching back, she thought he was going to pull out his gun and shoot her and Jason dead and dead.

CHAPTER SEVEN

J.D. was lord of the city. He was sitting on top of a dream of his youth, a 1968 Mustang Mach 1 with maroon primer paint and cams, and he had blood on his arm and a hard-on in his soul and you could walk those mixed blessings down a helluva lot of roads.

The clearness of the syringe became muddy with his fluid. "I am a fucking white cowboy and I've lost my girl and my horse," he sang to himself as he gently withdrew the needle from the large vein. He had gone in light, half a load, because he needed control for what he was going to do.

He also needed this, God but he needed it; the kick was already coursing through him, lifting him past disappointment and despair. The rush swirled through his head. Clenching his fists, he squeezed his eyes shut to slow its pace. Black devils danced on heavy cloven feet before his sealed off vision. Total Nude. My my my. I am a fucking . . . what the fuck am I? He squeezed his eyes shut tighter. I am sitting on the roof of a '68 Ford wearing a nine saddle bronc Stetson and I'm seeing Elvis and every other fluffed up saint and I'm seeing charred snow and damn but it's turning to peanut butter slush, and

89

now I am seeing the bullet twist her, opening her, and my mouth is open but I can't scream.

J.D. shook his head fiercely to shed the unconnected visions. His eyes were on fire. Brushing at his lashes, he was amazed there weren't any flames. He drew down his eyelids with his fingertips and red dots spun through the blindness. The dots became coins slipping through his fingers, then the dots became poker chips, and inside his eyes his hands were dealing out cards fast as a machine, and he needed a queen to fill an inside straight, but no matter how many cards he dealt, he couldn't find a lady for his life.

J.D. sucked in his breath and held the air as long as he could, which wasn't long, then exhaled. Maybe he'd gone in heavier than he thought, or maybe it was the mix of Johnnie Walker and nickel scag. He had this knack of bringing himself down if he concentrated hard enough. Assuming the lotus position, he lowered his head, kept his eyes closed, gave the images more agreeable shapes. He saw himself squatting in a boxcar, watching the country blur by, absently shuffling a deck as he gazed out at fallow fields through the half-open door. One time in Vegas, while passing through, he'd won over four thousand dollars in a whiskey driven drama of seven-card stud and believed luck had finally turned onto his corner. Next day he left town so broke, he had to pawn his zebra-striped fedora.

Pressing his hands down on his knees, he took another bracing breath. He felt better. I am under control. He willed himself to say the words, said them slowly and out loud until they were true. From somewhere close a cooing noise climbed up from the pavement like the heat.

That's not me.

I don't think.

I am under control.

He opened his eyes and swiped at the sweat. Must be near nine but the day's heat had hung around. His feet and neck and sides felt sticky. He stretched out his legs, flattening them against the Mustang's roof, and opened his coat, taking care with the buttons, as though this was a ritual that must be done right. Patting his shirt, he was amazed by the extent of the dampness; he was soaked. I can live with this, he told himself. It's only me, what I am. He gazed at the sky, at the closed eye of the moon, winked at it, thought he saw the moon wink back; both got our secrets, don't we, chum.

The cooing returned and he lowered his sight to the street. East whatever. Three parked cars, barred dark shops, a gas station and a pigeon, the source of the cooing. The pigeon was strutting along the sidewalk, one wary eye on J.D., the other eye keen for crumbs. "Hi there, motherfucker," J.D. said. For this creature he had nothing but love in his heart. The bird flew off at the sound of his voice and landed a short distance away. J.D. sighed. Next time you're dead, motherfucker. He stared idly down at his boots. Time to hump. Tucking his works back inside his coat, he jumped to the ground, the cement stinging the balls of his feet. Starting down the sidewalk, he caught his dark reflection in a pawn-shop window. Looked real mean: Long, loose coat, Clint Eastwood in a spaghetti western. He faced himself in the window, pushed back his coat and fast drew the .32 out of his waistband. "Pow," he said. "Pow."

When she was shot, the blood had burst through her hair like a flower.

Pow. He kept the gun sighted on his dead image. On hers. I am a fucking cowboy in love with the idea of love and that idea goes back twenty years. I am a fucking child.

Sticking the .32 back in his waistband, he resumed walking, clocking the street and the area beyond. Where the fuck is everybody? Staying inside or away, even the cops. Keeping a low profile, trying not to provoke things. Sensible tactic. Should work, except with someone who doesn't give fuck all.

Her hair was down to her waist yet the blood had covered its length.

He heard the low growl of an engine. Looking over his shoulder he saw headlights crawling toward him and two men silhouetted behind a windshield. J.D. carelessly buttoned the lower half of his coat, concealing the gun, and kept on walking. The headlights stretched gradually past him as the growl crept closer until it seemed like it was in his hip pocket. He sensed more than saw the car stop, level with him. "Say there?" a voice called. He kept walking. The car followed. "Hey bro?" He stopped and waited, not looking over even after he heard the engine idle.

"Say there, we're kinda lost."

J.D. faced the speaker; the man's head was sticking out the partially open window.

"You wouldn't happen to know where Strathern is, now would you?"

Both men were black, both were wearing gray sweats. Could be citizens, could be undercover. The passenger was young but with more wrinkles than the driver, who looked about forty. Their car was a brown and tan Plymouth with swept back fins and nickel plating. J.D. didn't see a dome light.

"Strathern and what?"

"East Sixty-third," the passenger said.

J.D. motioned north with his left hand. "Think it's somewhere that way, down near the railroad tracks."

"Thanks," the driver said.

J.D. resumed walking. Pow. The sound was a beast prowling through his brain and the black devils then Elvis held the leash. That's not me, I don't think, I am under control, he told himself, willing the images to disappear. The Plymouth went a few feet past him.

"Say?"

J.D. and the car stopped. The driver turned off his engine and rolled his window down the rest of the way. J.D. scanned the interior of the car. Styrofoam containers and greasy wrappers were on the back seat.

"Where you going?" the driver asked.

"Home," J.D. answered. He wondered why the car's upholstery was turning into lava, why the plating was drooling.

"Where's home?"

"Not far."

The beast had moved down to his back.

"You want a ride?"

"No, man, I'm fine. Like I said, it's not far."

The driver didn't say anything but didn't look ready to leave. His friend leaned in slow motion toward J.D.

"You sure? You don't want to get busted. You know there's a curfew tonight."

Definitely undercover, J.D. thought. "No. I didn't know," he replied. The beast crawled down his legs.

The young one laughed in a way that could give laughter a bad name. "Man, where *have* you been?"

"Minding my own business," J.D. answered. His skin was on fire, but only he could see the flames.

"Exactly what is your business?" the driver asked politely.

"I'm a purveyor of love."

The young one's brow furrowed and his blank chocolate eyes narrowed. "A purveyor of what?"

"Pick up what and where I can. Scuff and sweat." The beast was on the ground. J.D. tried to nudge it away with a foot.

"What're you doing?" the driver asked with an uncomfortable laugh. J.D. stopped moving his boot.

"Nothing."

The young one's eyes got so small, J.D. couldn't see them. "You on something?" he asked J.D. J.D. leaned in closer, but still couldn't see the eyes; perhaps the pigeon had pecked them out. He worked at braking the slide of his speech and his mind.

"Run that by me again?"

The young one raised his voice and emphasized his words. "I said are you on something?"

"Fuck no," J.D. swore, a little too loud. The .32 in his pocket was an option. He blinked and the man's eyes returned to their normal size. J.D. smiled and said, "What do you think?" as he eased his hand away from his coat.

The young one frowned. "I don't know."

"Anyway," the driver said nervously, "there is a curfew."

"Since eight," his friend added.

The driver said, "It's been on the radio."

"Guess I better hurry along then."

The driver leaned out the window. "You said it's close?"

"Two blocks."

The driver's gaze took in J.D.'s fatigues.

"You do a tour?"

"Uh uh. These are from Surplus."

"Guess we're holding you up," the young one said.

"Yeah," J.D. said amiably. He was in control, the holder of the leash; the knowledge swept coolly over him.

The driver faced the road and turned on the ignition. "Okay," he said. "Get home safe."

"You too."

J.D. watched the unmarked car drive off. When the Plymouth reached the intersection just before the gas station, the car stopped even though the light was green. He could see the dark forms of the two cops. The passenger leaned in close to the driver, who nodded and adjusted his rearview. He seemed to be studying J.D. in the mirror. The driver remained motionless for a moment, then the light turned red and the Plymouth swung a left, picked up speed and disappeared from sight. J.D. made sure they were gone when he reached the intersection, then crossed to the station, a mom-and-pop operation, two beat-up red pumps and a glass shack, deep South funk in another part of the nation. All the lights were out.

J.D. felt combat ready. Traveling unencumbered. Snake patrol. Strike and draw back. Most the time in Nam you hefted sixty plus pounds. And humped. Man, the miles. Grunts earned the name. He took off his cap and blew on its creases for luck before putting it back on. Over there you wore your cap in the safer zones. In country, government issued steel stayed on your head even when the heat turned your hair into a swamp.

He took out the .32 and balanced it in his palm. Moonlight glanced off its silver bossing like magic, like the way a horn shone when the jazz was jamming just right. J.D. laughed at himself; well, motherfucker, you are juicing this situation past all reason. Music and magic, shit. The .32 was pussy heat for chicks' shoulder bags, and you are a fool chasing something that's been dead for twenty years. Fuck it, he told himself. Fuck it, he told the chemicals and needs that were skidding across his nerves.

The bus token from Welfare was still in his pocket. That would get him back to The Paradise where he belonged. Do a gallery with Bobby. Bang out riffs of delusion on his crazy ofay skull, maybe frag a roach or two. Leave all the memories behind.

When she was shot, her eyes had grazed him for a second before they went blank.

He was walking. There was a bench out there somewhere, a place to rest. Maybe the two plainclothes brothers would swing back and give him a lift. Cells could be comfort stops. Bunk camaraderie. Not much different from a hooch. Trading off whispers and items of mild mercy, the rag ends of hope.

He had printed KIA on the snapshots of her that he had in his rucksack, on hers and Henry's.

There was a train whistle in the distance, forlorn, as all train whistles were meant to be. The whistle made him pause. He saw it as a sign. He looked up at the moon. Its perfect roundness was draped in black clouds. He saw this too as a sign. That bus would have to wait.

Walking back to the station he took out the .32. He could shoot directly into a pump but the result would be uncertain. Maybe only a ricochet or a bent shell drowning. There had to be a way to do it clean, do it right.

He placed the gun's barrel against one of the pumps, the muzzle on the key lock. Drawing breath he pulled the trigger, felt the kick travel halfway up his arm as the gun popped. When he opened his eyes, the lock was gone and the red paint was scored and smoke and cordite were in his nostrils. He shoved the handle from off to on and watched the meter's numbers roll to zeroes.

His eyes roamed the station and fixed on a plastic bucket with a squeegee and brown stained water. This is meant to be, he told himself, things are there for me. He tossed aside the squeegee and emptied the bucket, stepping back so that the water wouldn't touch his feet; keep it clean. Removing the hose's grip from its hook, he stuck the nozzle in the bucket and squeezed the grip's trigger, releasing the pressure when the bucket was full. The meter stopped at a buck seventy-nine.

J.D. placed the hose on the ground and walked the bucket away from the pump, pouring an even trail of gasoline on the pavement. He liked the rich, metallic fermented smell; machines could get drunk same as people. "I am a poor lonesome Harley and I've lost my saddle and my wheels," he sang softly until the bucket was empty. The moon was directly overhead. He felt steeped in holy light.

He needed something with a cutting edge. A rusted, punctured oil drum was on a flank of the shack and he went there and picked through the greasy paper towels and crumpled soda-pop cans until he found a bent windshield wiper blade. Things were there for him. He was blessed. The gasoline's spoor stretched forty or so feet back to the hose. Pulling the rubber off the blade like a wing off a fly, he retraced his steps. Cocking the .32 he fired again. The bullet sliced through the hose but not entirely. He bent down and awkwardly sawed with the wiper blade until he was able to separate the hose from the nozzle. Then he placed the ragged end of the hose on the ground, at the shoreline of gas. The air was getting cooler. Where his coat was open, he could feel it seeping through to his skin. Be so much easier to catch that bus back to The Paradise, he thought suddenly. He was on one knee now, the book of liquor store matches in his hand. He'd been down there before.

First time was when he was eight months. Had these urges to walk, only on the knees was easier. Got some rug burns to remember for his efforts. His momma found it funny. Called him Short Step, said hobbling 'long like that would stunt his growth. She had this strange, fucked up sense of humor. J.D. guessed that came from his father leaving before he was born. His momma called his daddy Walk Round. Had the wanderlust. Momma said one of these days he'd walk round 'til he fell off the world. Said she hoped there wasn't no net to stop his fall.

J.D. could forgive her her bitterness. She raised him best she could. Supported them slaving as a clerk typist. Flying fingers. Man, but she was fast. If she could've glued love to a keyboard, she might have kept up with his old man. Not that she was perfect. Sex was her downfall, sex and liquor. A lot of uncles and bottles passed through that door. He would hear the sounds in her room at night. A few of the cats were good enough to make her beat on the walls. 'God, you bastard, God;' this litany of profanity and prayer. Fuck me, daddy, eight to the bar.

He got on the sauce himself when he was fourteen, Ripple the older guys bought as a favor. Helped him sleep through the long nights. Momma was consumed by a fury when she started smelling it on his morning breath. Bounced him off the walls. Sobbed and slapped him around with those fast hands. The tears dried up pretty quick. After all, who was she to lecture?

Got to where they'd drink together. Once in a while, when the demon was really coiled around her loins, she'd even flirt. Slide on down her chair with the Johnnie Walker tucked between her breasts and play Lets-count-toes under the kitchen table. Never went any further, though a few times she had him wondering.

Despite his habits J.D. was good in school. He was smart, smart enough to cruise through any damn lesson on fumes. He made his teachers nervous but they passed him. At times he felt like this thing that walked through the nightmares of everyone around him.

He cut down on the booze when he was seventeen. That was enough to get him into Howard on a prayer and a hope. Howard was this small black college in D.C. with this king sized rep. Most the kids were proper niggers, acted like Yalies sniffing out bad smells, noses in the air, working at keeping the dialects out of their voices; look at me America, am I not shuffling fast enough sir? J.D. was going through a phase of pleasing people; I am whatever you want me to be. He had just about fit in when Uncle Sam slammed his ass into Southeast Asia. Uncles were people you couldn't fucking trust.

His tour was '70 to '71. Two years of riding a bullet. It took some adjustment. Rice paddies and living jungles weren't exactly his goal in life. One good thing. Nam got him off his high aspirations, brought him back down to where he belonged. 'Fuck you, man. My boot in your shit-can.' This was sweet language for his deprived soul. 'Course it depended on the speaker. One time he had to fight this John Reb swinging dick. Cat had got in his face saying, 'When I see you I see shit walking.' They'd punched through exhaustion to a draw. Still hated each other but at least they'd earned respect. J.D. almost teared up when the Reb bought it in the Mekong delta.

He lost a lot of friends, boon and cats you'd just wave to. Theo and Melvin in Firebase Lorraine. George and Lloyd in a village. Mathew to friendly fire. Horny Al to a Section 8 for running naked through the PX scattering MC scrip. Ken and Lewis and Ralphie on search and destroy. Matinee Andy at a no-name grid, Andy who'd had his picture in Stars and Stripes dancing the frug with Joey Heatherton on a Bob Hope blow by. And then there was Henry Rodriguez. Henry.

Henry was this tough little Mex J.D. got tight with. Henry would share his chow, an admirable trait. He had fragged an officer, which was also something to applaud. The officer was a fuck who kept getting men killed. Something had to be done and Henry had done it. Henry would laugh and say, 'Damn it all, bro, maybe I shouldn't, maybe God's looking to put me in the ground.' J.D. didn't know about God, but Charlie sure had some designs. They grabbed poor Henry during some screaming Fuck me Who the Fuck Where is Everybody? melee. Tied him to a tree and sliced off some skin and left him for the beetles and ants. J.D. was the first to find him. That day he'd cried. Crazy thing was, Henry had lived through it. Triage and grafting then six weeks of sack time with nickel ride nurses and Henry was back. A week later he was dead, but then that was another story.

The drugs helped cover the losses. You'd hose down the blood after a dust-off then hunker on down in your hooch for solace. Sometimes there'd be too much relief before you even got inside—Hell, man, that shoulda been me, I mean I got all these charms like these fucking teeth round my neck but damn I never had no kinda luck else I wouldn't be in this lousy stinking hole waiting to be sucked down to fuck all wherever while I'm traveling on down this brick road where ain't nobody gonna stop for my thumb—and you're talking this way even before the pot or the scag or the reds or whites or whatever good shit you're taking wafts you above the else or fuck all or six kinds of terror.

There was another way to ease the pain; the Saigon Sallys you'd meet on R & R. They'd be on polished stools in dusky bars, women with the bodies of girls, sweet lines of diversion with supple, subtle moves. 'Hi there, Joe, buy me a drink?' A tidy introduction that cut through the crap. Most had kids and habits to support. You either ended up paying for milk or powder. The sex was quick but good. Afterwards they'd wipe you off and send you on your way. It was like bandaging a wound.

He met Le on his second break out of country. She wouldn't tell him her age but he could see she was very young. The slit skirt and the Here-I-Am walk like the rest, but she was different. No baby, no habit, vulnerable, not hard. She had long silken hair to wrap a man's desires in, but her gentleness mixed the heat with something resembling love. J.D. had less than two weeks with her. During that short time he decided she was what he wanted out of life. He sent his mother a postcard saying as much. His momma wrote back saying, Keep on cranking, baby; his mother really was a wicked woman.

The day Le was killed, she and J.D. were strolling hand in hand down Tu Do Street, mingling with the rash Hondas, the ARVNs wearing red berets, and the monks in singed saffron. It was J.D.'s last day in Saigon, a quiet stretch before he went back to the dying and the drugs. The boy had come pedaling along in that loose way they had, the front wheel of his bicycle casually twisting to the side and then back. He had materialized through the heat waves that shimmered off the street; weaving through traffic, a bouquet of roses in one hand, an AK-47 strapped over his shoulder. Later, J.D. decided he wasn't Charlie, that he was probably just an ARVN recruit on his way to see his sweetheart—the mood was right—the summer air had the fragrance of jasmine instead of blood. No, he wasn't Charlie. What he did, he'd done on impulse.

Something in a shop window had attracted Le and she had released J.D.'s hand and gone back to look. For some reason his eyes had stayed on the boy, catching the change in his expression from indifference to annoyance. Maybe he knew Le and harbored some grudge, maybe the sight of this particular girl with this particular American had triggered some sort of hate. All J.D. knew was that the boy's arm shifted so that the rifle was suddenly off his shoulder and firing. The burst had spun Le away from the glass, her eyes briefly asking why before losing their light. The boy was gone before J.D. could react. If he could have caught him, he would've tied him to a tree and looked for a long knife.

After that it was fuck all. J.D. finished his stint and took his habits and grief back to the States. Got the wanderlust fast once he was home. Just like your old man, his momma said bitterly as she threw his shit out on the street. She was on a toot and fucking day laborers.

Gathering up his things, he went looking for the rim of the world. Hitched a few rides with truckers rabid on bennies and saw six states. Almost killed a man in Topeka, almost got killed himself in Austin. When he got bored, he rode the rails, the appeal of knowing where you were going but not where you'd get off. The trains went through towns that offered cheap meals and easy tolerance. And hoboes were good people; they didn't spread their misery out for all eyes to see. For a while it was the life. He knew if he stuck with it he could be happy, so he moved on. Picked up scuff and sweat jobs and collected Relief. Had a woman when it was convenient, most the time it was not. Twenty years seemed to go by so fast, he barely noticed.

J.D. buttoned his coat. He lit the match.

It was sweet fucking time.

CHAPTER EIGHT

Arletha Mae wasn't believing it. I'm not seeing what I'm seeing, she told herself, her hand to her mouth. Jus' ain't real, the Man with his pants down reaching on back for his piece in this stinking ol' room. Gasping, she flung herself and Jason out of the doorway and back against the outside wall.

"Wait, please wait," the voice from inside called out. "Goddamn it, I need help!"

"You jus' trying to get me in range," Arletha Mae called back. She was working real hard at controlling her heart. Jason's unhappy face was scrunched up. Her only child whimpered and clutched at her top. Cupping his head in her hand, she held him tight to her breast.

"Range? What . . . what the hell are you talking about?" The voice was young, disgusted, confused, losing whatever it was reaching for.

"I ain't looking. I know you got your gun pointing right at that there door."

The man laughed so bitterly, he nearly sobbed.

"I don't have a goddamn gun."

No way Arletha Mae was believing him. "You a cop, now ain't you?"

"I lost it," the cop whined. "I lost my gun and I lost my hat." That same bitter laugh. Hat and a gun were what an officer was all 'bout. Arletha Mae almost felt sorry for the fool.

"You sure?"

"Of course I'm sure. You think that's something I'd make up, that I want to be in this fucking shithole?" Losing it again. And pissed to beat all. Arletha Mae felt like she'd slammed into somebody else's parking space.

"I'm goin' now."

She started to walk. Angle on round to where he couldn't see her. Should be easy. Except for what the moon was giving up, most everything round her was dark.

"Fine, just get the hell away from me."

Arletha Mae went a few steps with that in mind.

"No, wait! Please. I'm hurt."

Arletha Mae stopped.

"I still ain't looking."

"What . . . ? Jesus . . . are you listening, are you goddamn listening to what I'm saying?"

"You don't settle on down, I'm goin'."

"O.K. Alright. We'll talk, whatever you want. Just stay here."

Arletha Mae sighed. Jason's fingers were kneading her blouse and the skin underneath. She kissed him on the head, then returned to the wall by the doorway. Her shadow was larger than life on the stucco.

"You made me spill my groc'ries."

"I'm sorry, O.K.?"

"Not O.K."

"I'm sorry."

"Carton's broke. Milk's all over." The white puddle was just short of her toes.

"What in God's name do you want me to say?"

Arletha Mae sighed again. She stilled Jason's hands then touched her shadow, as if it had some say in the matter.

"How'd you lose your hat and gun?" she finally asked.

The cop's voice shot past control.

"How'd I lose my hat and gun? I'll tell you how I lost my hat and gun. Your goddamn people killed my partner and tried to kill me!"

"You ain't goin' a long way to making me feel charitable."

"O.K., I'm sorry, but Jesus!"

There was a stifled sob from inside the room, followed by silence. Arletha Mae's attention went to Jason during the respite. She could see he wanted to nurse and she unbuttoned the top of her blouse and gave him her nipple.

"You still there?" There was some real serious panic now in the cop's voice.

"Huh huh," Arletha Mae said.

"What's that noise?"

"My baby's hungry."

"Oh."

"You mind?"

Arletha Mae looked down at her child. It seemed as though the darkness had smoothed out his skin. His mouth made her feel warm all over. Michael would be out soon. Then they could be a family.

"I'm sorry 'bout your partner."

"What?"

"I said I'm sorry."

"Oh."

Jason had Michael's eyes. This was a blessing, since Michael was a fine looking man.

"You the one on the TV?" Arletha Mae asked. She leaned toward the door. When she drew back, she touched her shadow again.

"What?"

"Why you keep saying that? I'm speaking up."

"I'm hurt, for Chrisake. You say they're looking?"

"I guess." Michael's eyes and his mouth.

"I'm surprised they noticed." Sarcastic this time. And sorry, so sorry for himself.

"How you hurt?"

"My leg, my ankle, I don't know, I just hurt, hurt all over. Would you help me?"

"You sure you ain't gonna shoot me?"

"Why the hell, why in God's name do you think I'd shoot you?"

"I wouldn't be the first."

Jason had had enough. Arletha Mae held him pressed against her as she rebuttoned the top of her blouse. She did more considering, then she placed Jason down by the wall. He squirmed and reached up for her, the way he'd reached for Slope's keys. "Don't fuss," she whispered.

"What?"

She didn't answer. Taking a deep breath, she cautiously stuck her head around the door's frame.

The cop was off the toilet now, sitting with his head down and an arm resting on the rim of the bowl. His trousers were pulled up, but she couldn't tell if they were zipped. There wasn't much moonlight to shape him. In the near darkness he could've been black.

"What's your name?" Arletha Mae asked shyly.

Larry looked up and saw her standing half in the doorway, silhouetted against the sky. The girl sounded awfully young.

"Larry. My name is Larry. Where's your baby?"

"Staying safe."

Larry showed his empty hands.

"I told you, I lost my gun."

"Look that way."

The baby gurgled and the girl left the doorway. When she returned, she was holding the child.

"I've never knowed a Larry. Not one. Now ain't that strange?"

Larry didn't reply. It suddenly occurred to him that she might have a knife or some other kind of weapon hidden in her purse or behind the kid.

"I'm Arletha Mae. Bet you ain't never knowed one neither."

Larry imagined her smile flashing a fierce whiteness as she laughed. She could even have a gun. He stiffened as she moved carefully into the room, one timid foot followed by the rest of her.

"You got a badge?"

He fumbled with his shield, trying to unpin it from his chest. "Here, take it, you can have it," he said hastily.

"Don't you be funning with me," she laughed. "Sides, I don't want it. Jus' that badges, they so pretty. You know, all shiny and what not."

Larry decided it was important to assume a position of authority. Gripping the rim, he hoisted himself back onto the bowl. "See here . . ." he began, but the pain snaked through his leg and he cried out. The baby burped.

"There, there, there," Arletha Mae said, comforting Jason. She lifted her eyes to the cop. "You O.K.?"

"I'm just fine," Larry said defiantly. He squeezed the rim with both hands to stop from falling off. Rubber soles scraping over the concrete, Arletha Mae moved a little closer and he instinctively sniffed—in the locker room, blacks usually had their own peculiar odor—but all he could smell was himself. He was foul, all that sweat and urine and blood pooling together. He maneuvered so his perch wasn't quite so precarious.

"I'm . . ." Having forgotten what he was going to say, he didn't finish. The girl moved a little closer and rested a hip lightly against the shopping cart. She was in silhouette again, framed against what little light came through the window and doorway.

"That don't look comfortable."

"I'm fine."

"They shoot you?"

"No, I fell. I was running and I fell."

"Break something?"

"My ankle, probably. I'm not sure."

"Can you walk?"

"Right, I can walk. That's why I'm still here."

Arletha Mae didn't like the ugliness in his voice. She looked away and rocked Jason and tapped her foot.

"Look, I need you to help," Larry said, gearing down. "Please?"

She let him suffer some before she said, "What you be wanting from me?"

"I need you to call the police, tell them where I am."

Arletha Mae put her free hand to her mouth and chewed on a cuticle. "I don't know, I could get myself in a whole heap of trouble."

"There's no way my people are going to be angry if you help them find me."

"Wasn't your people I was 'xactly thinking 'bout."

"All you have to do is make a call. You listening?"

"Uh huh," Arletha Mae said, but to Larry she seemed to be staring out at the sky. He needed to get her focused.

"You live around here?"

"Ain't nothing here 'cept falling down buildings."

"I mean close."

"Not far."

"Please?"

Arletha Mae sighed. This could bring some grief sliding into her life, but it was her spiritual absolute duty. 'Sides, if she was any later, her granny would kill her dead. "Alright," she said, "but I ain't too good at remembering no numbers."

"All you have to do is call nine one one."

"That one I know."

"Nine one one. They'll put you right through."

Jason was a wearing load on Arletha Mae's side. She shifted him to her other hip. Jason objected then settled into utterances of contentment. She'd enjoyed carrying him when she was pregnant, liked to feel him bumping round inside even when he got to pressing 'gainst her spine; now sometimes, she could use a little less weight and movement.

"He's a good baby, isn't he," Larry said. "Quiet." He hoped this was what she wanted to hear.

"Most the time." She started toward the door. "I'm goin' now."

Larry leaned forward, had to grip the bowl once more to avoid slipping off.

"You're going to do it, aren't you?"

"Gave you my word now as a Christian, now didn't I," she said petulantly.

"I can trust you, can't I?"

"I told you."

She was almost outside. Leaning too far, Larry lost his grip and fell heavily to the floor. "There might be a reward!" Down on his side, clutching at the pain shooting through his leg, he had to fight his hysteria.

"I'm goin'," Arletha Mae said, then the explosion stopped her when she was on the far side of the doorway. There was a brief brightness set against the sky, followed by a rumble close enough to thunder, she was sure the heavens had cracked open. "Sweet Jesus," she mumbled.

"What was that? What the fuck was that?"

Larry's voice was the squeal of a car losing control.

Ben knew he was somewhere he shouldn't be even before the blast, so when the flash and cracking sound arrived a block up ahead, it came as a confirmation. He braked and watched as the brilliance faded until only light and mushrooming smoke remained. I have to get out of here, he thought, I have to get the hell out of here. He clutched, geared and sped into reverse at a high, weaving speed that left treadmarks vanishing under his headlights.

Reaching a cross street he hit the brakes and ashes from the butt tray blew into his lap. The car slewed and the shocks coursed through his legs. Twisting the wheel to the left, he careened away from the light and the smoke. Keep the needle at forty, he told himself, no need to panic, just leave. The deserted streets reassured him, made the explosion seem like an aberration. He couldn't imagine what it was. Maybe an accident. Accidents happened where people didn't belong.

He realized that ashes were all over him, even on his shoes, and he let up on the gas and brushed them off before driving by a neon that flashed TOTAL NUDE then another that flashed FAT JACK'S, no people, just letters and numbers, and he was trying to figure out just where in God's name he was when the second explosion struck. Even though the jolt was well behind him, Ben slammed on his brakes again and ducked. When he looked up, people were spilling out of doors and into the street. "I'm praying for you, David," he said out loud. I'm praying for myself, a louder voice said inside his head.

The radio said things seemed to be quieting down.

The second blast caught J.D. by surprise. He spun around the way he had when Le was shot, got this subliminal flash of her blood and brains in the soft air before she dropped, then the present kicked in and all he saw was flame and billowing smoke a hundred feet away, the heat sharp against his skin.

He'd expected this when he lowered the match to the gas, one explosion on top of the other, but it hadn't happened that way. The flame had sprung waist high so fast it had seared his hands. The first pump had blown while he was still running. He knew how to dive, tuck and roll, but the concrete had still been brutal. Belly down he had turned to see a bulb of blue-red flame climbing, shedding parts, the whoosh and thump echoing in his head. Then mangled metal was clattering all around like iron leaves and he buried his face in his arms. Something hot bounced off his leg, something else struck his back, and for a moment he thought the rim of the world had come to him, then a heavy silence had descended. When he raised his head, a fine metallic dust was hanging in the air and the rankness of burning gas and wild odors he couldn't define filled his nostrils. Band-Aids, change, the .32 and cracker crumbs were scattered among broken glass and gnarled steamy metal. Spot fires were burning in puddles of gas and larger flames flared where the pump had stood; a lick teased the other pump, which was charred but intact. J.D. braced for another eruption but nothing had happened. Nothing was happening anywhere. Apartments flanked the street to his right, lights were coming on, and a guy in a third storey window was leaning out, facing J.D., but the street stayed empty. He found this as inexplicable as the fact that he was still alive. Puzzled, hurting, he'd gathered up his things and left what he'd wrought, saying, 'Fuck it, fuck this fucking soft city, ain't nobody got no kinda balls no more,' and then the second blast had spun him and in that instant he'd seen Le and then nothing but fire and smoke.

Two mega fires, that's what he was seeing now, a spectacle, a fucking show, juice me, daddy, eight to the bar. The scag was still working him, no rush, just lacing his veins, and he laughed crazily at the sight. Turning to the apartments, he spread his arms and shouted, "What the fuck is it with you, what do I have to goddamn do, blow my brains out, what the fuck does it take?" but all he was getting back were these faces in windows staring, then all of a happy second, there she was.

The music came first. Wilson Pickett doing *Midnight Hour,* loud even at a distance. The girl followed, funky strutting as she came down some steps, boom box up on her bony shoulder. Couldn't have been more than eight, just a kid, but showing class down to the pink umbrella she was holding up high with her other hand. The umbrella was tattered and old and so was her dress, but she owned the street, sharing it with Wilson.

Head down, mouthing the lyrics, bouncing the beat off her hips, she was coming toward J.D., locked in whatever trance and vision she was playing out. He swung his head back to the windows, saw lights but no faces. They were coming out into the streets, collecting courage from the music and the girl and the flames, and J.D. laughed until he could laugh no more.

The explosions from less than a mile kept rolling over Larry. Just kept coming in waves long after they were gone, flattening his nerves. Whump, whump, two, there could be more. Something fierce out there was mocking him, saying, "You ain't never getting out your shit, you ain't getting out alive, motherfucker." He hugged the bowl, praying for salvation, squeezed shut his eyes to keep back the tears. His blindness fed flights. The raggedy angel was the one mocking him, tickling his feet with a big boa feather and growling, "Such a long way down," and it was, sky and clouds and the only net this black bitch and her listless brat that was probably drug poisoned.

"Man oh man."

Larry opened his eyes to her voice. She was standing in the doorway, facing outside, caught in the wonder of the blasts.

"That's really profound, that really says it," he said with a tremor and so much viciousness it embarrassed him. Not wanting to lose that edge, Larry scowled when she turned to him.

"Why you gotta be so mean?"

"Because I'm scared. How hard is it to figure out?" What was in him was a scream but he managed to keep his voice down, knowing if he didn't someone would come along and push him so far he would never stop falling.

The sonabitch was back on the floor on his side. Arletha Mae watched him lift and ease back until he sat with a groan, propped up by the john. She figured there was ten feet between them and that was as close as she wanted to get. She stared at the white cop with resentment and confusion, talked to him cautiously, the way she would to a crazy, no minding child.

"I'm scared too."

Larry laughed crazily.

"What the fuck have you got to be scared about? They won't do anything to you when they find us. You'll probably even fucking help them."

"Help who? Help who do what?"

"Jesus," Larry swore. He realized he was squeezing his hand open and shut, open and shut, but he couldn't seem to stop. "Jesus," he said. "My head's on a goddamn spit and I have to listen to this?"

I am being tested. God give me patience, Arletha Mae told herself. Maybe he's been drinking on top of the rest. Little kids and drunks talked shit. Only way to keep things normal, have a conversation, was to pretend they were making sense.

"Spit?"

"Yeah, like what's on my chin, on your sidewalks." He was stringing out the sarcasm, couldn't stop his hand, couldn't stop his mouth. He felt like he was auditioning for the role of Karl coaxing sheet time from the dispatcher. These are manifestations of fear, he thought. Suddenly drained, he let his hand and voice fall.

"I'm afraid."

Arletha Mae felt herself softening toward him.

"So am I."

Jason rustled about and pulled at her blouse. His insistence was so light, it might as well not been there at all. "So am I," she repeated wearily. The officer nodded, but she wasn't sure he had even heard her. His voice stayed distant.

"It really has gotten quiet out there, hasn't it." Larry said hopefully.

"I guess." Jason tugged loose the top button of her blouse. She put it back in place. The silence seemed unnatural. There never was much silence in her life.

"You were going to help."

The hope in the cop's voice might as well not been there at all.

"Still am. Nine one one, right?"

"Right."

She started out the door.

"No, don't leave."

She turned back to him.

"Can't help if I don't go."

There was a tightness in Larry's throat and his mouth felt fuzzy. "I'm afraid . . . I don't want to be left alone."

Arletha Mae didn't know what to do. She had Jason and by now granny was waiting with an axe.

"I'll get you some help, what you want." If she moved fast, she might be gone before his fear could stop her.

"Wait!"

She stopped but didn't face him. Just stood there, half of her already gone, the other half holding back; the half that felt him reaching out.

"Maybe I can walk. You get me something. You know, that I can put under my arm, use like a crutch, maybe I can."

His voice was so weak. Arletha Mae looked back over her shoulder. He was this dark shape, arms and legs quivering, straining to lift himself back up onto the toilet. State he was in, even an act this ridiculous took courage.

Arletha Mae brushed off a spot on the floor with her hand and set Jason down, then she went to see what she could do about helping this pitiful child man. When she braced her hands under his armpits, she felt him stiffen and draw back. She knew he didn't like a black face next to his. They were all like that. She didn't let it bother her none.

He wasn't fat but he had heavy bones. The tension swept up her arms and she grunted with the effort as she got him up and balanced on the bowl. He smelled something awful, worse than Jason had when he had the grippe. No liquor on his breath though. "There," she said, once he was secure. She kept a hand on his shoulder to steady him, didn't need him falling again. She thought she sensed his gratitude but he didn't thank her. Jus' sat there holding on tight to the rim. His breathing was fast. When it slowed enough to stop being scary, she removed her hand from his shoulder as gently as she would release something that might break.

"You're strong," he said resentfully.

" 'Cept for Jason, you wouldn't be needing no crutch."

"I need something."

"Maybe I can just wheel you on out on that there cart." This tickled her but not him.

"Please, just look."

He was getting whiny again. Time his courage had lasted, wasn't worth mentioning.

Jason was kicking and beating on the air. Arletha Mae went and scooped him up.

"What're you doing?" Larry asked anxiously.

She gave Jason her breast. "People always be asking me that question. Feeding my baby. What's it look like?" She winced. Jason was a hard nurser. Sometimes her nipple would be swollen and bright red after.

"Is he almost done?" Jesus H. Christ, Larry thought. How long does it take?

"He don't keep no watch." It was hard keeping patience with this man, but she would try. "Getting there." Her nipple felt like rubber. The determined mouth left. She set Jason down where he had been and buttoned her blouse.

"Funny, ain't it. We here talking and I can't see your face and you can't see mine."

"That's not what's important."

"Maybe not to you." Patience. "You watch him close. I be right back."

"Where're you going?"

"No time t'all."

"Hurry, please."

She went out the door without feeling the need to say any more. If there was something close, she'd help him 'long. Take him home and watch granny's eyes get big. If there wasn't, she'd get Jason and scoot. Pick up a phone and call those numbers. That was taking her absolute spiritual duty far as it needed to go, Amen.

Larry felt panic ripple through him. She'd left the baby and walked out without a word. For all he knew, the kid wasn't even hers. She might just keep on walking, never make that call, never come back. They were different colors, on different sides. She didn't have a single damn reason to do him any favors. She was part of the vision that kept sloshing around inside his head. See how far whitey can drop.

The pressure in his bowels was suddenly overwhelming and he shoved down his pants and relieved himself both ways. Better, he smiled. That's so much better. He pulled up his pants and looked at the kid. Jesus, but he was quiet, a bundle in a corner. Probably a fetal alcohol birth, not drugs. When Larry was a baby, he could never stop bawling. That was healthy. Normal, even if his old man didn't think so. The only other time his father had hit him hard enough to break anything, he'd busted an eardrum; sometimes, late at night, Larry would still get a murmur in the ear, as though he were down by the sea. A murmur and a hollow ringing. He was getting that sensation now, the noises slurring together with another sound, one that renewed his hope.

Arletha Mae was scrounging around a falling down wall when she heard the sirens coming nine ways from everywhere, flat, doubled up bleats like a toy trying to catch its breath. Tracing the bleats with her ears, she went to where she could see light and smoke sprouting. That's where the sirens were going, maybe a mile away. Some hard truths were being played out, but there was no point staring. Ain't nothing here to help the lame hobble. Time to scoot.

She was making her way back through the rubble when she saw the lantern rooted with some other trash. Jus' a sorry old thing, all tarnished and dirty. She knelt and turned the knob. Light rose through the glass. With the faith deep inside her, she knew she had received a God given sign.

Ben had once seen an accident happening and it had been happening to him. He was out for a drive with Maggie and David in marginal country, a one-note road with just enough scenery to let you think you were clear of the city. They were nearing the crest of a grade when a pickup bounced over the top, straddling the center line. The kid behind the wheel had gone right, Ben had gone left, tires grabbing shoulder dirt, and when it was over, Ben knew he'd seen the face of death, and now it was happening again, only this time there was nowhere to swerve.

Locking his doors, Ben desperately scanned the street. Christ, where were they all coming from? Not massed but in knots. Some running, some stopping to stare. Skinny and fat, jeans and teeshirts and print dresses the size of tents, more surprise than anger in the black faces. There were sirens somewhere but not close enough.

He braked to avoid driving into the loose crowd. He had some room to maneuver but not much. Rage was overtaking shock. Epithets assailed him. "Motherfucker, Get the Bastard, Damn It, Do the Sonabitch!" "Please God No!" he shouted, holding up his arms to shield himself from what he could see and what he couldn't. Something hard smacked into his fender followed by rocks and bottles striking his car like heavy hail. His windshield splintered. A side window shattered, covering the back seat with glass. Gripping the wheel with one hand, he slammed the shift into reverse and the engine shrilled and the knots unraveled as those in his path fell back, then the mob closed ranks and even before he hit the brakes, a giant in a football jersey heaved a bowling ball through the passenger window to laughter and cheers. More glass flew and the ball bounced once on the seat, thumped into Ben's leg and fell between his feet.

Ben stared in disbelief at the ball then up at the giant, who was yanking on the handle of the passenger door. There was an opening in the crowd to Ben's left and he backed up hard and fast, shedding the enormous man and momentarily buying space before he braked then shot through the crowd. Lithe bodies braved his speed then sprung free of his vision. He kept on a straight line into and through an alley with the bowling ball rolling, jarring his feet. The Buick sideswiped a trash can which bounced off a wall then off Ben's car then suddenly he was clear, nothing but open road and the night up ahead. Wind and his engine were in his ears and he felt a joy past expression racing through him. City shapes blurred by, round and square, and the few people he saw seemed small. He grinned maniacally at them, thinking, You can't touch me, and the rush around and in him kept gathering a momentum. Then headlights burned across his vision as a four wheeler came at him like déjà vu, shooting deliberately into his path from a side street. Ben swerved, saw faces from his past as metal smacked metal. Darkness and light swirled and he fought the wheel and then his car struck something and shuddered then leaned and righted itself, screeching along the curb before coming to rest, the engine coughing before cutting out.

Ben shut his eyes. I'm still alive. He breathed deeply, each inhalation an expression of gratitude. Suddenly, footsteps were pounding toward him and his eyes snapped open as relief turned to fear. Frantically, he twisted the key in the ignition but the engine wouldn't catch. Black faces flared through his windows, through the splintered and broken glass, rapidly moving mouths and blood-eager eyes. He lunged for a lock that was no longer down but a hand snaked through an opening and clutched his hair, yanking him back so hard it seemed his roots were being ripped from the skin, and he screamed, everything pitched to a scream now as his door was flung open and hands dragged him out by the hair and collar, anywhere he could be tugged at and torn. Then someone wrenched his arm, slamming him into the car, the impact shooting up his spine, numbing him, and a voice was saying, This is happening to someone else, and the voice was his own in his head; he could see himself there untouched, floating free, and the voice said soothingly, Put up your arms, your hands, and he did, protectively in front of his face, but then the voice was gone as stronger hands knocked his arms aside. A fist suddenly filled his vision, twisting his face into a wing window, splattering his blood on what was left of the glass. Then he was punched in the belly and in the jaw, dropping him hard and flat out on the street. He could hear his attackers grunting as they kicked him in the sides and legs, digging deep into his flesh, and he willed the voice back, saying, This isn't my body, this isn't my pain, and the words were a litany he kept repeating until he drifted away to a place where neither the past nor the present could touch him and he could see the face of death.

CHAPTER NINE

This is fuck all promising, J.D. thought, after he recovered from his joyous laughter. The sidewalks were packed with people watching the kid lead a conga line, hands on swaying hips, twenty-some cats following the bouncing umbrella and the bruising rhythm. A rusted, oxidized aquamarine Volvo fell in behind the line. A head and shoulders poked up through the Volvo's sunroof; the brother put his lips to a dented trumpet and started belting out hot licks with Wilson P., getting the notes but not the timing right, kiss and smack. The girl with the blaster and rain stopper grinned and grinned and never stopped moving, just kept right on down the street doing the drunk chicken, dipping low and high. Other cats' heads turned back, digging the ragged accompaniment. "You ain't no Dizzy," one of them shouted. "Safest car in the U and S and A," another yelled with the rising spirit of dangerous fellowship. The Volvo's fat driver braked, revved his engine in mock menace, then eased into first once more as the procession kept going, kept going. They were heading toward the station, where the fires continued to burn with a blue passion. A trim hipster sporting Wing Walkers waved to J.D.:

"Join us, cuz, we're going straight to fucking hell!"

J.D. shook his head. "I'm just an observer of the parade." The sirens were getting close and he wanted to witness the next stage from a distance. He was feeling good. The drugs and booze had brought him to a state of neutral derangement.

"Here they come!" someone hollered.

Claghorn shrieking, the fire engine was the first, followed by three black and whites angling in from different streets in a frenzy of red and blue strobes. The conga line and the car and the trumpet faltered but didn't stop. J.D. sidled over to a wall where he could gauge the potential and check the action on his piece. He clocked the faces and colors in the crowd. There were bangers among the brothers. He could see they were considering the possibilities too.

The firemen were rapidly unraveling their two hoses, the cops were out of their cars. The ranking officer, black, with graying hair, lifted a bullhorn and cleared his throat. The horn was amplified; the sound of his congestion was a heavy metal burp.

"Better try fucking keyboard!" a sister yelled.

A fireman snickered but the cops didn't join in the laughter. The conga line and the Volvo and the hot licks halted, and the girl turned down her boom box to hear what the black officer had to say. The hoses went about their business, blanketing the flames with spray and foam.

"This is an illegal gathering," the officer said solemnly. "I am ordering you to disperse." He had a big grave voice capable of commanding respect, but the formality of his language and his color encouraged ridicule.

A skag saucily planted her hands on her hips.

"Say what?"

"I am ordering you to disperse."

"Rather play the numbers with you, baby," a young chick said, mocking him flirtatiously.

"I am ordering you."

The trumpet belched an E flat.

"Your mama so ugly, she use brillo for makeup."

The Volvo's driver rapped his steering with a drummer's rimshot.

"You have two minutes."

"Say what?"

"Two minutes."

"Lawd have mercy, I done forgot my watch."

The trumpet dropped a staggered D.

The crowd was reaching for its party rhythm, held back by the presence of the Law. The trumpet player kissed the air with a few sloppy notes, then resting his arms and his instrument on the Volvo's roof, waited to see what would happen next. A brother and a sister exchanged a glancing high five. The eight year old twirled her umbrella and smiled boldly at J.D. He smiled back shyly. The crowd engaged in other displays of defiance, but their eyes kept returning to the cops, who were grim and edgy, with the heat of anger coloring their faces. J.D. admired the detachment of the firefighters, although he noticed they were wearing flak jackets.

A scrawny banger with a red bandana around his head wandered over to J.D. and offered a gallon of Gallo. Using the finger hole to lift the rounded bottle to his mouth, J.D. took a long hit. The cheap wine went down smooth, mingling with the other vices that had accumulated in his stomach.

"This is the way it started this morning," the banger said, his gaze moving from the cops to the crowd. "Some fooling round, then gonna be blood."

"Way most things begin and end," J.D. remarked, handing the bottle back. The banger smiled and rubbed one foot with the toe of the other; his sneakers were black and had 8 TREY painted in white on the sides.

The black cop with the bullhorn made a show of looking at his watch.

"You have one minute."

"Or what?"

"Less than a minute."

"So mean, brillo to wipe."

"I'm counting."

"Mercy, mercy."

Two uniforms—one Hispanic, one white—with bodybuilder arms hauled double gauges out of their cars and held the shotguns slanted across their chests.

"I'm counting," the black cop repeated.

"Fuck you, house nigger."

"Forty seconds."

"Fuck you."

"Thirty five."

"Fuck you."

The flames were almost out. The foam and spray formed a cream-colored mist through which the wreckage on the street became visible. The barrels of the shotguns gleamed.

"Thirty and counting."

The shotguns moved down to the bodybuilders' hips. People began to grudgingly leave. The trumpet player laid down a bar of *Taps*.

"This might not be happening after all," the banger said to J.D. J.D. shrugged and took another hit.

"I see you got a strap."

"A strap?" The nomenclature of the young was becoming increasingly obscure to him, a foreign tongue.

"A piece," the banger explained.

"I'm not in the mood." J.D. wasn't. For the moment he'd lost his edge.

"Ten seconds," the black officer warned.

"That's okay," the banger said to J.D. "I understand."

J.D. watched with a mix of disgust and admiration as the banger took out his own piece and fired repeatedly in the direction of the cops. Screaming, people ran every which way and the cops were firing, the black cop down on one knee; the screams became cries of anguish muffled by the Volvo's engine as it weaved in reverse at high speed.

A pretty teenager was shot in the back. She fell on her face, losing a high-heeled shoe. Her shoeless foot twitched and blood ran from her mouth and from under her stomach. The Volvo disappeared into an alley, a blur of chrome and oxidized blue. A bullet spun a lanky, shirtless child into a parked car. Eyes enormous, the boy grabbed a side mirror to keep from going down. Gathering himself, he staggered a few feet then dropped to one knee, got up and stumbled a few more feet before he went down to all fours, head lowered, gasping for breath.

J.D. had gone flat with the first shots, but the banger stayed up firing until he was hit in the side. His arm flew up, the gun flew out of his hand and he fell on his back, moaning and writhing and kicking out against the pain. His blood mingled with the wine leaking from his shattered bottle.

J.D. squirmed behind the cover of a brick building, got up on his haunches and took in things. Except for the five who were down, no one was near him. The mist of spray and foam drifted, making everything ghostly and ethereal. The street was emptying out but the cops kept firing at any backs they could see.

At least seven people were down now. The pretty teenager's foot had stopped twitching, the shirtless boy was trying to crawl under a car, the boom box and the pink umbrella were in a gutter. The firemen had gone to cover behind their truck. Their hoses whipped furiously back and forth, indiscriminately spraying the remnants of the flames, which hissed and sizzled and cast sparks. Streams and puddles were forming in the street and someone was sobbing. The black cop was almost smiling as he squeezed off another round.

J.D. lifted up slightly and yanked the .32 out of his waistband. He was back in country, down in the muck of a rice paddy with friends bleeding beside him, their blood foaming in pink patterns over the fronds. Charlie was coming through a low mist and J.D. was sighting on him and then he pulled the trigger back tenderly and put a round through the black cop's throat. The man's thin neck turned red and his smile slipped and his mouth went slack. Eyes wide with shock he groped for the ground with a hand and lurched back into a sitting position, one leg twisted under him, the other straight out. Trembling, he reached up and covered his throat. Bloody bubbles squeezed through his fingers and J.D. shot him in the head and blood misted in the air as he fell back with a sigh.

The bodybuilders stared down at the body and at each other, then at what little they could see of J.D. He guessed they'd seen the same movies when their shotguns simultaneously rose to their hips; they were both so solid through the thighs, the recoils didn't budge them. The shotguns went whump and shed blue-white flames and he spun behind the wall, rested his head against brick and laughed. This is some merry time, he thought, smiling with something like love. He took in air, let it out and peered around the corner of the building. Down the street, cops were popping up Jack-in-the-box quick from behind their cars, returning a brother's fire.

J.D.'s eyes swept the rest of the scene. The ferocity of the hoses continued unabated, dancing and bucking through the shifting mist which was split and brightened by the muzzle flashes. The firefight intensified, then a cop flung open a car door and snaked inside, while one of the bodybuilders reached out and gripped the nearest part of the officer who was down, his hair. The big man started to drag the body to him, back behind a black and white; the dead officer's graying hair was short and the bodybuilder had trouble maintaining his grip. J.D. put a hole in his forearm. The cop swore and whipped his hand back as though he'd been stung.

"I'm a fucking white cowboy!" J.D. shouted.

The cops paused before shooting back. The banger was still moaning and a sister lying in the street was starting to shape anguish with her screams and J.D. could hear the shrill plea of the cop in the car.

"Get Us Some Goddamn Help!"

J.D. would've blown him a kiss to get him where he lived, but there wasn't time. Too many sirens were humping toward him, and the spotlight of a chopper was crisscrossing the sky. J.D. wiped his brow and eased away to find where the rest of this night would go.

From deep in the alley the trumpeter began playing God Bless America in a wickedly derisive manner, while down the block, a brother shouted, "This ain't ending this time," a sentiment sufficiently direct to erase all doubt.

Larry didn't like one damn thing he was hearing. The way things were going, he'd be on this lousy rim until it started to spin, and the spin it would take would be vertigo.

Suddenly, light filled the doorway. Larry flinched then realized it was her. "Where'd you get that?" he said with a grimace.

"Sure wasn't Pic n' Save." Arletha Mae came into the room and held the lantern over the baby. "He been good?"

"Good? I don't know, damn it, they're shooting out there, don't you hear it?"

"Sound to me like they done stopped."

"Right, just like the goddamn explosions. They stop then they start. Stop and start." Larry could hear his teeth chattering.

Arletha Mae sighed. "Way of things, I guess."

She came closer. He could see now that she was very black and very young, with full lips, hair in cornrows and large brown eyes already creased with worry lines.

Arletha Mae held the lantern out so she could see the white face. The cop was nice enough looking for a man who couldn't stop being angry or scared. His straight, short hair was blond, his fair face was smooth and his eyes were a blue that was nearly green. He didn't remind her of any particular television star. She realized this was probably jus' as well.

"You're young," Arletha Mae remarked.

Larry snorted. *"I'm* young. What about you?" He realized she wasn't carrying anything besides the lantern, adding to his disgust.

"You didn't find anything? There must have been *something* out there."

"Jus' this here light. We be safer staying in here." Arletha Mae walked back to her baby. "Like you said, stop and start."

Larry watched her squat down and adjust the comforter around the baby's neck. She had a good figure. Not much in the chest, but long in the body and legs. Larry looked beyond her as he heard more sirens.

"See what I mean," she said. She sat beside her child and rested her chin on her knees and looked at Larry, who was barely touched by the lantern's glow.

"My granny's gonna kill me." Her gaze was level, her voice composed.

"Yeah, I know." Larry didn't know and didn't care. Too much of him ached and he couldn't stop smelling himself, but he wouldn't have cared anyway.

"I got this here question," Arletha Mae said. I can't wait, Larry thought.

"How old 'xactly are you?"

Larry viewed this as some sort of challenge which had to be thrown back.

"Twenty four. How old are you?"

"Fifteen."

Screwing up his face, Larry looked away and nodded; he wasn't surprised. "Fifteen," he repeated.

"Sixteen in two weeks."

"O.K.," Larry said. "When I was fifteen, I was shagging fly balls and making ice cream runs."

"Meaning you wasn't having no babies."

"Each to his own." Larry still didn't like anything he was hearing. The sirens were getting fainter and this welfare sleaze wasn't about to shut up.

It looked like it was going to be a long night.

CHAPTER TEN

"Jesus, Maggie," Ben said. He was on the country road again, swerving to avoid the head-on. She was gripping the seat and staring in horror and Ben was bracing for the crunch and tumble that would end with everyone in pieces, and those were the words that came out of his mouth at the instant he knew they were all going to die.

"Who's Maggie?" The man's deep voice was in front and above him.

"What?" Ben's own voice occupied a darkness he couldn't see.

"You said, Jesus, Maggie."

"What?"

"Never mind. Just take it easy."

"Who are you?"

"It's not important."

Ben vaguely understood he was lying down. He had an image of himself in a deep hole with people shoveling in dirt, but he was in a car, traveling, he could feel the motion. The engine was well tuned. He wanted to open his eyes but someone had taped them shut. He hurt all over. Keeping himself still, he concentrated on tossing off the pain, but the pain kept jumping around, he couldn't grasp it. He licked his dry lips, tasted blood in his mouth.

"I'm in an ambulance?"

"If you like."

"Are they dead?"

"You were alone."

"Maggie and David."

"Just try to relax."

Ben swallowed. A little of the pain seemed to leave with the blood washing down his throat. "That's better." He still wanted to open his eyes but was afraid the face belonging to the voice would be angry and black. "I'm sorry," he said.

There was an incredulous laugh from up front, a laugh too small for the deep voice.

"For what?"

"For everything."

The man didn't reply. Ben realized he was on the back seat without enough room for his legs. Drawing his knees up, he braced his feet against the door and draped a forearm over his eyes. The stale air buzzed with the car's engine and a distant siren and a sense of the city trying to define itself.

Everything was cracked or broken. He touched his eyelids with the tips of a thumb and middle finger. The skin felt fat and tender and shifting; he was at the mercy of the whims of his flesh. Groaning, he leaned with the car as it turned left. Delicately prying open his lids, he tried to focus through dancing specks and the blurred ceiling of the car. When he rubbed his eyes, his vision improved.

Jesus, but they'd ripped him up. Blood was everywhere, on his torn shirt, his pants, the seat. Blood came off on his hands as he patted his pockets.

"I can't find my cigarettes," he said plaintively. "And my wallet's gone."

"Thought you'd drifted off again."

"I guess. I don't know."

"We're almost there."

"What?"

The back of the man's head, large, round and black, loomed over the front seat. His hair was thin, making his big ears look even larger. Ben turned away and stared at his shoes, where there was more blood.

"Where're we going?"

"There's a hospital. We're close."

There were particles of something or other on one of his socks. He wondered what the particles were even as he hazily recalled his benefactor beating off his attackers with flaying indignation.

"Why'd you help me?"

The man didn't answer. Ben's eyes shifted to him.

"I don't know," the man said at last. He sounded like he was starting to regret it.

"Thanks anyway."

"Forget it."

"I'm Ben."

"Did I ask?"

Ben studied his shoes again. "You've got a radio?"

"Yeah?"

"Could we hear the news?"

"I'd rather not."

Ben closed his eyes. Images of the accident flashed again before him; David flattened out on the seat, not crying, not screaming, but gripping the upholstery so tightly, it had taken ten minutes of soothing before Ben could pry his fingers loose.

"Another block," the driver said. Ben barely had time to shake himself back into the present before the car stopped. He heard the driver's door open and close, then the door by his head swung free and the driver got him under the arms and helped him out. They were parked behind an ambulance in front of the emergency entrance to a hospital. Whoever the ambulance had been carrying had been removed in a hurry; the rear doors were still open and the dome lights swam before Ben's clouded vision.

"I'm dizzy," he said, once he was on his feet.

"Imagine that," was the response.

The black man draped Ben's arm over a fleshy shoulder and his own arm around Ben's waist and made him walk. Ben took stiff, cautious steps, felt like a drunk. All of the man was large, like his head. He had on a jacket that didn't go with his pants and he smelled of mouthwash and nerves. His weight jostled and bullied Ben. The interior of the ambulance reeked of blood and antiseptic as they lurched past.

"There's a lot of blood on me," Ben said, panic stirring within him.

"Not so much," the black man said matter-of-factly.

"Not so much? Look at me, for God's sake!"

"I don't want to."

They were trudging toward the emergency entrance when brakes squealed and a white Oldsmobile screeched into the lot. For an instant Ben thought the car was targeting them, but the headlights quickly veered off and the Olds slewed to a thudding stop forty feet away, engine idling loudly, headlights still on. Eyes battered shut, face caked with blood, his chest still, a fat Oriental was slumped against a side window. Behind the wheel an Oriental woman was staring at her passenger in shock.

"Damn," the black man muttered.

Ben nodded dreamily and touched his own swollen cheek. "Shouldn't we help?" he heard himself say.

"I got enough damn trouble," the black man replied.

Ben let his benefactor drag him away. "My God!" the woman shrieked and his eyes returned to her. She was shaking her friend furiously by the shoulder. "My God, he's dead!" she yelled at the unconscious man, as though she were describing someone else; for a moment, in his daze, Ben thought she was talking about him.

Two paramedics came rapidly out of the hospital's Emergency entrance. "See?" the black man said. "That's *their* job." Ben nodded, watching as the paramedics strode past the Olds, slammed the ambulance's rear doors shut, then got in up front and sped off.

The black man shook his head as he watched the ambulance leave, then he turned to Ben and said, "Pick up your feet."

"Huh?"

"Before you trip."

Ben nodded again. In the background the woman's shrieks sounded like a parody of fright. The black man got Ben through the entrance's sliding glass doors. He tried to concentrate on what was in front of him; if he could objectify, he might be able to forget how much he was hurting.

They were in a hallway harried by overhead fluorescent tubes that buzzed and flickered. Plastic chairs flanked the aisle. Only a few of the orange bucket seats weren't taken. Most of the casualties looked as bad as Ben knew he looked, but they were strangely passive, a mood of silent resignation having settled over them.

The black man helped Ben lurch to the front desk where the receptionist barely looked up from the forms she was shuffling.

"Do you have insurance?"

"Sort of," Ben answered.

"Have a seat. A doctor will see you as soon as he can."

The black man frowned. "When's soon?"

The receptionist motioned to the chairs then returned to her forms without replying. An elderly Latina dressed like a domestic moved over so Ben and the black man could sit together. Ben slid down as far as he could without falling off the seat and stretched out his legs. The black man leaned over his big belly, his arms on his thighs, his hands loosely joined.

"I could use a cigarette," Ben said.

"You lost them," the black man reminded him impatiently.

"Maybe I could bum one."

"You can't smoke in here."

"Maybe—"

Pointing to the wall, the black man cut him off. "Look at the sign."

Mouth mashed beyond repair, the old Latina smiled at Ben and nodded sagely. Ben decided what he could really use was a drink, a foot tall and straight up, but there was probably a goddamn sign for that too. He tried to find somewhere to place his pain that was clear of his body. Set it down, shake his finger at it from a distance. Loan it to a friendly martyr. That would be nice. His father would have accepted it without hesitation. Here, your flesh is my flesh. Biblical equations, indecipherable in this room.

Blinking, Ben tried to focus on his feet. From a distance that seemed great, he studied his sock. The particles in the fabric were fragments of glass, small as motes. They had smashed a window of his car. Maybe from that. His vision drifted to a long scuff mark, dirty white against the brown leather, on the side of his left shoe. The image of one of his attackers grinding his foot with methodical savagery into the pavement came back, briefly the rest too, the shouts, the thumps and thuds, the murderous eyes.

"Here."

Ben flinched before he realized where he was. The black man was offering a Kleenex.

"Your nose is bleeding again."

"I'm sorry."

"Forget it."

Ben took the Kleenex with the conviction that none of this was real.

"Philip."

"Huh?"

"My name's Philip."

Ben nodded and wiped the bright blood from his nostrils and upper lip and snuffled. He wadded up the tissue, which stuck to his hand, and placed it on the floor. Things floated around him, sounds that were near seemed to come from another room. Philip coughed, took out another Kleenex, and blew his own nose loudly. The elderly Latina tapped one of her remaining teeth, appeared to be testing its stability. A nurse came along with a clipboard and whispered to an old white man who looked like he'd been scalped. Bewildered, the old man shook his head. The nurse whispered something else, got him to his feet and led him shuffling down a corridor.

Ben's attention shifted to someone swearing in Spanish. He drew back his feet as a tough-looking Latino wearing a gold earring shoved through the sliding doors. One of his eyes was hanging out of the socket and the Latino tried to hold it in place as he rushed past the receptionist, who jabbed a buzzer. A small sunburned orderly appeared and laid hands on the Latino but the man pushed him into a wall. The orderly looked stricken, then he followed the Latino, staying at his heels but not touching him again. With a curious anticipation Ben watched them, but all they did was disappear down the aisle, so he stretched his legs out again and watched the fluorescents flicker. He knew he should call the police station and ask about David, but he couldn't seem to get to his feet. The only energy in the lobby came from the receptionist, who was on the phone, her voice erratic with indignation. After a moment angry voices shouted in Spanish and English from deep in the building.

The shouts subsided, the injured went back to waiting, then the Oriental woman came through the doors alone, wild eyed, but she didn't raise her voice when she went to the counter. A black with dreadlocks and a dangling arm gave in to the pain and began whimpering. Blood dripped lazily from Ben's nose onto his pants. Philip gave him another Kleenex and Ben pressed it to his nostrils. A doctor was paged, a sloe-eyed child hummed tonelessly to herself and scraped the floor with her shoes. There were low professional voices from a corridor. The Oriental woman took a seat. More casualities filtered in and were forced to sit on the floor.

Through the glass doors the darkness over the city was broken by the glow from several fires. Sirens keened. After a while a nurse took Ben into a room, helped him up onto a stainless steel table, washed the blood from his face, then left. Ben gripped the cold sides of the table and stared at the ceiling in horror.

Ambling onto East 93rd, yet another boulevard of pillaged hopes, J.D. found himself a shadow where he could stand hipshot and unnoticed and take in the sights. People were everywhere, alone, in pairs, mobbed up, chanting, "Join us! Join us!" singing out full-throated to the night; J.D. tried this in cadence but the rhythm wasn't there, so leaning against the source of the shadow, a greasy spoon that looked like it might fall down if he leaned too hard, he felt up his bruises. His hands were flame-blackened from when he'd put the match to the gas, the heat so intense, his palms were split. Parts of him ached from hitting the pavement and his calf was stiff where a fragment from the pump had struck it. The half a load he'd mainlined kept most of the hurt confined to his head.

J.D. watched impassively as the parade passed him by. Decked out in garish cheerleader outfits two spiky-haired young sisters brought up the rear, giggling and doing a low-volume yell; "Two, four, six, eight, who do we appreciate?" Got places to go myself, J.D. thought, figure out where as I walk. He crossed the littered street and strolled through a vacant lot of trampled crabgrass to an avenue lined by barred stores and potted palms.

Fires were burning, he counted five, two east, two west, one south. J.D. hadn't heard any of them go up, so he knew it was amateur hour; kids jazzing their natural juices, gas on a mattress, strike a match and sprint, whoops and cheers, two, four, six, eight. Got the job done though, if given the time, only the sirens wouldn't allow that. Pitched to a shriek, they were coming with an urge to do some violence.

J.D. focused on the nearest blaze, a convenience store or some such. Smoke and soot and tear gas were in the air, although not enough to trouble the eyes from half a mile. There wasn't any wind to sway the flames, whose tranquility he found oddly disturbing.

A series of sudden explosions brought back his smile, flat, crumping sounds similar to a mortar barrage. He could see flames rolling angrily a couple of blocks down. The fractional intervals between the blasts spoke of incendiary devices and precision, of cats bringing knowledge to their sport. Might be his imagination, but J.D. thought he heard the sirens falter, as if sensing that the power was shifting to the other side.

He looked for a direction to go. One was as good as another; this shit was spreading. Toss a coin, follow your feet. Isolated gunshots echoed in the distance and he sang a little as he walked. *Somewhere Over the Rainbow*. Doing Garland's big gestures but scatting the lyrics and flatting the sharps. He was tired of this white fucking cowboy bull. Somewhere over that sucker, bluebirds fly, right. Pull their feathers, see how far the sweetness goes. A three sixty degree flutter. He heard more crumping sounds. The war was in good hands.

He yawned and stretched. Starting a revolution was just plain hell on a man his age. He could use a little R & R, freshen up for the next round.

A shrubbery flanked gate on the nearest corner got his bleary attention. Taller than J.D. and with a lock. And beyond the gate, a one storey stucco building shaped like a horseshoe. Giving a perfunctory thumbs-up to a chunky, barefoot Chicano torching the potted palms, he trundled down the block until he could make out the sign over the building's entrance. Hazelwood. An inviting enough name for someone who needed a while to rest.

J.D. went over and fingered the lock. Industrial steel. Nothing that could be picked. He wearily dug the .32 out of his pocket, singing low, "Why, oh, why, can't I?"—standard Saturday night rebop. Demonstrating skills offensive to the race, he pulled the trigger. The gun flashed and popped, the lock spun and dangled. "I am the bane of locks," he growled as he pushed open the gate that opened onto a courtyard of pebbled tiles, potted plants and tables with metal umbrellas poking up through their middles. Even with just the moonlight to go by, J.D. could see that the tables and tiles were dirty; bird droppings added to the effect. He checked out the horseshoe as he walked toward the entrance. Maybe thirty windows altogether, all dark except for two, where light shone through drawn drapes.

The entrance consisted of two glass doors flanked by glass panels. He tried the handles, but there wasn't any give. Through the panels he could see a poorly lit, uncarpeted hallway and what appeared to be an office; the door was open, but the room was dark. He knocked on the glass. No one home. He knocked harder and a golden retriever appeared in the hallway, padding lazily out of a deep shadow. Tongue lolling, the dog sat and looked up at J.D., as though expecting a treat.

"Me too," J.D. said.

Acknowledged, the retriever smiled and began sweeping its tail over the shiny linoleum floor. A voice rooted in nasal complaints came from the shadow the dog had inhabited:

"What the fuck?"

The voice took the shape of a young, small black in orderly whites; pants and short-sleeved shirt. He stopped when he saw J.D. and his eyes widened with annoyance and maybe some fear. J.D. smiled and opened out his arms to show he was harmless. The attendant's eyes narrowed then he snickered. Muttering to himself, he strode to the entrance.

"What the fuck, man?"

"That about says it all," J.D. replied. "O.K. if I come in?"

"Visiting hours are over."

J.D. made a demonstration of hugging himself.

"Gimme a break. It's cold out here."

"No it ain't."

"O.K., but it's loud."

The attendant shook his head. "Man, you're something. Really something." Trying to push the retriever aside, he unlocked a door with one of the keys he had hooked on his belt. The dog wouldn't budge; just kept sitting there looking happy and dumb.

"I ain't scared of you, see?" the attendant said, once J.D. was inside.

"Why would you be?" J.D. responded. He looked around. The walls and floor and the attendant's clothes gave off agreeable aromas, old paint and fresh wax and bleach.

"Yeah, well," the attendant said. The dog was clearly getting on his nerves. He peevishly tugged on his crotch then twisted a doggie biscuit out of his pocket, tapped the retriever on the snout with it and tossed the biscuit into a corner. The dog ambled over, sniffed the gift indifferently, then lay down.

"Figures," the attendant snorted. Facing J.D. he blinked, as though seeing him for the first time. "I heard this pop," he said. "Close, like somebody shooting off a piece. That's what you were wanting to get away from, right?"

"Right."

The attendant fidgeted with his keys.

"How'd you get in? Climb the fence?"

"Somebody had shot off the lock."

The attendant's gaze went to the darkness. "I ain't scared of them neither."

The dog made a sort of rippling moan. Its head was on its paws and its eyes were closed.

"He protection or company?" J.D. asked.

"He ain't nothing," the attendant sneered. "He belongs to one of the residents."

"This a retirement home?"

"More like where they stick the ones gone in the head." The

attendant was walking, his shiny fresh-off-the-shelf-looking shoes squeaking over the slick floor. J.D. followed him past closed doors.

"We got eight or nine do nothing except shit themselves. Rest, you don't want to know."

"You here alone?"

"That's right. I'm what you call the fucking night shift."

"Where we going?"

"I'm on my break."

"You watching what's been happening on TV?"

"Fuck that. Right now I'm pretending I'm one of them. Sit and stare and diddle myself. Guard gets called in, it's over by morning."

There was a pool of urine on the floor. "Jesus, watch your step," the attendant warned.

"The dog?"

The attendant shook his head in disgust.

"Mister Skinner."

The attendant went into what seemed to be an employees' lounge. A lamp sat on a nightstand next to a worn sofa. Scattered about, there were popular magazines, empty soft drink cans and a TV. Comic books were spread out on a rickety wooden table like a deck of cards, glossy covers offering gouts of blood and heroes and villains on steroids, the standard selection. The attendant picked up the nearest, sat on the couch, put his heels up on the table and started to flip the pages.

J.D. stayed by the doorway. "You a fan?" he asked.

The attendant kept flipping. "This shit? C'mon, man, don't insult my intelligence. I'm a collector. Mint condition, these get top dollar. Ten years from now I can fucking retire."

"You reserve a room?"

The attendant wasn't listening. He had already lost whatever interest he had in J.D., who might as well have been furniture or a resident or the dog. See how far the sweetness goes.

"Mind if I look around?"

The attendant didn't look up.

"For what?"

"For whatever."

"You a collector too?"

"In a manner of speaking."

The attendant didn't seem to notice when J.D. left the room. Sweat had pooled in his socks and his feet made slurping sounds as he walked down the hallway, past more shadows and more closed doors. His body ached, the effects of the way he lived. Where he was at wasn't helping. The corridor was musty, stifling, no more agreeable aromas, the truth behind all facades. He could hear sirens roaming, but not much else; only his feet and the violent breathing of a sleeper. His shadow stretched along the floor, and in his present mood he felt like he was watching his soul depart.

Reaching into his coat pocket, he touched the gun, had a few thoughts. The mind was a camera, a recorder of desires and images. He saw his shadow lift on the wall as he brought the revolver to his head. He would take the moment seriously, show serendipity some respect. He was among the lame and the dying, what better place? He would consider alternatives as he cocked the hammer: If he made it to old age, he would be crippled by time and the years of fuck all abuse. Shuffle in robe and paper slippers, barely able to urge his feet forward. Sing the forgotten songs, lose the words. He would see all this and nod and smile. Then his smile would wobble and he would pull the trigger. He would see light flash as his brains replaced his shadow on the wall. His blood would ease into the darkness. The retriever would find his body, nuzzle his limp hand and sit and wait, hoping for a treat. Hoping.

J.D. watched his shadow fill a wall as he went down the corridor. He felt like he was walking back into his life, all the misdirection. Maybe he could stay here until dawn, avoid the bad moves for one night. But he knew he wouldn't, of course, knew he would just keep walking. His life was on rails, no stopping this motherfucking train.

Been like that for so long. Le had briefly given him hope that things could be otherwise, but she was dead. What stayed alive was the guilt, the sense of having sinned dogging him since the first time his momma tickled his thigh.

"Joseph, is that you?"

J.D. stopped and blinked. It took a moment to realize that the raspy voice wasn't in his head.

"Is that you, Joe?"

J.D. walked to the only room in the corridor that showed light. He could hear anxious breathing. He nudged the door open with his foot.

Thin to the point of extinction, all wild electric hair and haunted eyes, an old white woman was sitting on a disheveled bed in a transparent nightgown with her dinner on it. In the soft light from her bedside lamp, he could see her drooping breasts and pubic hair and the bruises on her arms. She fixed him with a ferocious glare and drew back, her shrunken body curving in on itself.

"There isn't a drain in my shower," she said.

"Mine either." He took in the unadorned room, which was about the size of a large closet.

"Mister Skinner wants to fuck me."

"Meant to be a compliment, I'm sure."

The old woman's expression became flirtatious, then grim.

"Who are you?" Her eyes took up most of her face and her jowls and arms trembled as she spoke.

"Nobody," J.D. told her.

She cocked her head and studied him warily.

"Are you sure?"

"Known it for years."

"You aren't Joe?"

"No."

The old woman picked at her hair and what was on her gown as she weighed her disappointment. Time to move on, J.D. thought.

"There's money under the mattress," she hissed with some urgency, as though reading his mind. "I'll give it to you if you'll take care of me." Smiling flirtatiously she jiggled her legs in anticipation. The straps of her shoes were unbuckled, her feet were swollen. Toiletries and a shower nozzle and the rest of her dinner were on the threadbare, unvacuumed carpet.

"Please?"

J.D. looked away from her insistent eyes. He realized with uneasy shock that she probably wasn't much older than his mother. He had no idea what to say. In the adjoining room someone began whooping like a sick dog. The old woman squeezed her eyes shut and she began to moan.

"Joe, I need you. Please, Joe, come on back, please, come on home."

J.D. cleared his throat, but he might as well have been furniture. Her eyes stayed closed, her face corkscrewed, and she was wringing her nightgown where it covered her lap.

The whooping continued unabated in the next room.

"Joe, oh, Joe, why?"

J.D. didn't need this. He started to walk.

"Lord, let me go," the old woman suddenly wailed. "Lord, let me die. Lord."

"Here's the door," J.D. said and he kept on walking out into the familiar night.

CHAPTER ELEVEN

"**M**ight as well talk," Arletha Mae said. "Ain't got much else to do no how."

"Might as well," Larry agreed. In the Academy one of the instructors liked to joke around when the cadets were worn down to the nub and cussing about it. 'Dead man talking,' the asshole would say. That's me, Larry told himself now. Corpse carrying on in the boneyard.

"Where you from?" Arletha Mae asked him.

"Here."

"Growing up, what I'm saying."

"I know. Here. I mean, outlying, but the city." The more he talked, the more he might forget the pain.

"Me too," Arletha Mae replied.

"Fancy that," Larry said dryly; dryness was the state of his mouth and his mood. The girl's chin was still on her knees. Her eyes were enormous in the glow from the lantern. To Larry, she looked like a native on the fringe of a fire.

"When you was a kid, you like to play games?" Arletha Mae asked.

"Games?" Her gaze was boring too deeply into him. Larry wondered if she was plotting some mischief.

"You know, games. Shagging, you said."

She reached back and laid a hand on Jason's chest. Sometimes when he was colicky, his breathing seemed to lift his heart right out of his body. His heart was calm, praise Jesus.

"What're you doing now?" Larry asked, glancing at her.

"Jus' seeing. Making sure."

Larry nodded uncertainly but her fussing over the baby made him feel a little better; the distraction would make it harder for her to consider harming him in some way.

"What kinda games?" Arletha Mae asked.

"Baseball mostly." In baseball you didn't get knocked down that much.

"Was you good at it?"

"Not bad." In his last year in Pony league, his team had made the regionals. They'd lost the championship game 6–5 in extra innings. Larry was weak at the plate, mostly a bench warmer, but that day he'd timed a couple of curves and gotten two hits. His father wasn't impressed. All he mentioned was the error Larry made that cost his team a run.

"Mister Emmett down at the Pic n' Save, he played pro."

"Uh huh," Larry said.

"Hurt his knee. Made him mean. Me, I like swinging on 'em bars."

Sure, you and all your family going way back, Larry thought. Scratch under your arms and chatter while hanging from a limb.

"What you call 'em?" Arletha Mae asked.

"Jungle gyms." Bet she still spends time doing loop a loops. Helluva note, her having a kid.

Arletha Mae stared at Larry, trying to witness the direction of his soul, 'nother mystery deeper'n Sherlock. One thing certain. She was right seeing him as a man child. Not all his fault. Hard to be a man when everything was handed to you, 'specially the color of your eyes, your hair, your skin. She tried to imagine him as a father. If he could keep it on daytime, he be fine. Read his lines, smile, walk away. Do it for real, uh uh. Be whining more'n his blue eyed baby.

"Your folks, they living?"

"Sure. They're not that old. Fifties. Though my father's not in the best of health," Larry said with some satisfaction.

"What's the matter with him?"

"His lungs. He had to have one scraped last year."

"Scraped?"

"Get rid of scar tissue." Might as well humor her. "What about your parents?"

Arletha Mae took a deep breath and lowered her gaze. "My mama's somewhere, my daddy's somewhere else. My granny's done raised me. Her and my auntie."

"Uh huh."

Larry looked past her and her sleeping baby. The sky was lighter, although not with the promise of morning. The fires were spreading, their smoke mixing with and masking the artificial brightness and the horizon, and a subtle heat had infested the air.

"I get letters," Arletha Mae was saying.

"What?" His leg hurt so damned much, and somewhere out there people were prowling with a stick for his head.

"From my mama," Arletha Mae told him. "She live in Dallas–Fort Worth. She sent me this postcard a coupla months back. All these big tall buildings. She wrote real nice, asking me 'bout Jason."

"Jason?"

"The baby." It was plain this man couldn't think 'bout nothing 'cept himself, as though his pain was the only hurt in the world. She pushed the lantern forward a mite to see more of the blues of his eyes, the pretty color; she wanted to hide the selfishness, hide what he really was.

"Why'd you do that?" Larry said, briefly shielding his eyes.

"No reason." Arletha Mae smoothed a wrinkle in Jason's comforter. "Was you scared?" Only way to keep the white boy happy was to keep turning things back his way.

"I don't know what you're talking about," Larry said.

"When it happened this morning."

"Of course I was scared," Larry snapped. "I'm scared now. Isn't it obvious?"

"What did you do to make 'em so hateful?"

"I didn't do a thing, not one damned fucking thing."

Arletha Mae felt anger stirring within her. Why wouldn't he admit what was clear? His eyes had narrowed to razor gleams, the blue had almost disappeared. Arletha Mae drew back the lantern.

"You musta done something, said something," she insisted, jus' as hard as him.

"Right, there's two of us and a hundred of you—"

"I wasn't there."

"—so naturally we smacked our clubs in our hands and said Fuck you, you black bastards. Is that what you want to hear?"

"Want to hear the truth, that's all." If he didn't quit with the sass, if she didn't like what she heard, she was going to scoop up Jason and hurry on home.

Larry blinked over the set of her dark eyes, decided it was wise to conceal his hostility. "There was this guy with an umbrella, walking up on a wire." And in my head, I'm up there too. "People were smiling. It was like a party. I don't understand what happened." He could see the small, grizzled black man silhouetted against the sun, hear the brittle exchanges, the crowd laughing. Why couldn't the bastard have kept his balance? Taken a few more steps to the ledge and climbed down?

"I mean, I do," Larry said. "He fell and people went crazy." Like ants when you stir up their hill.

"Don't see why, less'n you done something. Maybe your partner?"

Larry shook his head but realized she was right. Karl had said something, or maybe just laughed when the guy had hit the pavement. That was all it took. Damn him, damn him all to hell.

"It wasn't me."

"But him?"

Larry nodded. "Yeah."

Satisfied, Arletha Mae smiled. Something don't come out of nothing, no more'n babies come out of the air.

Now she was smiling. God, Larry thought, they're a funny bunch. Knife at your throat then let's be pals. He looked at the sky. There seemed to be more fires, some not too far away.

"Are you sure it's safe here?" he asked nervously.

Arletha Mae lifted her shoulders and let them fall. "Safe as anyplace. Ain't nothing here to loot or burn, 'cept maybe you."

Larry took this as a somewhat friendly joke. He managed a short laugh that didn't make him feel any less anxious as he stared outside, where the sirens, his solace, were remote.

As he lay there on the stainless steel table, Ben sketched scenes from his past on the ceiling. Fragments, that's what always came back; he never could get the pieces to fit into a pattern.

When he was two, his father's, not his mother's, comforting hands. Hands like his, office soft and pale. The long, thin fingers, the short lifelines.

When he was four, he had pried snails from the driveway and placed them one by one on his father's hairless chest. His father was sleeping on a blanket under the midday sun. Ben had stood there watching the snails weave disgusting trails across the pink flesh.

Thought it was funny. When he woke up, his father's eyes got large but he didn't get mad. He'd just carefully picked the snails off him and told Ben not to do it again. Ben saw his father's patience as evidence of his love.

An elevator bell chimed and Ben turned to hushed footsteps, voices and laughter going by the room where he had been abandoned. According to the clock on the wall it was eleven. He had been here nearly an hour. He didn't know what was so goddamned funny. Where the fuck was a doctor?

He faced the ceiling's dull light again. When he was sixteen, he'd laughed out loud when a classmate crashed his bike into a wall. The boy had been showing off, doing wheelies in the playground, so he didn't feel too guilty. After the boy got his senses back, he had beaten Ben up. This, Ben's father told him, wasn't right but it was understandable. He hadn't spoken to his father for a week.

The door opened. The nurse who had left him in the room returned with a clipboard. She adjusted a switch by the door so that the ceiling light brightened.

"Hey," Ben objected, shielding his eyes.

The nurse dimmed the light slightly. "You need to fill this out," she said. She handed him the clipboard, which had a cheap, scarred pen dangling from a chain. He felt all his joints tighten as he sat up.

"What is this?"

"A standard form. Every patient has to fill one out."

"Goddamn it, I've been here for an hour!"

The nurse looked up at the clock and kept her composure. "Not quite." She was young, with large, clear glasses and blond hair tied up in a bun. Ben's eyes went from her to his ruined clothes.

"I mean, look at me, I've got blood all over."

"There are people here in worse shape. We have priorities."

"Yeah, well, this is a hospital, isn't it?" He didn't care for the heights his voice was reaching. His father had taught him that staying calm was the greatest virtue in life. Used both himself and Ben's mother as examples. Ben knew his mother had to work at it. Sometimes he'd catch her sneaking a drink to tamp down her rage.

"Don't forget to sign it," the nurse told him as she walked away.

"Where're you going?"

"A doctor will see you soon," she said, closing the door behind her.

"Shit," Ben swore.

He glared at the form. The words blurred, shifted in and out of focus. Most of the questions seemed to be about insurance. Squeezing the pen so hard his hand trembled, he filled out his name, address and phone number, then he flung the clipboard against the wall. It struck with an inordinately loud noise and clattered to the floor. Ben listened for footsteps from the corridor, but no one seemed to have noticed. Disgusted, he lay back on the table and returned to his past: As he grew older, he watched his mother develop a taste for Cutty Sark. In the dark light of early morning, David's eyes were the color of gin. When Maggie was drunk, she liked to be done from behind.

The door opened. A man in a long white smock came into the room and turned up the light. Ben flung an arm over his eyes. "Hey."

The doctor didn't turn the light down. He glanced indifferently at Ben, then focused on him. "Do you know you have an erection?" he told Ben with revulsion.

Ben looked down. His pants were tented. "Sorry." The fabric shrank and he felt better. When he was thirteen, his mother had caught him masturbating and he'd experienced the same kind of shame. That was the first time he'd seen her have a drink. As far as he could tell, her drinking never got out of control.

"Never mind," the doctor said disdainfully. He was lank and pale, with a wispy goatee and the sour expression of a drained intellectual. The name tag on his shirt read Shapiro.

"Where's the form the nurse gave you to fill out?"

"I don't know," Ben said guiltily. Shapiro's dark eyes searched the room briefly before he spotted the clipboard.

"Why is that on the floor?"

Ben's gaze returned to the ceiling.

"I lost my temper."

"Lost your temper?" Shapiro enunciated each word.

"I've been here for over an hour. Look at me."

The doctor didn't look. He went over and picked up the clipboard instead.

"This isn't completed."

"I told you, I lost my temper."

Shapiro sighed and put the clipboard down by Ben's feet.

"Lie back."

Taking Ben's jaw gently in his hand, Shapiro turned his head from one side to the other. Ben caught a whiff of disinfectant.

"Somebody sure did a number on you, didn't they." Shapiro said, letting out a low whistle.

"There were at least three of them."

The doctor released Ben's jaw.

"Open your right eye as wide as you can."

"It's swollen."

"Try." Shapiro used his fingers to help. Ben flinched. The doctor shone a pencil flashlight into his eye then released the lid.

"Now the left."

They repeated the process. Shapiro switched off his flashlight. "Where else did they hurt you?"

"All over."

"Be specific."

Ben placed his hands on his sides and on his legs. "Here and here. And here."

The doctor unbuttoned Ben's shirt and pulled his pants down to his ankles. Ben looked down apprehensively. There were numerous contusions on his sides and legs where he'd been kicked, red streaks and knotty blue bruises. Ben flopped back and covered his face with an arm. He suddenly felt queasy and clammy and short of breath. Shapiro put a calming hand on his stomach.

"If it was as bad as it looks, you wouldn't be able to walk." Shapiro removed his hand and snapped on a pair of throwaway latex gloves.

"You sure?" Ben asked.

"More or less."

Ben decided to believe him. The alternative was worse. Shapiro began to probe Ben's injuries with his thumbs.

"Does this have a purpose?" Ben asked.

"A scale of one to ten, let me know any pain that's at the top."

"Oh Jesus," Ben said, gritting his teeth as Shapiro pressed down on his side.

"Would it help if I told you a joke?"

"No," Ben gasped, fighting off Shapiro's hands.

"It's Halloween. There's these two dead guys, one's Jewish, the other's black . . ."

"Anyone ever tell you you have a goddamn lousy bedside manner?"

"Try the hours. The personality goes fast."

Shapiro finished with a flourish and dogged consistency, a couple of pinches and an absence of charm.

"See, I told you. Nothing broken."

Ben felt his left eye, the one that could still open, grow wide with astonishment.

"Am I out the door?"

Shapiro pulled off the gloves and dropped them in a wastebasket.

"How's your insurance?"

"Bad."

The doctor frowned and scribbled a few things down on a chart.

"Do you have a ride home?"

"I think so."

"Good." Shapiro glanced at the clock. "I have to run, I'm off my shift. The nurse will give you some Neosporin and codeine, then you'll be on your way. My advice is, spend about a week in bed with someone feeding you chicken noodle. If you start hemorrhaging, give us a call."

"That's a joke, isn't it?"

"No."

Ben sighed. The queasiness returned. "Thanks," he muttered.

"Don't mention it." Shapiro started out the door.

"Could she hurry? I have to—"

"She'll be right with you."

"I have to find my son." But his life would be so much simpler if he didn't.

The doctor looked at him curiously. "Well, good luck."

Ben attempted to shove Shapiro's hand away, then realized he was just trying to pat him on the shoulder. He tolerated the perfunctory gesture then Shapiro left, dimming the overhead light and closing the door behind him.

Ben lay there staring at the ceiling. Out in the corridor the elevator's bell chimed, an intercom coaxed a doctor, hushed voices and footsteps went by. Someone cursed in Spanish. The overhead illumination took up the length and width of the ceiling. The light seemed to drip down on Ben's face. A fly buzzed somewhere. The past whispered. After half an hour the young nurse came into the room and turned up the light. She put salve on his wounds and pulled his pants up over his underwear and his erection without comment or embarrassment. She helped him button his shirt. She made him finish the form. She gave him some codeine and Neosporin. She helped him out to Reception.

Philip was gone. After paying his bill with plastic, Ben went out through the sliding glass doors and scanned the parking lot to make sure. "Shit," he swore. He shuffled back inside. The lobby seemed to swim abstractly around him. I have to focus, I have to find my son, he told himself, the words a weak litany.

He had change in his pocket. He made it to a pay phone in the corridor and called a neighbor, asked if David had come home. The woman took the pay phone's number and went to check. Ben rested his arm against the wall, his forehead on his arm, while he waited. Muted footsteps and voices passed behind him. The phone rang, Ben's neighbor told him David wasn't there. He asked if she was sure, had she looked in the linen closet? She said "What?" then repeated that David wasn't there. Ben swore again and punched the wall with his elbow and his neighbor hung up.

He called the police station and listened to the phone ring for a long time before a recording finally told him all the circuits were busy, try later. Ben muttered, "Thanks a whole fucking lot," and clumsily replaced the receiver. He returned to the lobby at a loss. Sport for AT&T.

The Oriental woman was sitting in one of the plastic chairs. Ben limped over, sat next to her, and buried his face in his hands. "Shit," he said. He looked at the woman. She was staring straight ahead. Ben stared with her. People came in, others went out. An orderly mopped blood off the floor. The bell chimed. In a dead voice Ben asked the woman if she had a cigarette. She opened her purse and gave him a Benson & Hedges without looking at him. He fired up the smoke. No one stopped him. He dropped the match on the floor and asked about the woman's friend. In a dead voice she told him she was waiting for news. Ben nodded slowly. They watched the mop glide over the floor, watched the water in the orderly's bucket turn pink then red.

After a while a pudgy doctor came out and called the woman over, took her hands in his and whispered words Ben couldn't hear. She lowered her head and nodded. She didn't cry. Taking her keys out of her purse, she walked briskly toward the door. Ben told her he needed a lift as she went by. She stopped and stared at him in astonishment, then she nodded. He followed her outside. Sirens wailed, fires blossomed, springing moods loose in the night.

CHAPTER TWELVE

J.D. was counting change, playing Jack the Monkey with nickels and dimes. He was in a thoroughly vandalized phone booth on East 98th, the receiver snug between his shoulder and ear. The directory was ripped out, graffiti was spray-painted and scratched into the glass and the box, and the light was out. Across the street a black and white was belly up and burning. The only other fire was a few pops of flame from a shoeshine stand. One of the quieter blocks.

The operator's deep fried voice came back on the line, livening things up.

"I'm waiting."

"What's your name?" J.D. was feeling convivial, a friend in every port, all that shit.

"Sir?" the operator said.

"That wouldn't have been my first guess. Where y'all from? Mobile? Austin? Louisiana, mojo land?"

"I'm waiting."

"Ain't we all." J.D. sighed. "Ain't we all." He finished spreading his coins out on the tray. He had enough, a nickel to spare.

"Thirty five cents," the operator told him.

J.D. was feeding dimes into the slot when a tap on the glass stopped him. Turning, he saw a banger—baseball cap on backwards, red hanky in his right pocket, pullover down to his knees—leaning against the booth. The gangly teenager had a lead pipe in one hand and he looked vexed. J.D. opened the door to see what the punk wanted. "Fifteen cents," the operator said. "Hold on," J.D. told her, then to the kid, "What the fuck, man?" The banger impatiently scuffed his dirty sneakers.

"Gotta make a call, man."

"So do I."

"Ain't my problem," the banger sneered.

"Look, man," J.D. said, starting to lose his temper. The operator said, "Savannah," and broke the connection. "Shit," J.D. swore. "See what you made me do?" He slammed the door in the banger's face, was no longer feeling so convivial. He smacked the box with the heel of his hand, listened for his dimes to drop into the return. Nothing. He smacked the box harder. Nothing. Swearing, he felt his pockets for any change he might have missed. Nothing. "Fuck," J.D. said.

The banger rattled the booth with the pipe, two sharp knocks. J.D. tied a ribbon around his patience, reminded himself that he was almost an educated man. The banger knocked harder, splintering a panel. No need to be snobbish, J.D. thought. Far better, an act of social grace, to communicate with people on their level. Yanking out the .32 he opened the door and waved the gun in the punk's face. "This is what happens when you don't fucking go to school." The banger's Adam's apple dipsy-doodled as he gulped audibly and dropped the pipe on his own foot.

"Now that we've established a dialogue," J.D. said, rapping on a panel with the barrel of the .32, two sharp knocks. The banger nodded dumbly then showed J.D. his back.

"Hey!" J.D. said and the kid froze. "Got some change?"

The kid was flush. Three ones, three dimes and four quarters. J.D. gave him back the green and a dime.

"Go buy yourself a book. Bring you luck."

The kid goggled at J.D. then scampered off for points unknown. "My, my, my," J.D. said to himself as he fed the box and dialed by the light from the flaming car.

After a couple of rings the cat who worked The Paradise's front desk, a gump named Rokowski given over to flights of asthma, wheezed in J.D.'s ear. J.D. asked for Bobby, hummed *The Man I Love* while the gump went to find him. The cop car exploded mildly, shedding a few surface parts. "Someday he'll come along, he'll be big and strong," J.D. sang raw and soft, Joe Cocker on downers. He heard someone lurch into the desk on the other end of the line.

"Bobby?"

There was a strangulated giggle.

"Man," Bobby said, drawing out the word.

"You shoot into the neck, babe?" J.D. was glad he'd only gone in half a load himself. He wanted to do the rest of the night straight, at least as straight as this night would allow.

Bobby laughed aimlessly for a while. This is my life, J.D. thought. The operator, a different one, told him his three minutes were up, so J.D. and Bobby got her to agree to bill the call to The Paradise.

"So where the fuck are you, pardon my English?" Bobby inquired, after the operator rang off. Bobby had gotten himself somewhat together. J.D. guessed it was the stale air in The Paradise's lobby, which discouraged euphoria, or maybe it was just the gump.

"East side," J.D. answered.

Bobby found this funny.

"What the fuck for?"

"I'm not sure," J.D. said truthfully. He could smell burning rubber from a tire that had been wickedly blown off. J.D. empathized with the car.

"So what's down there?" Bobby asked.

"The revolution, more or less," J.D. said.

"Jeez," Bobby swore, amazed. "I thought all that shit was fucking over."

"No, Bobby," J.D. said patiently. "It isn't." He opened out the .32's cylinder. The sharp, clean gun smelled of oil and chamois cloth. There was only one shell left in a chamber. One was enough.

"So what're you doing?" Bobby asked.

J.D. wasn't sure the question was directed at him; he could hear the gump wheezing in the background.

"Making new friends," J.D. said.

"Guess what I'm doing."

He could see Bobby smirking, getting downright smug. "I can't imagine," J.D. admitted. "Making new friends?"

"Making old ones." Bobby giggled some more. "Fucking, fucking righteous."

Bobby temporarily lost control, laughing maniacally and pounding the receiver on the desk. J.D. could hear the gump trying to restrain him, saying, "Hey, pal, hey!" Yes, definitely in the neck, J.D. thought, and more than once. Bobby apologized to Rokowski in a manner of speaking and returned to the conversation.

"Jesus, the promises you gotta make," Bobby said. "So you lonely?"

"No," J.D. said.

"Shit," Bobby swore. "Shit!"

There was a long pause, broken by some scuffling on Bobby's end of the line. Keeping the receiver tucked under his chin, J.D. struck gunfighter poses, admiring his slick moves reflected in the cracked glass. The scuffling continued, so he started singing *God Bless America* in a wickedly derisive manner while he removed the shell from the .32 and scratched his initials imperfectly on a panel.

Three bloods carrying ill gains ran by the booth, grinning and waving as best they could; one of the bloods was wearing a blond wig and a bridal veil at a disrespectful angle. J.D. grinned and waved back, saying in his head, Where's the groom? The black and white exploded again, so meekly, nothing flew off. In his ear J.D. heard a loud thunk that sounded suspiciously like a body hitting the floor. Returning the shell to its chamber, he closed the cylinder and stuffed the gun back in his coat pocket.

"So where were we?" Bobby said. His breathing had gaps.

"You been working out?" J.D. asked.

"Huh?"

"Nothing."

A green parakeet fluttered by the booth.

"There's this thing been bugging me," Bobby said.

Rokowski wheezed.

"Yes, Bobby?" J.D. asked cautiously.

Rokowski gagged.

"You think the office is gonna be open tomorrow?" Bobby asked. "I mean, you know."

Rokowski possibly threw up.

"I don't know," J.D. said. "I sorta doubt it. Tomorrow's Sunday."

"Oh man," Bobby whined. "But it's fucking check day!"

"Monday, Bobby. Monday's check day. Besides . . ." The fifth of the month. Social Services reception mobbed up. Shoving and swearing and a few fistfights. Another kind of revolution.

"Besides what?" Bobby wanted to know.

"Just besides." J.D. could hear groaning over the wire. The groaning was close in key and pitch to his rendition of *God Bless America.*

"See, here's the thing," Bobby was saying. "I didn't do my fucking workfare. Jesus, man, they had me down at Plummer Park, stab the leaves, all that shit, hours and fucking hours."

"Time's the essence of God," J.D. reminded him.

"Yeah, I know, right, but you know that prick foreman they got there, that fucking prick Abrams?"

The groaning went on and another parakeet flew by, riding the tail of a wisp of smoke as Bobby affected a girlish voice:

"Bobby, over there, you missed a leaf, Goddamn it, Bobby, your bag's only half full. Jesus, I mean, God," Bobby swore, getting himself into a state, "how much am I supposed to take?! So I did the righteous thing. Ripped off the bag and threw the stabber at him. Only grazed him, just this fucking nick, you know, but it really pissed him off. Sucker chased me half a block. Christ, you see what I'm talking about, what the fuck I'm getting at?"

There was more scuffling on Bobby's end. Bobby cursed and Rokowski retched. There was a thump and the commotion stopped. A raccoon put its long nails up on the phone booth, peered through the glass at J.D., then scurried away.

"Here's the thing," Bobby panted, "they got me by the fucking balls. I go in, my worker, Jennings, that fuck, that miserable fuck, he's gonna sit there smiling and leaning back and saying, Where's your workfare, huh, Bobby, huh? and I'm gonna be sitting there going duh with my fucking hands between my fucking legs. So I'm figuring maybe I'll try and cop a fucking cold, I been practising, trying to sound like Rokowski here, Jesus, bastard's got ahold of my leg now. So what do you think? You think Jennings, that cruddy shit, will buy it?"

"What?" J.D. was watching the raccoon move on down the street. Nice ass, he had to admit. A perfect roundness.

"You're right," Bobby said, then, "Jesus fucking Christ, Rokowski, leggo!"

A struggle of serious dimensions was commencing but J.D. wasn't really paying attention. A good-sized snake was sashaying his way from the direction the parakeets and the raccoon had come from. Wondering if half a load had been too much, he hung up with Bobby's curses and Rokowski's wheezing climbing toward dementia.

J.D. strolled out to the middle of the street and squatted to check out the snake, whose pace was half a lap faster than a turtle's. The thing was about three feet long, with sleek black skin and red circular stripes. Not a Two Step, but definitely not indigenous to these parts and probably poisonous enough. Its tongue sinuously working the asphalt, the snake circumvented J.D., moving with such purpose that J.D. thought it must have some sanctuary in mind, somewhere dark and deep where it could curl up beyond the reach of predatory strangers. This was the snake's nature. J.D.'s nature was to walk to the rim of the world.

Pushing up out of his crouch, he trudged toward the next block. Distant gunshots and sirens reminded him of what he'd started. He inhaled odors; smoke, soot, the booze on his breath and a trace of cordite. Several puppies of various breeds raced toward him, prancing by with their tongues hanging out. There were more shots and sirens and an aborted high C from a trumpet. Water was flowing heavily somewhere. All this would pass with dawn. Sunshine and headlines and television highlights then sweep away the dead. Maybe Bobby was right. Maybe the office *would* be open Monday. A day of body counts and rest, then welcome back the old habits, the ragged anger, the dreary exclusions. J.D. took some pride in the fact he'd done his workfare last week. Not that he'd be around to collect his check.

He heard the black and white shudder behind him. Turning, he saw what remained of the car shudder again, giving off an effluvium of fire and smoke. Death spasms, not unlike those of man. Bodies in their throes came back. Charlie. Le. Henry Rodriguez. The cop he'd shot. Some died as softly as snow. Others seemed to wrench themselves out of their skin, their bodies lifting, swelling, reaching for the indifferent air. Came down to the same thing. A stillness, the light emptying out of the eyes, that white line you couldn't cross. These, J.D. knew, were maudlin reflections. At the moment he wished he smoked.

A dog barked; one of the puppies, a fluffy white spaniel, had found the snake. The puppy played tentatively with the snake's tail, touching a pale paw to the expendable black skin. The reptile curved back on itself and displayed its fangs. Confused, the puppy whimpered and drew back. The snake slithered off, making good speed. The puppy sat on its haunches and cocked a curious head, watching the snake disappear down a rain gutter.

J.D. resumed walking. A canary fluttered into sight and settled atop a lamppost. A dachshund wet the same post. A shotgun went whump whump in the night. Somebody screamed. A chopper did wheelies in the distance. He kept on walking, preoccupied, trying to remember the lyrics to an ancient song. A well-groomed cat of the animal persuasion skulked away to his right. A car downshifted behind him, raising the decibel level of the bass jolts from its radio. Just for the hell of it, he put out his thumb and the car pulled up alongside him. J.D. waved the driver off. The car left, taking the jolts with it. He kept on walking. Head slowly bobbing, a palm-sized turtle approached, offering proof of his theory regarding the relative speed of snakes and tortoises.

This is my life, I am my father's son, J.D. thought, although those weren't the lyrics. He heard the flapping of erratic wings and looked up at the sky. Through moonlight white as milk, a parrot of wild, wondrous colors swooped down and clumsily tried to land on his shoulder. J.D. endured the attempts without resistance, although he avoided the self-indulgent gesture of resting his head on his shoulder and spreading out his arms. After some swoops and stalls the parrot flew away, no doubt seeking a more stable perch. J.D. sighed and kept on walking. He was passing by a poster of hard drinking pleasures when the lyrics came back: "You can't always get what you want, but if you try sometimes, you might find, you can get what you need." Too bad he didn't have someone here, a companion in need, to catch the curves these fucking A words tossed.

Something else was coming down the street, streaks of water that died in the gutters. J.D. could hear the extraordinary sounds of the night, and the parrot, the voice of an old woman, shrieking, "Feed me, you mother, feed me!" The water was more concentrated now, reaching his feet. He could see the source up ahead, a fire hydrant gushing a heady stream. A brother was sitting by the hydrant, arms loose over his knees, a man J.D.'s age, wearing dungarees, a flannel shirt and a three day stubble. His bloodshot eyes followed J.D. as he approached. When he was close, the man nodded and patted the curb, which was in a red zone. Accepting the invitation, J.D. sat next to him, mirroring the man's pose. They watched the water splash and spread down the pavement.

"Those things ever get round to stopping?" J.D. asked after a short time.

"Got me." The man shrugged and took out a fucked up pack of Lucky Strikes. J.D. lifted an index finger to the hydrant.

"You do that?"

The man shook his head. "Somebody else. Me, I'm just passing by."

"Slowly."

The man smiled, revealing bad teeth. "Yeah." He had a voice life had taken too much out of. Firing up a bent smoke, he offered the pack to J.D. who gave it some consideration before declining. The man shook out his match and returned the pack to his shirt pocket.

"Be the death of me," the man coughed.

"One of those choices," J.D. replied.

"Ain't many." The man squinted up at the sky. So did J.D. The chopper was still circling in the distance.

"Look at that."

"I see it."

"Sucker's got a hard-on for something," the man said, the cigarette drooping from his lips.

"Long as it ain't us," J.D. added.

The man's congested laugh caused him to choke on his phlegm. He coughed savagely and wiped the mucus from his mouth with a sleeve.

"Getting a little colder. Could use something for the head."

"I had this hat I favored once," J.D. told him.

"What happened to it?"

"Lost it drawing to an inside straight."

The man nodded as though this had happened to him too.

An old Ford Fairlane, with a plate reading WATEVER and crammed with bangers, lurched down the street, holed muffler snorting, trans grinding with despair. The cats flaunted serious weapons and the joy of violent encounters in their young eyes. The driver honked and enthusiastically waved a baseball bat out his window.

"A Louisville slugger," J.D.'s companion remarked.

"Come again?"

"The bat. My eyes are good, even if the rest of me's not much."

The bangers smiled and waved and made bewildering gang signs. J.D. and the man smiled and waved and clumsily gave some of the signs back. The banger with the Louisville slugger energetically pounded the bat on the side of the car, denting a door, then the Ford was gone in an explosion of water and black exhaust.

"Kids," the man said stoically. J.D. nodded in agreement. Encouraged, the man went on.

"When I was their age, it was fists and feet, maybe an occasional knife. Occasionally things would go too far and some poor fool would end up dead or missing a limb, but that was pretty damn rare."

"Times change," J.D. said.

The man took a final drag and dropped his cigarette into the water. "Don't they though," he said as J.D. watched the cigarette float away.

The sound of rapid fire came to them from a few blocks down, the rat-a-tat-tat of automatic weapons. The man shook his head sadly then took out another cigarette and lit up. He and J.D. were tracking the wayward plumes of smoke and listening to the energy of the water when the parrot returned, fluttering to a landing near them on the sidewalk. The bird approached then backed away, approached then backed away. "Awk," it screeched, then, "Feed me!"

"Yours?" J.D. asked. The man exhaled smoke, coughed and shook his head. "Fuck you," the parrot said, ruffling its feathers.

"Although I wouldn't mind." The man gestured with a lazy hand to a pet store down the block. "He's from there. Someone liberated the place. You wouldn't believe what's loose."

"Yes I would." J.D. looked at the store. A lot of its glass was on the ground; display window and the door. A Siamese cat was out front playing, batting shards.

"Kinda quiet," J.D. noted.

The man gave him a puzzled look.

"Ain't that why you're here?"

"Well, sort of," J.D. admitted. "I been doing a lot of walking, and my feet and what all needed a breather."

The man tapped a long ash from his cigarette.

"So you're ready to move on?"

"Pretty much."

The man nodded. He didn't seem to care if J.D. stayed or left. J.D. took off his cap and held it out to him.

"Here you go. For your head."

"No, man, I couldn't."

"Got a new one waiting for me at home."

The brother didn't resist as J.D. put the cap on his head.

"Thanks, man."

"Don't mention it."

"O.K. I won't."

In every direction J.D. looked, there were flames. He felt his blood rise as he pushed himself up from the curb. The man pointed with his cigarette to where the helicopter continued to prowl.

"If you're looking for cheap thrills," he said.

"Well, maybe I'll see you around."

"Maybe during the next one," the man answered.

J.D. nodded then walked. He glanced back once. The man was

trying to coax the parrot onto his arm. The parrot responded with a common obscenity and backed away.

The shortest route to cheap thrills was back through the water. As J.D. trudged along, he felt the dampness through his boots and let his mind stray to a Biblical distortion: his feet were being washed, cleansed, to absolve him of his sins. "Ain't gonna happen," he told what flowed around him.

Going under a traffic light that was blindly blinking, the dead eye of the machine, he started down a block where the kinks had knotted up: Either a dwarf or a stocky child in a Darth Vader costume was lobbing Molotov cocktails into a Food Stamp outlet; two bums were French-kissing on a bus bench; a plumber's snake was tied around a lamppost; another post was festooned with toilet paper spray-painted black; a familiar trumpet was lying flattened in the street, alongside two mannequins from the smashed display window of a bridal shop. The groom, whose elbow was out for his lady to take, was on his back in his tux, his bow tie placed neatly over his smile, his smiling eyes marker-blackened. His bride was facedown and naked except for the bridal bouquet, which covered her buttocks. "I'm the best man," J.D. whispered, stepping over the dummies. Voices, excited, multiple, varying in gender and volume, were curving around a surplus store at the end of the block. "Get what you need," J.D. growled as he went around the corner.

The action was pretty spry. There were a dozen establishments. All but one, for office supplies, were being vigorously looted. Almost all of the looters were black; J.D. spotted a few Hispanics and a young blonde in minishorts with varicose veins streaking her flabby white legs. People were hauling out whatever could be carried, food, portable TVs, appliances, booze. The heavy items, furniture and washing machines, were being hefted by pairs and teams. A lot of the looters were dressed for around home; women had their hair in curlers, men were bare-chested and barefoot. There were a surprising number of children, some clinging to their mothers' hemlines, some staggering under the weight of whatever, others standing around thumbs-in-mouths like What the fuck is going on?—same as the two uniforms parked down the street in a black and white.

J.D. placed a flat hand over his naked brow and craned his neck to get a better perspective. The cops had marine sidewalls and this problem about what to do with their faces. Like, where does my thumb go or how do I get my jaw off my gut or should I look fucking pissed? Mostly they were settling for the latter, glaring at the citizens, working them with the evil eye. Most weren't buying the cops' menace. Just went about their business, bend and load, eat my shit, motherfuckers. The squad car's radio was on. J.D. couldn't quite catch what she was saying, but the dispatcher seemed to be trying to boost morale; the uniforms didn't look like they were believing word one.

Sauntering down the street, J.D. showed some nifty open-field moves as he sidestepped the brothers and sisters, who didn't pay him no mind either. He tousled the hair of an intelligent looking child who was blowing up then popping balloons with a darning needle. A young man slumped in a motorized wheelchair angrily slowed to give J.D. the right of way. J.D. tipped him a nickel for his courtesy, avoided the temptation to ask him how fast that sucker would go. When J.D. was halfway down the block, a blood behind the wheel of a slamdangle VW wagon waved him over; it was nice to be wanted.

"Yeah?" J.D. said, ducking his head down so he could see the cat, who had a frantic face, a webbed cap on backwards, frayed workman's gloves with the fingers cut off, and an interesting way of expressing himself; part rap, part drugstore cowboy:

"This is a high old time now ain't it," the cat said happily, "box-seat prowl, providing you got, and I'll say it loud, make sure the ears can hear, providing you got yourself the ticket." What have I wrought? J.D. asked himself, with a mix of pride and sorrow, adding this is what I do; guilt and a stroll toward the ultimate punishment, diseases of the mind and heart.

"We just here to exchange observations," he muttered, "or you got the fuck something else in mind?" He noticed that the rear seats had been removed. The back of the VW was cluttered with a range; guns of all sorts—gauges and high pop and Saturday night specials— and goods of a household persuasion, tags still on. Although there was no one close enough to hear, the cat dropped his voice to a conspiratorial whisper.

"Hey, lookit here. I got what you want, I got what you need."

"Hate to mention this, babe," J.D. said, "but under these strange and unusual circumstances, there don't seem to be much need for people to be laying out cash."

The cat frowned.

"You ain't lookin' at the broader picture, no, you jus' ain't. I got what is called a damn, shit, fuck selection, all of them quality items the Johnny come lates kickin' theirselves, and I say it again, kickin' theirselves over for not gettin' to grab." The cat's bony fingers clutched J.D.'s arm. With difficulty, J.D. broke the surprisingly strong grip.

"Let me see now, oh let me see, this has jus' gotta suit you, stroke you, don't you pay them pigs no mind, they ain't lookin', they got their balls in their throats. Let me see, you look like you go high gauge. I got a beaut back here, a prince, short stock, no numbers, not nothin' to fear." The cat reached back and rummaged through the mess. Objects clanked and pinged and clanged as he tossed aside what didn't suit him.

"No thanks," J.D. told him. The cat stayed his quick hand and twisted his lean, wild face J.D.'s way.

"No? Then how 'bout something fit your pocket?"

"Sorry, but I'm already packing."

J.D. checked the sky. The chopper was still there.

"Well, how 'bout that," the cat said, "I shoulda knowed, a man of your distinction. Then how 'bout things for the home? Price is cheap, I buy wholesale." The cat poked through merchandise that wouldn't quite take off your head. "I got these here hammers, a power stapler, locks keep you safe, toaster, mixer, dress for marryin', this here juice squeezer guaranteed give you all the essential vitamins, feel tha' fuckin' blade, make your finger disappear." He tucked a forefinger into his gloved palm fast as a wink and looked eagerly up at J.D. "You hitched, conformin', carryin' tha' ball and chain?"

"No," J.D. said. "Not that particular one."

"Well, that's alright, the single life, bachelor party, goof dog gig, way I do too. Let me see now, got your prayers—Sheiks, Excita, Double X, twin ribbed, lubed, add to your pleasure." The cat took short note of the two cops driving off in a state of high disgust.

"Like I was saying, in their throat," the cat chortled, "nobody here 'cept friends and neighbors and relations now. Like we was sayin', what you can afford? Name your price, I'm a reasonable man."

"Sorry, I'm busted."

The cat's face dropped then climbed past disappointment. "Well, that's alright too, been there myself." He rummaged some more, came out of the disarray with a fingerprint-smeared can of spray cologne. "For good lovin', guaranteed, on the house. What the hell, that kinda night."

J.D. thanked him, stuffed the can in his packrat pocket, shook hands then strolled on down the sidewalk. A squat, shaggy bum, so dirty he was of indeterminate race, thrust a homemade sign reading WILL FUCKING WORK FOR FOOD in his face. Saying, "Good for loving, guaranteed," J.D. handed him the cologne, kept on walking, felt the can hit his back. He didn't turn; it was what he deserved. Fact was, he deserved a bullet.

Looking up at the slate sky, he saw the chopper circling over a tall building half a mile away. Muzzle flashes suddenly flared from the rooftop toward the machine, their brightness quickly lost in the helicopter's spotlight. "My, my my." J.D. smiled, swinging his arms and the words in cadence. "Time to hump."

CHAPTER THIRTEEN

The sirens were gone, as though they had never been there. All that remained was what could kill him, the night.

With his back resting against the toilet—what he'd come to bitterly regard as his station—Larry stared through the doorway. The ruins of other abandoned buildings blocked much of his view. Beyond the warp of crumbling mortar and dangling crossbeams, the shape of destruction loomed. There were so many fires, the sky had taken on their color, an ominous bloody shade that the smoke couldn't obscure.

Jason's half formed laughter brought him back to Arletha Mae. She was sitting a few yards away on the floor, playing koochie koo with the baby, who was lying beside her, laughing and trying to fend off her stalking fingers with his tiny hands and his covered feet. The glow from the lantern seemed to have softened their black skin.

"That was funny, what you said."

Arletha Mae kept at the baby, whose limbs continued to jutter with happy resistance.

" 'Bout the burning and looting and you?" she asked.

"Uh huh."

"Couldn't have been *that* funny." She imitated the short laugh he'd let out. "Sounded more like you had something caught in your throat."

"Yeah, well, that's pretty close to the truth."

Arletha Mae stopped her fooling round and watched Larry. His eyes were filling all up with damp. Same old shit. Poor me-ing himself again. "You ain't 'xactly dying, now are you?" She wasn't about to start coddling him now; better to try and bully all the feeling sorry outta him.

Larry swiped at an eye with a dirty sleeve and steadied his voice. "No, but you know."

Jason was tugging at the hem of Arletha Mae's blouse. She opened her purse for his pacifier, then remembered what he liked even more. She dug out her house keys and placed them under Jason's chin. Jason looked down and fingered the gift.

"What is it I'm supposed know?" Arletha Mae asked firmly.

Larry didn't care for her tone. He tried to force-feed himself some patience, but couldn't keep the annoyance out of his voice. "I just keep thinking someone's going to come along and find me."

Me. Thinking only of himself. That wasn't changing either. "What you're meaning, bad not good?"

Larry nodded. "Then what?" His head on a stick. That was the image that kept tugging at him.

"Then guess we got ourselves some serious trouble."

"What have you got to worry about? I mean, hell, you can just walk away."

"You're pretty dumb, ain't you, even for a cop," Arletha Mae said. His face showed his confusion. She would have to spell it out for him. "They find me with you, ain't neither one of us walking."

Larry suddenly realized what she was risking. It should have been obvious before, but his mind had been clamped to his pain and his bad nerves and visions.

"But with the baby . . . ?"

Arletha Mae shook her head pityingly.

"You jus' don't know, do you? You jus' don't unnerstand, no way, no how."

Larry ran a hand through his hair then rubbed his eyes in one quick motion, fingers tight to the skin.

"Jesus, you're right. I don't understand. Why *are* you staying?"

" 'Cause I should."

"I still don't understand."

Arletha Mae had a fair idea he wouldn't no matter what she said. Outside a siren scorched the darkness before fading away. Releasing the keys Jason turned his head and giggled at the sound then belched.

Larry barely noticed. "Jesus," he said, running his soiled hand through his hair once more. "Jesus." Hearing movement he looked up. Arletha Mae was over the lantern, lowering its light, which seemed the color of his hair. She saw him watching her. "No use drawing no moths," she said with a vanishing smile.

In the milder light her worry lines gave the appearance of character. Embarrassed, he avoided her gaze. His voice was subdued. "I'm sorry."

"For what?"

"For what I was thinking." Her scheming. Her up in a tree. Scratching and chattering and hanging. "For that," he said, with the solitude of regret.

Arletha Mae couldn't begin to guess what he was talking 'bout. She figured he was hoarding secrets to get back for when she'd confused him. Tit for tat.

Jason had the keys in his mouth. "Here now," she said irritably, taking the keys from him. "Gawd almighty." Jason's face squeezed into ugliness and bawling and he squirmed and flailed with his arms and feet. Arletha Mae got out his pacifier but it was too late.

"I gotta change him."

Larry watched Arletha Mae remove a new diaper from her large purse and replace the old one, which she dropped outside a window, all of this done with a deftness and ease he couldn't fathom. Then she gathered up Jason and, barely touched by the light from the lantern, sat with her back against a wall and her baby cradled in her lap.

"Think he's going on back to sleep. It's what he do best, that and eating. Same as me when I was his age. Least that's what my granny say." Her heavy lids slipped over her eyes for a second then lifted. "Feeling pretty darn tired myself."

"Me too." Larry could hear both their voices thickening with the long hours. His back ached where it was braced by the toilet and he shifted in an attempt to lessen the throbbing. "Only I'm afraid if I go to sleep, I'll never wake up," he said, wincing.

Arletha Mae nodded. "We ain't got us no coffee, so we might jus' as well talk, keep us awake."

The throbbing wasn't quite as bad. "Might as well," he said.

"What's your fav'rite holiday?"

Larry found her choice of a topic unusual. "Holiday?" he snorted.

"Something to say, that's all."

"Hell, I don't know." Larry rubbed the side of his face, the raw stubble. "They're all about the same. A day off."

Arletha Mae drew up her knees slightly and Jason almost vanished from Larry's sight.

"Me, I like Christmas," she said. "Presents to open." Once she'd left candied apples she'd special made for baby Jesus in a stocking. Her granny thought that was nice. Others thought it was weird. "Things to open and that angel on up there at the top of the tree." She reached up with a hand. "So high up, you never no way can touch it."

"I don't know," Larry said. "Last Christmas there was some yelling." He and his father had almost come to blows before Larry backed down. "Maybe Thanksgiving. That'd get my vote."

"Thanksgiving, it's O.K." Arletha Mae yawned, though not because she was tired; the white boy, he wasn't bringing much to this. "Wonder what time it is?" she said.

"I couldn't even guess."

"Maybe one. Maybe two."

"You think it's that late?"

"Maybe."

"That's good," Larry said. "It's getting close to morning. I mean, day's better than night."

"Sometimes."

Arletha Mae leaned down into the reach of the lantern's light and gently kissed Jason's forehead. The infant stirred but didn't wake. Her baby brought back her interest and she faced Larry.

"You like music?"

"Music?"

Arletha Mae smiled. "I ain't got no radio neither. Jus' talking, you know."

Larry knew. He nodded. "Who doesn't? Like music, I mean."

"Man, you'd be surprised," she said, laughing. "What kind?"

His lids momentarily felt leaden and he delicately pushed up the skin between his eyes, removing the weight. "What kind of music?" he asked Arletha Mae.

"That was the question."

"I don't know," Larry answered. "All kinds." He doubted that talking was going to work. "Something with a beat." He didn't know why he said that. Songs that thumped tended to get on his nerves.

"Me," Arletha Mae said, "I like something that reaches on down to your soul."

"Soul music?"

"That too." Arletha Mae lowered her knees a little and danced her fingers lightly over Jason's chest. Larry had gotten quiet, so she poked round for something else to discuss. "What you gonna be doing with yourself? You know, a job?"

"I've got a job," Larry replied. In some strange way she'd nailed it though. Even before today, he'd been considering other things. Law school, if he could bring up his grades. Or something with an office and a secretary. Anything to make his father proud.

Arletha Mae said, "I was hoping something else. Me, I'm gonna be a singer, you know."

"I didn't."

"Hmm hmm. Gonna have my own band. Guitar, piano, drums, maybe two backup. My auntie say I got this voice made in Heaven. 'Course it wouldn't be no kinda right, I say it myself."

"No, it wouldn't," Larry agreed.

Watching them travel, Arletha Mae gracefully drew her hands down over her shoulders and breasts. "Gonna get myself some dresses like Whitney and Janet got."

"Whitney Houston?"

"And Janet Jackson. Dresses that be so fine, all pretty and smooth with them things on 'em, what you call 'em, so small and sparkly . . . ?"

"Sequins?"

"Sequins, shiny as stars."

Larry tried to imagine her up on a stage, tracked by a spotlight. She had nice eyes and a figure that would look good in tight, toney gowns, but Whitney Houston and Janet Jackson were attractive women and she was plain in a way no amount of makeup and flattering lighting could fix. He thought he might be doing her a favor by telling her she didn't have a chance, but he no longer felt like being cruel. His forbearance gave him some satisfaction, as though he were protecting her.

"Everyone has to have their dreams," he said.

"Ain't no dream. It's what's gonna happen."

"Well, good luck."

Arletha Mae shivered. The night was getting colder, slipping into her bones, and wisps of smoke from the fires had found the room. She hugged Jason to her, cheek to her chin. "One of these days," she whispered. "Then I'm gonna buy you things you ain't gonna believe."

Larry watched her with pity, which he attempted to conceal: "You're right. Hard work is what it takes." He was probably fooling himself. Even if he had the grades, he didn't think he could pass the bar. "Besides, hard work is its own reward." He felt his stomach muscles cramp as he leaned forward to probe his ankle. The skin was spongy and tender, but maybe the ankle wasn't broken. One thing he was certain of, it wouldn't support his weight. Leaning back against the toilet, he heard then saw a chopper skimming low under the dark clouds. He watched its green and white guide lights vanish.

"Getting chilly."

"Sure is," Arletha Mae agreed.

"He alright?"

Arletha Mae nodded. "Weather don't bother him much." She studied Larry some. Now that he wasn't being angry or scared, he was near to fine on the eyes. Scrub and dress him up and he'd be looking good goin' on down an aisle.

"You got a girl?"

The question rattled Larry. "Why do you want to know?" he asked sharply. He wondered if she thought he was gay.

"Jus' asking."

"Sure. I've got a girl."

Arletha Mae grinned and shook her head. "You ain't got no girl."

"Why do you say that?" Larry asked nervously. Once, when an aunt deep into religion had dragged him to Midnight Mass, he'd been approached by a subtle fag. Coupled with his father's abuse, this had gotten Larry to wondering how others perceived his soft features.

"Jus' don't believe you do," Arletha Mae told him.

"I think you have to really like someone." Sometimes he wished his nose or mouth was crooked. "I went steady in college."

"Huh huh." Arletha Mae's smile didn't retreat. Nine years older, but he didn't know half as much 'bout life.

"Her name was Sharon."

"Pretty name. Pretty girl?"

"Very."

"White?"

"What?"

"I'm jus' funning with you. Was she nice?"

"I guess." She was blond and blue eyed like him. People would ask if they were brother and sister. Neither was comfortable with their lovemaking. She preferred being on top. That way she could press into his neck so he couldn't see her face. The noises she made were hesitant and unspecific. One night she admitted she had never had an orgasm. A month later she'd left him for a football player. Since then his relationships had consisted of a few drunken bar pick-ups and three months of dating an older woman who wouldn't sleep with him, which suited him just fine; he was sorry when she'd gotten a job in another city. Sometimes when he went to his parents' house, his mother would corner him and ask, with that worried expression she kept handy for most occasions, when was he going to find the right girl and settle down? One of these days, he'd always tell her. One of these days.

"She just wasn't the right one," Larry told Arletha Mae.

"You always know," Arletha Mae said. "Me, I found him."

"Oh?"

"Huh huh. His name is Michael."

"Is he black?" Larry wasn't about to let her realize how uptight he was about the opposite sex.

"As the ace," Arletha Mae laughed.

Larry indicated the baby. "He's, ah . . ."

"Jason."

"Jason's father?" Larry asked warily.

"That's right. I wasn't messing with no other."

"You're married? I don't see a ring."

"Close." Despite the cold she could feel Michael inside her, the reach of him.

Larry wasn't comfortable having this conversation. "So where is he?"

"Around."

Larry decided not to press it. "O.K."

"We got the wedding all planned," she said.

"Congratulations," he said reluctantly.

"Lots of folks, family and friends."

"That's nice." He preferred feeling sorry for her. "I'd say it's closer to two. You know, the time." He gestured to the space surrounding them. "What were these? Apartments?"

"Lincoln Heights project. They had this fire."

"A fire? That's funny."

"No it ain't."

Larry suppressed his laughter. "I'm sorry."

"It was all coming down anyways," Arletha Mae said. "What wasn't burned, weren't worth saving."

"Where'd the people go?"

"Somewhere else. Wherever they could."

Larry had been holding up pretty well, but now the nerve ends centered in his forehead and eyes were pressing in. He yawned elaborately. Arletha Mae was talking to him. Her voice seemed distant.

"You okay?"

"Yeah," he said, yawning again.

"Hang in."

Larry nodded. Somewhere out in the darkness either an old woman or a parrot shrieked, "Feed me!" When he tried to lift his head, his chin froze on his chest and his eyes closed.

"Larry?"

"Huh?" His head jerked up and his eyes opened.

"You awake?"

Larry nodded again. "Got so tired, all of a sudden." His words traveled even slower than his thoughts. I sound like a drunk, he told himself. Where's blond and blue eyed Sharon? Where's my fucking hard-on?

"Maybe I should do all the talking," Arletha Mae suggested. "Michael and me, that's what we do time we drove to Vegas. Hundreds and hundreds and hundreds miles, him driving, me keeping him on the road."

Larry blinked and looked startled.

"What?"

"Yeah, think I should." Arletha Mae paused to gather a subject.

"Ain't so bad living where I do, 'cepting my auntie, she ain't home much, and my granny, she so old. Old and hard. My auntie say she useta be dif'rent, maybe not much, but a tad, back when she was young living on down there in Selma. My auntie says it gotta be my gramps made her that way, you know, a little better. See, my auntie done tole me these here stories my granny done tole her, 'bout when they was spooning. My gramps, he useta take granny on down to the 'Bama river. They'd set up there on Pettis bridge, jus' watching the water run and run. My gramps, he had himself this way of seeing, useta tell her these things. Said river was this smooth carpet, ride you anywheres. 'Course, after they was hitched and he got to knowing her little better, he said river was this short walk for people don't wanta live no more, but my auntie says he was a real good man, and her own mama, my granny's sister—prettiest woman you ever seen, I got pictures—she said the same. And even granny, she admit that some. She say he never raised a hand and was tol'rable long as you wasn't downwind of him. See, he done worked in this here slaughter place killing poor, dumb animals, brought that smell on home. He played mouth harp and done some singing. I figure that's where I get that from too." Arletha Mae sighed. "Yeah, what I unnerstand, a real good man, even though he never did read the Book. Died 'fore he was forty. Natural death."

Larry's head went back to his chest. He hadn't heard a word for quite a while. "Don't kill me," he murmured.

"Maybe you should jus' go on to sleep. I'm here, I ain't goin', you be safe."

Arletha Mae's voice was at the far end of a tunnel, then it was whisked away by the darkness of passage. Larry was in a technicolor dream, splashes of sharp focus hues, no clouds, no wire, no wasted angel hawking menace in his ear. He was behind the wheel of his cruiser, following the center line down a lonely desert stretch, taking in the tall cactuses, scrub brush and heat lightning sparking behind distant hills. Someone had given the souped-up Chevy Caprice a sunroof which was open; the overhead Mars lights were revolving in slow motion, blue and red flashing at 33 RPM. Karl's naked body was on the back seat, tossing when the tires hit the ruts. Insistent sunlight through the roof framed the corpse, which was bloated and turning black. Angling the rearview down, Larry kept checking for the revolting or the macabre—loud gas, hands dripping flesh around his neck—but all he got were rabbits darting across the road where less fortunate cousins and neighbors were melting into the molten asphalt. At first, the rabbits appeared one at a time, a bolt of fur braving Larry's wheels. Then, after a while, they started coming in pairs, then three or four, then in bunches. Most made it safely to the other side, but now and then Larry would hear a mild thud and feel the car shudder, and in the side mirror he would see a rabbit motionless or thrashing toward death behind him. Then suddenly the creatures were leaping from all angles onto the car, blanketing the windows and gnawing on the glass until their mouths and teeth were thick with blood and foam. Larry didn't scream, didn't throw up a defensive arm, he just kept driving down a road he could no longer see or understand.

Arletha Mae sat there watching him sleep. From the ugly smile on his face she figured he was dreaming 'bout the steady he'd loved and lost. Must've made the wrong moves. Easy to see why. White boys

never knew jackshit 'bout cutting on loose from their mama's strings.
'Course there was 'vantages to that. Kept 'em polite, you didn't always gotta be watching their hands or their zippers. Black boys like
to slap your brains to 'Bama you don't get down. What was she, not
yet eleven when Jimmie Jay forced her head where it had no damn
intention of wanting to go, in the weeds in the lot behind Marcus
Garvey Elementary. She had long hair then and he'd twisted it in his
strong hand, holding her in place, making her lick his cock. 'Get to
pretending it's a lollipop,' he'd told her. She'd shut her eyes tight and
tried, but all she could see was this ugly black rod that jerked to the
touch of her tongue. 'Suck it, bitch.' That was next. She'd done that
too, no damn choice, taking the thing in her hand to steady it, taking
it in her mouth, feeling its heat and separate life, tasting its sweat and
salt, trying not to gag, trying to hold back her vomit, keeping her eyes
clamped shut, thinking I am paying for something, I don't know
what. After Jimmie Jay was done, after she'd thought all the pain was
past, he'd gone up her head, cutting her ear and yelling she'd 'bout
ruined him with her teeth. Then he'd left her there to walk round,
moving jus' to move, hugging herself and washing out the hurt with
her tears. Took her awhile to ride out her shame after that. Spent a
week home sick from school, avoiding her granny's stares and suspi-
cions. When she went back, there were other eyes flashing new interest, word had gotten round. So she'd cut her hair and figured what
the fuck, I ain't worth shit no how. Got to doing whoever'd ask, got
to doing it pretty fair. Learned to keep her eyes open and her teeth
outta the way. By the time she turned twelve, she'd done most Marcus
Garvey, telling herself, honey, this either a slide to Hell or please,
please, to love. 'Bout the time she realized neither was charging her
way, her auntie got wind and put her right. Said, 'Girl, you making
more enemies than true found friends, you gonna give it out, might as
well get paid, help on out with what gotta go on the kitchen table.'
Arletha Mae took this hard advice to her heart. Spent the next couple
years learning her ABC's whoring, replaced boys with men. Got near

perfect at doing what had got her a tore up ear. Price was ten for sucking and a hand and wipe finish, fifteen if they insisted on coming in her mouth. Fucking never had a rate, she never let a single joy boy stud inside her. This way she felt she kept part of herself pure. 'Course even at that it took some damn hard work convincing herself she wasn't a bucket of slop. Pretending helped. That much she could thank Jimmie Jay for. Pops and cones and slurpees, these were the tastes she put into her mind when she went down. For the ones she could almost like, she shut her eyes and gave 'em faces. Imagined she was blowing some picture-cover hero like the oh so fine cats on TV. Most the time though it was living on down there in the slop, same as with Jimmie Jay. All kinds demands. 'Lick my balls, bitch, faster, cunt, Oh Gawd, oh Gawd, oh Gawd, you ho.' You had to keep your cool, let 'em shoot into your face, your eye, jus' smile and wipe the cum off. Otherwise things could get real rough. Could anyways even if you showed no mind. Black eye, bloody lip. One cat broke her jaw. Another broke her wrist. Another slashed her breast with a razor. Twelve stitches. Hurt like hell. Scar was still there. When the damage got real bad like this, it was good reminding herself of the hard truth no amount of pretending could chase away: she wasn't worth shit, no way, no how. She tried some new gigs, to see if they might make a dif'rence in her head. Got herself a mean pimp to keep the beaters sedate. Bryan K. Not one of your high boot, snakeskin and boa feather smoothies. Just a cat with an old Ford wagon and a fast blade. Got to where he turned the meanness on her; more hurt, few more scars, so she figured Mother Horse might ease the ride. Got caught at home with a needle in her arm and powder on a spoon. For granny that was the last absolute last. Kicked her out. Bryan K. wasn't the answer. Him and his bed, was like living on spikes. Nothing left 'cept the streets, new kinda walking. Home was anywheres you could curl up, alleys, stairs, grates with a little blessed steamheat. H and the life took off the pounds. Got down to eighty, maybe less. Bones ached, gums bled, skin started changing colors, spells and whims of the no place blues. That razor had left an impression. She'd see it in her deep dreams, big as a sled and flashing on down. One night it seemed the answer. Borrowed herself a rusty Gillette and went behind a dumpster. Her hands were shaking so much, at first all she could get was a nick, then she took a long breath and dug deep. Her blood ran black in the light from the moon and she did the other wrist. She musta made some noise, 'cause some fool found her. They rushed her to County General and wrapped her up. Granny got the word and took her back in. Wouldn't talk to her but wouldn't have her on her conscience. Auntie tried to pump up her flesh and spirits with refried beans and ignored advice. After a week the bandages were off. After another week she was looking for another rusty razor. Then one day Wanda Lee came visiting and changed her life.

Arletha Mae woke from her past to the sound of Larry stirring. She wondered what it would be like taking him in her mouth, more colors, black on white. He'd come fast. Kneeling between his legs, she'd hear him cry out and she'd lift her head and smile, knowing he'd never had it like this.

Larry's eyes snapped open. His foot lunged for the brake from his dream and he looked frantically around for buck teeth closing on his throat.

"Take it easy, you're alright," Arletha Mae assured him.

"Huh?" Larry mumbled, trying to get her in focus. She was smiling at him in the strangest way.

"You was dreaming, that's all."

"Who are you?" Larry said anxiously, then he remembered and his face and body relaxed. "Was I?"

"Hmm hmm."

"Did I do anything?" He was afraid he'd said something that would compromise the way he presented himself.

"You was twisting and turning and making these weird kinda noises, like some scared all to hell dog."

Larry was relieved; these were things she'd already seen in him. "Oh," he said.

Arletha Mae's smile widened. "I was only funning again." She turned and faced the fire and smoke and distant flaying sounds outside that made the night seem unreal. "Jus' dreaming," she said, her eyes mildly troubled.

CHAPTER FOURTEEN

"Is that where we get on? Up there?"

From the passenger seat of the white Olds, Ben glanced questioningly at the woman before he realized she meant the freeway onramp down the empty street. They were only a block from the hospital, but the silence had been so deep, it seemed like miles.

"That's right, the Four fifty-three south," he told her, "but I'd rather go to the police station first." He had to keep trying even if part of him didn't want to; trying was what fathers were supposed to do.

"Where is it?"

"Twenty-third and Maple, I think."

"I heard on the radio the police stations were cordoned off."

"The radio's wrong sometimes," Ben said.

"It doesn't matter. I want to go home. I'll take you to yours, but that's all."

Nothing in the woman's face allowed for argument or much else. Her inflection was dead and her eyes were somewhere Ben didn't want to be. He took her in a little more, kept looking for things to take his mind off David.

She was around forty, slender and tidy in a two-toned dress of wavy browns and reds. The glow from the dash panel exaggerated the sharpness of her features, the high forehead and high cheekbones. Her sleek black hair was pinned up in a bun and she was well groomed and would have been pretty except for the eyes and the tension in her face, and tense was the way she drove, holding the wheel almost at arm's length.

"Why do you want to go to the police?" she asked, turning onto the entrance to the freeway.

"It doesn't matter."

"Alright."

Ben sank lower in the seat. Maybe the circuits would be open when he got home. He would stay on the phone until he got through.

The woman stopped for the light at the top of the ramp. The light changed to green. The woman hesitated before she pressed down on the gas, as though afraid that an ambush awaited them. She had muscular legs in nylons, black stiletto high heels and aggressive perfume. Ben felt like he was on a date designed for abuse.

"What's your name?" the woman asked indifferently.

"Ben." Her proximity bothered him and he edged closer to the door.

"I'm Irene Cho."

"Stouder. Ben Stouder." After a few seconds he said, "Thanks for, you know, doing this." The words didn't come out easily. His vocal cords were constricting and his throat was dry.

Irene shrugged. Her response was similar to Philip's; people do what they think is right then start regretting it.

"I'm sorry about your . . . ?"

"My boss," Irene said quickly.

"I'm sorry."

The silence took over again. Even though there wasn't any traffic,

Irene kept her speed at a steady fifty-five. The Oldsmobile's engine was smooth.

On the other side of the center divider, headlights and spinning blue strobes suddenly blazed toward them and Ben instinctively shielded his eyes, then the two cop cars screamed past at a ridiculous movie speed. Irene logged their progress briefly in the rearview mirror before she spoke:

"What happened to you?"

The question seemed absurd. Nevertheless, Ben stated the obvious.

"I was beaten up."

"I meant the circumstances."

The circumstances still seemed unreal, he thought. "A car cut me off. They dragged me out and punched and kicked me silly. Then a man started yelling at them and they stopped and the man took me to the hospital."

"The man who helped you, was he white?"

"Excuse me?"

"His color."

"No. He was black."

"I'm surprised," Irene said.

Up ahead a number of buildings were burning just off the freeway. Smoke drifted across the lanes, so thick in places, it was like driving through fog. When the smoke cleared, Ben stared at the orange fires. "What happened with you?" he finally asked. Irene sucked in her breath and exhaled.

"I was giving my boss a ride home. He was sitting where you are."

"I know," Ben said. She had stretched a towel over the seat to cover up the blood, but splotches still showed through. He could feel the dampness through the seat of his pants.

"The street we were on was quiet, so I stopped for a light. Suddenly, this black man walked up and opened the door on your side before we knew what was happening. He started hitting Mr. Osawa in the face with his fist. He hit him very very hard. I can still hear the sound of him hitting. I screamed and drove away, very fast. The man didn't try and stop us. The door was open. I had to reach across Mr. Osawa to close it. It was a miracle we didn't crash." Irene took a deep breath before she went on.

"I thought he was going to be alright. He hadn't taken that many punches, although he was having trouble breathing. Then suddenly he slumped against the window. When we got to the hospital, I could see he was dead. A doctor told me he'd had a stroke. I told the doctor he had died of fright."

"I'm sorry."

"No, you're not," Irene said bluntly. "You didn't know him. He was a nice man." She shuddered. "I'm going to have to tell his family. What am I going to say?"

"I don't know," Ben said.

"Neither do I."

"Maybe somebody's already told them."

"I doubt it."

They went by the last of the closed ramps. An electronic message board up ahead was dark; Ben thought he could see bullet holes. A dirt and weeds embankment on his right was on fire, the flames nodding as gently as reeds in a breeze. More smoke threaded his vision and he looked away. He watched the needle fall to thirty as Irene dropped her speed.

"Where were you going?" she asked.

He might as well tell her. "I was looking for my son."

Irene wrinkled her brow. "Your son?"

"He got lost."

"Lost?"

"He wandered off."

Irene glanced at Ben in astonishment. "Why did you let him?"

Ben didn't feel like explaining. "I don't know."

"How old is he?"

"Ten," Ben told her.

"Did you find him?"

"Not yet."

"I don't have children," Irene said. "Maybe I just don't understand."

Ben shook his head. "Neither do I."

The moon was wrapped in dark clouds that mirrored the smoke floating across the windshield. Squinting, Irene leaned forward. Ben leaned with her. "Hard seeing, isn't it," he said.

"Yes," Irene replied.

Turning, Ben gazed out the side window. Reflected in the glass, his face was lumpy and swollen, his left eye had closed to a slit. He looked like a Halloween ghost. He recalled David's face when Schultz had turned on the power mower, and when they'd spun out on the country road. Both times Ben would've sworn David was about to die of fright.

"Where do we get off?" Irene asked.

"What's that?"

"Your exit."

"Langdon. About four miles." If the circuits stayed closed, he would be trapped at home. No car, too hurt to look for David on his own.

"Where do you live?" Ben asked.

"A few miles past you. Why?"

"I was just curious. What are you going to do when you get there?"

"I'll probably have a drink, then I'll try and get some sleep."

She had a car. If he stayed with her, he might be able to talk her into helping him in some manner.

"I could use a drink too."

"Then you should have one."

"Look," Ben said directly, "I don't want to go home."

Irene's face tightened.

"What are you saying?"

"That I don't want to be alone."

She shook her head.

"I'm sorry."

"Look, it's nothing like that," he assured her. "I just want some company and some time to think."

"You must have friends, a wife?"

"Not anymore."

Irene slowed as she approached his exit. She shook her head again. "I don't think so."

"Please? The shape I'm in, I couldn't do anything even if I wanted to."

Irene took her foot off the brake. The car coasted through the darkness.

"One drink then you have to go home."

"One drink."

The clock on the dash said it was 1:37 A.M.

Cutting through an alley where a slouched ratface was retailing lethal hardware to eight year olds, J.D. reached his destination, a two storey cinder-block lowrise with a moldering yellow facade. Far as he could tell, the building was abandoned; the windows were out, the interior unlit. Pressed against a wall, he looked up at the sky. The chopper was still circling, but the muzzle flashes from the roof had stopped. The possibility that the sniper had walked caused J.D. to experience a profound disappointment.

The chopper's searchlight was scanning the street, coming too close. J.D. slipped into the building's entrance, away from the light's reach. Several rapid shots came from the roof and he smiled as the light disappeared.

Passing through the space where dual doors had been, he found himself in an enormous room. Moonlight spent its dying light through the empty windows, revealing an interior that was barren— walls and slab floor stripped, insulation coils dangling like tentacles from the ceiling, and set in the far wall, stairs that gave off the odor of urine even from a distance. Still, some effort at renovation was in evidence; part of a copper-colored wall had been painted white, and on the floor by the wall there were white splotched dropcloths, two open cans of paint, a brush, and a stick for stirring. He heard the gunfire again, muffled by the ceiling.

J.D. went and climbed the stairs by feel. The grain of the railing was coarse and the walls and risers reeked of decay as well as piss, a stench redolent of war; socks rotting in the rain. When he reached the top of the stairs, the fading moonlight washed over the darkness. The second floor was like the first, open and unfurnished.

Someone had set up a small hooch as protection against the elements, plastic sheeting and cardboard cut and joined cleverly for shelter. J.D. lit a match then bent down and peered inside. There was a rumpled bedroll and a stash of supplies; cans of food, a razor, a bar of soap, a corroded bucket filled with water, a hand mirror, a toothbrush and paste, a tall plastic cup bearing the Big Mac emblem and a neat stack of cheap clothes.

The sound of the chopper was suddenly on him again. He quickly blew out the match and faced the throp and growl. Jesus, but the thing was almost in his face, hanging there by a window. Through the dust-clouded glass he could see the police logo and the pilot inside, a lean man so intent on the sniper, he was unaware of J.D. After a few seconds he swung the gear stick to the left and the helicopter climbed and banked. J.D. tracked it until it was out of sight. In Nam choppers were friends. Here they were enemies.

Another short flight of stairs led him to a small door that opened onto the flat concrete roof. It was high enough up for there to be a little wind, which didn't quite override the cooing of pigeons. Letting the door ease shut behind him, he walked to where he could see more.

A coop packed with at least a dozen birds was up against a side of the access housing. The pigeons stopped pacing long enough to regard J.D. as a possible supplier of food. He considered speaking to them in the droll manner he'd spoken to other semi-wildlife this night, but someone who clearly didn't welcome intrusions was armed up here.

Crouched down against the roof's ledge, the kid was twenty feet away, forcing a clip into a pistol, nervously checking the sky. Not wanting to startle him, J.D. cleared his throat. The kid wheeled about and dropped the gun in surprise, then retrieved it; while he didn't exactly point the weapon at J.D., he was coming pretty damned close. J.D. showed his palms to let the kid know he was harmless, but the boy stayed crouched and kept the gun ready.

"Hi," J.D. said casually. He had no idea if the safety was on or off.

"Who the hell are you?" the kid shot back. He was well shaven and good looking and his clogs and loose fitting trousers were clean. A warm-up jacket with the letters of another city's football team was keeping out the early morning chill. His skin was an uneven freckly brown, pigmentation that couldn't make up its mind.

"J. D. Lawson," J.D. replied, "but I think what you meant was what the fuck am I doing up here."

The boy's laugh was close to a hiccup. "Something like that," he said. The wind gusted, pressing his trousers against his thin legs, and the pigeons pushed against each other, looking for either warmth or room.

"I saw what was happening up here and I was curious," J.D. explained.

"Yeah?" the boy said warily, although he lowered the pistol slightly.

"Uh huh, and by the way, I think he's coming back."

The kid jerked his head up at the sky, where the bulbous shape of the chopper reappeared, approaching at a steady pace, searchlight streaming out from its nose. J.D. used the diversion to ease over and squat down beside the boy.

"Damn," the boy swore, "thought it was gone. Damn." Watching the chopper, he put the gun in his left hand and reached across his body and shook hands with J.D. "I'm Floyd." The boy had a good handshake, one that didn't try to prove anything.

"Pleased to meet you," J.D. said. "How old are you, son?"

"Nineteen," Floyd told him. J.D.'s smile was for himself. He had been nineteen when the Army had showed him how to kill with pride.

The chopper's rotors grew loud, then the searchlight blinded them. J.D. shielded his eyes and ducked. The boy returned the gun to his right hand but ducked too instead of shooting. Then the glare and the racket were gone, leaving only a backdraft and more nervous cooing from the pigeons. J.D. watched the helicopter's guide lights recede into the darkness. His legs felt tight but he stayed in the same crouch as the boy.

"It'll be back," Floyd said ruefully, wiping a sheen of sweat from his brow, "but I don't think he's armed."

"I already figured that out. What I can't figure out is why you're doing this?"

"Protecting my home. And my birds. What I can't figure out is why *he's* doing it."

"He's probably waiting for friends to come and shoot you," J.D. said candidly. "Plus, he seems to be stubborn."

"Think they will? His friends?"

"Probably not. The city's pretty busy at the moment."

The boy nodded. J.D. looked up with him as the chopper returned, its light fanning down like a carpet you could climb to heaven. The chopper was smaller than the big Hueys and Chinooks they had in Nam. During the day their shadows, the dark ghosts of the machines, had crossed the land with an inexorable purpose.

Floyd braced his arms on the ledge, took fastidious aim and released the safety. Flame flared from the muzzle and the pistol bucked and cartridges spun off to his right as he squeezed off several errant shots before the chopper got close. Hearing a commotion in the coop, J.D. turned and saw the pigeons beating the air and the wire with their wings; they had endured the bird-like machine, but the gunfire had set them off. The light swept over J.D. and Floyd and over the coop, where the wire was speckled now with the pigeons' blood, then the light was past, part of the sky.

"You need to lead him a little," J.D. volunteered.

Floyd's eyes had gotten large and fixed. His hand worked the zipper of his jacket, up then back down.

"Lead him?"

"Shoot where he's going to be a second later," J.D. whispered.

"I really don't want to hurt anybody," Floyd said. "I just want it to go away."

"Well . . ." J.D. was shivering; the wind had gotten worse and his head was cold. He regretted giving away his hat.

"Do you think I could?" Floyd asked.

"What's that?"

"Hurt it? Him?"

"With what you're shooting and what you're shooting at, it's not likely."

The boy made a show of frowning, but J.D. sensed he was relieved; his eyes returned to normal and he left his zipper alone. The chopper made another pass. Floyd led it. Wings flurried behind him. With his second shot the helicopter lurched and hung suspended for a beat before it wobbled away. J.D. watched the boy hold his breath as he tracked its flight, relaxing when the chopper steadied and straightened out.

"Maybe we should go inside," Floyd suggested, as the chopper started back toward them in a flat, hard, angry line, the pilot leaning into his stick. J.D. felt the tightness leave his legs as he got to his feet.

"Good idea."

Cooing and scrambling feet followed J.D. and Floyd as they walked past the coop. "Easy, it's alright," Floyd murmured, trying to soothe his flock before stooping through the short access door, which J.D. locked behind them.

"Why did you do that?" Floyd asked in the sudden darkness.

"Just in case he decides to land on the roof." J.D. could sense those eyes getting wide and fixed again.

"You think he'd do that?"

"Maybe," J.D. answered. "He seems to be taking this personally."

They listened to the chopper hover over the roof, its rotors drowning out the wind and the pigeons. Finally, the rotors receded then died out.

"He still might come back," Floyd said with a quaver in his voice.

"I wouldn't be at all surprised," J.D. said.

They went carefully down the stairs, using the walls for direction and balance.

"I've got a flashlight, but it needs batteries," Floyd said.

When they reached the second floor, Floyd asked J.D. if he wanted something to eat and J.D. said, "Why not." He gave his matches to the boy and followed him to the hooch, waiting while Floyd struck a flame and ducked inside.

"What would you like?"

"Something fresh."

Floyd returned with a can of peaches and a fork. He dug an opener out of a pocket of his jacket and twisted off the can's lid. After handing the can and fork to J.D., Floyd lowered himself to the floor, where he sat cross-legged. J.D. joined him. The slices were cold and good. When he'd had enough, J.D. offered the can to Floyd, but the boy shook his head.

"I don't seem to have any appetite."

J.D. nodded and ate another slice. "Always that way after your first time in combat. Where'd you get the gun?"

"From this guy in a van. He sold it cheap. I only wanted it for protection."

"Your home."

"That's right."

J.D. finished, gulping down the syrupy juice after the peaches were gone. He belched and rubbed his stomach.

"That was good. Thanks."

"You're welcome."

J.D. looked around at the pockets of shadow and dim light. Through the window he could see the fading moon. "How long have you lived here?"

"A little over a year. I had a job at McDonald's, assistant manager, but I got laid off. My unemployment ran out eight months ago. I lived out of my car for a while. When I moved in here, I sold it for salvage."

J.D. shook his head sympathetically then stretched out his legs and leaned back on his elbows. "So how do you get by?"

"Recycling bottles and cans. I won't panhandle," Floyd said earnestly.

"I believe you. You seem like a nice young man."

Floyd smiled.

"You wouldn't have a beer?" J.D. asked.

"I don't drink." Picking up the pistol, Floyd placed it in his palm and examined it, as though the weapon contained some sort of explicable truth. "And I don't like guns. I don't know why I bought this."

"Protection."

"I know, but . . ." His voice trailing off, Floyd put the gun carefully down and looked away. Some of the cold from outside had climbed through the floor. J.D. took this as a sign.

"I should be going."

"You're welcome to spend the night."

J.D. realized there was nothing sexual in the invitation, but he wasn't interested in sleep.

"Thanks, but I've got places I've got to be."

"Could you stay a little while?" Floyd asked politely. "I don't get much company. That's why I've got the pigeons. One or two at a time. You know, just throwing out crumbs. I really enjoy them, although they're not the cleanest birds, it takes a lot of scrubbing to get out where they mess. I was hoping there would be some chicks, or whatever you call them, but they don't seem very interested in mating. Maybe at night, when I'm asleep?"

J.D. nodded but he wasn't really listening. It was annoyingly quiet outside. Wrinkling his nose, as though he'd just discovered a bad odor, J.D. leaned back on his elbows. "Maybe," he muttered. Automatic weapons fire from somewhere smoothed his expression.

The boy waited out the burst, then shook his head. When he spoke, his voice was sad. "It's not much different from any other night—just slightly worse."

"Well . . ."

Floyd abruptly cheered up. "Since you're staying, we could make this a party."

J.D. wondered if he'd misread the boy's intentions.

"A party?"

"Yes," Floyd said happily. "I've got a couple of cans of grapes that aren't so fresh. They've probably fermented. That way you can—"

J.D. finished for him. "Have my drink."

"Exactly." Springing to his feet, Floyd ducked back into the hooch. J.D. saw the faint glow from another match, heard him rummaging around. Floyd reminded him of Henry Rodriguez. Henry was a walking hard-on, but in some ways he was as guileless as this boy.

When Floyd returned he poured the grapes into the empty can of peaches, leaving only the juice. The taste was tolerable, sweet turning sour, just like so many other things J.D. had put into his stomach over the last few hours, over the many years.

"How is it?" Floyd wanted to know.

"Good," J.D. said.

Pleased, Floyd sat opposite him, legs angled out, supporting himself with a hand. J.D. gave him the can. The boy drank, shared communion.

"Guess it's pretty silly, isn't it, drinking old juice, pretending it's something else. Same as shooting at that old helicopter."

"Oh, I don't know," J.D. replied.

They talked for a few more minutes before J.D. left. Floyd told him some of the things he had learned while living alone, about how you could soft boil eggs with wire mesh, a match and a coffee can, or dry your clothes by scotch-taping them to a sill facing the sun. J.D. didn't tell him these were standard riffs of the vagrant life. Better to let him believe that his discoveries were priming the basics.

Back out on the street, J.D. looked for a new direction. Any would do. He started walking, not knowing where. He hadn't gone far before he heard the chopper return to the boy's home. Leaning against a lamppost, resting his suddenly heavy bones, he watched the helicopter settle over the rooftop, a provocation, a challenge. J.D. walked away from the image and what it called to mind, soft focus snaps from Nam, those memories that kept turning in his stomach, twisting him away from any kind of a normal life. In his mind he was slogging through the jungle, searching for Henry, working his way with an increasing urgency through the high grass, all the juices in his belly going sour as the slow knowledge came on him that he'd fucked up, that Henry was probably out there dead because of him.

J.D. ran into an overturned trash barrel, realized he had been walking with his eyes closed. He set his sights straight on, fixed on the street, the city, the night, shifting impressions of horror and short promise hauling him in.

He kept walking.

Kept on.

CHAPTER FIFTEEN

Irene lived in a neighborhood of suspect security. The houses were small and flimsy, hers beige with a shingle roof and roses in the garden. After parking in the narrow driveway, she took Ben through the front door and flicked a switch. The light from a Tiffany lamp bathed the living room. The furniture was modern American, folksy geometry, but the doodads and paintings were Asian. Ben watched Irene consider then reject opening the bay window curtains before walking briskly to the kitchen.

"Coffee?"

"Thought we were having a drink?"

"Just one."

"I know. Can I use your phone?"

"Behind you. On the stand."

Ben tried the station. The circuits were still busy so he called the neighbor he'd phoned earlier. The phone kept ringing. Through the kitchen doorway he saw Irene empty two glasses into the sink, washing what little liquor remained down the drain. After drying her hands she turned off the faucets and got two clean tumblers out of a cabinet.

"What would you like?" she asked.

Ben replaced the receiver with a long sigh and ran a hand down his bruised face. He felt like giving up. The impulse also made him feel guilty; his kid could be dead out there. "I don't know," he said wearily. "Do you have any Scotch?"

"I think so."

"Straight up."

If he rested, maybe the guilt would leave him alone. He gravitated toward a velour sofa. He wanted to stretch out but didn't want to give Irene Cho the wrong idea regarding his intentions, so he stuck a hand in his pants pocket then realized he looked about as nonchalant as a car wreck. Besides, the stance was throwing him off balance. Roaming currents in his skull suggested he might topple over.

Irene returned to the living room holding the liquor away from her, as if she might spill it, although the tumblers were only half full. She gave Ben one of the glasses.

"No luck?"

"I couldn't reach anyone." He was beginning to tilt. Irene noticed with alarm.

"I'll be right back."

Sipping his Scotch, he watched her walk down a short hallway and disappear into a bedroom. She had watered down his drink. He should have known.

"You should lie down," Irene said, returning with an old blanket and spreading it out on the sofa. "Your clothes, you know."

He lay down splayed, a foot on the carpet, a leg bent, the glass tipped in his cupped hands. There was blood on the tumbler from his fingers. Irene sat facing him in a polished chrome chair. "Is that better?" she asked.

"Sort of," he replied with some truth; he didn't feel so woozy. "Can I use your phone again?"

She brought it to him and Ben got through to the station this time. A cop found his paperwork and told him they would look for David tomorrow. When Ben tried to argue, the cop said he would call him back. Ben gave Irene's number but had the impression the cop was just trying to get him off the line. He had to exercise restraint when he replaced the receiver.

"Not what you wanted to hear?" Irene asked.

Ben shook his head. Despair was upon him. The feeling wasn't entirely unpleasant. He reached for a little rapport, the depersonalized intimacy of small talk, before it went too deep.

"You have a very nice house."

Irene didn't reply. Ben jiggled his glass, then remembered there wasn't any ice. "You live here alone?" There was a conspicuous pause before she answered.

"Yes."

"I'll pay you," Ben blurted out.

"To do what?"

"Drive me around, look for my son."

"No."

Irene's eyes had the cast of coming to terms with trauma. Ben sipped the diluted Scotch. "Do you want to watch the news, see what's going on?" he asked. If things were calmer, David had a better chance. He might even show up on the screen, on the fringe of some local color.

Irene indifferently switched on the television. An angry hash flared on the screen then calmed into a picture of a man and a woman engaged in post-coital banter. Irene changed to another station. A female field reporter was holding a mike out at arm's length to a large black man who gesticulated fiercely as he described how today was a social upheaval, not a riot. In the background, flanked by stray smoke and littered sidewalks, people were waving their arms and making faces at the camera. Irene sighed and turned off the TV. "You should go home," she said.

"I know." Parts of Ben were growing numb and he shifted his weight, jarring loose some worrisome sensations. Touching his side he felt the heat of his swollen skin. "On a scale of one to ten," he said to himself.

"What?"

"You want to hear a joke? It's Halloween and there's these two dead guys and . . ."

Irene stared at him hard. Ben glanced at himself in a wall mirror. His smile was a rictus. "Never mind." He swallowed more liquor. He was down to the dregs.

Irene absently smoothed her skirt. "He was a jeweler. I work for him." She squeezed the fabric and released it. "Worked. His name was Osawa."

Ben nodded dully. His left foot was dead.

"He was a good boss. Very fair. I wonder what the funeral will be like."

Ben quickly finished what was in his glass. "Okay if I have another?"

"We agreed just one."

"I'll make it small. I'll even get it." He needed to know if he could walk. If he could walk, he could look for David. He had to push off twice and suppress a groan and grab his left knee to steady himself once he was up. "I'll be right back," he said, through clenched teeth. In the kitchen he filled his glass with Scotch, straight up. Knowing he could lurch without any support gave him the strength to sit instead of lying down when he returned to the sofa. His smile faded when he realized that her eyes were misting over.

"Helluva note, isn't it," Ben said.

"I'm alright." Irene wiped her eyes. "Do you think they'll call back?"

"I don't know."

"He'll probably make it home on his own."

"I don't think so." Ben grimly inhaled some Scotch.

"What do you do?"

Ben's eyes shifted to her.

"Hmm?"

"For a living?"

"I'm an engineer. Unemployed," he said bitterly.

"These are hard times."

"Getting harder."

Irene had left the door open and the light on in her bedroom. Beyond the darkness of the hallway, he noticed a man's large jacket lying neatly on the bed. The face of a smiling, overweight man in a photograph on the coffee table was suddenly familiar. Ben's gaze went from the picture to Irene.

"It wasn't that serious. Like I told you, he was a nice man." She took a sip from her drink then gazed at the curtains shrouding her front window. "I don't think they're going to call back."

"I know." Ben realized he hadn't had a cigarette since almost yesterday.

Slope and his joy boys were down on East 89th, jamming some sprightly fear up some firemen asses, seeing if the personnel could keep their mud.

They were fighting a blaze in a humongous warehouse that took up the better part of the block. Whoever had set it had a notion about combustibles. The fire had shot through the building in no time flat, rolling waves that whooshed and curled and spread. Way Slope saw it, turf was first arrived and the Nine Deuce Crips had beat the shiny red trucks by a sprint, give or take, so what did the fuckers expect, 'cept what they were getting, rocks and bottles and whatever abuse.

"It's ours!" Slope shouted good naturedly as he sidearmed an empty pint of vodka liberated from Triple A Liquor. The bottle clipped a hoseman, causing him to lose control of his equipment.

Water whipped the feet of friends and associates, getting the desired response from the Nine Deuce, peals and whoops of laughter.

"My, my, my," Slope remarked. "It look like we done run outta missiles to try out our skills."

Separated from the helmets and yellow slickers by the empty street, Slope stuck his hands in his jean pockets, leaned back against his pink, buffed '82 Caddy and watched. His homes did the same, taking on the role of fans rooting for their side. Although their eyes were red and stinging from the ashes and smoke, they were having fun. Near much fun as Arletha Mae going down. That smooth busy mouth.

Little Peter stopped bouncing a ball off a paddle long enough to shout, "Yay, fire," and raise a power fist.

"Good pick," Slope told him. Fact was, the fire was winning, burping up all the foam and wet the hoses could lay on it.

"I'm placing two to one," said Fat Tyrone.

"Don't know," said Web, who was named for his feet. "Water, it always come out on top."

They stopped rapping to get a read. The sprays were mobbed up in a spot where the flames were highest. So much water and smoke, no way of telling exactly what was going on. Then the water started dragging down the bright heat. The Nine Deuce goggled, prayed, lost faith, then suddenly the flames rocketed up again, challenging the sky, and all the cats cheered and lowered their heads and raised power fists into the smoky air.

"Sucker got heart," Sweet Leo remarked. Others nodded, saying, "Amen, amen."

"Hey man!" 9-T yelled at the fire fighters. "How you like that shit? Métete eso donde te quepa." One of the firemen turned to the Nine Deuce in terror. His eyes looked haunted in his white face and his thin lips were moving.

"What he saying?" Cobey asked.

Slope said, "Saying where's the police?"

Homeboys volunteered some possibilities.

"In their mamas."

"In Mississippi."

"Heading for Hollywood."

"The beach."

"The stars."

"Òjalá que llueva!"

"Waxing their four wheels."

"Brillo to wipe."

"Unner their beds."

"Doing Sister Bernice."

"I got this long barrel dream," 9-T crooned.

"Shit," Slope swore, shaking his head. "Trade all you niggers in for Eight Trey Rangers." When he saw that his boys looked hurt, he added, "Jus' funnin'." To pretend that's all he was doing, Slope took out his glass eye and yelled at the firemen, "Sure look pretty in the moonlight, don't it?" The few firemen who turned displayed revulsion along with their fear. Slope grinned at them and popped the glass back into its socket.

9-T had had enough of stationary funning. Never could stay still. He ran across the littered street and touched the nearest fireman on the shoulder. The fireman jumped and screamed like a woman. 9-T ran back across the street cackling and clutching his sides.

Scrap Iron, who had a bridal veil high on his shaved skull, was busy examining the intricacies of a juice squeezer, but 9-T's antics got his firm attention. "What the fuck?" he said.

"Injuns," 9-T answered. He was in a spinning seizure of giggles, his soiled Nikes flashing red reflector lights.

"Say what, nigger?"

"Injuns," 9-T repeated. He wasn't slowing down, so Scrap Iron slammed him in the hamstring with a tire iron. 9-T dropped with a shriek that jerked the firemen's heads back in their direction. Cobey shot the firemen with his thumb and forefinger and Little Peter sidearmed the paddle at them.

"Indians you was saying?" Scrap Iron grinned as 9-T picked himself and his tagger Magic Marker up and jammed his hands in the pockets of his tight bluejeans.

"Indians," 9-T said sullenly. "Do their enemies that way."

"Why the fuck?"

"Chinga tu madre," 9-T spit out.

Scrap Iron's eyes bulged.

"Say what?"

"Chinga tu madre," 9-T hissed, limping. "Vete al carajo."

Scrap Iron's eyes were close to coming out of his head. "What that white nigger saying?" he asked Slope.

"Something you don't wanta hear."

Scrap Iron reached for the tire iron again. 9-T jumped back, stumbling because his hands were still in his pockets. Pushing off from his car, Slope gripped Scrap Iron's twenty-inch biceps, holding him back. "The words, they jus' come out," Slope told him. "Don't mean nothing, nothing t'all." Scrap Iron crippled 9-T with his eyes, but backed off.

"Coup," Slope told Scrap Iron. "It's called counting coup."

"Coup what?"

"Ain't important," Slope said. He watched a chopper buzz a building a couple of miles away. Muzzle flashes flew up from the rooftop, followed by a frenzy of pigeons. "Yay," Little Peter said faintly. He twirled a finger carelessly in the air, as if to say, it ain't no thing.

Slope shrugged and rippled the muscles of his bare arm. When he'd had enough of watching his tattoo wink at him, he turned his attention to 9-T, who was moping in an exaggerated manner. During this dispute two weeks back, brought on by 9-T branding an 8-Trey Ranger's cat with a curling iron, the Ranger had got a blade up against 9-T's throat. Slope had flung the Ranger off. Saving 9-T caused him some regret; the kid was a few pops short. Didn't know which from what and always had that meanness ready to spring, Lord knows the reason; Nine's folks wasn't split and his old man had gainful employ, which was more than Slope could boast 'bout his sorry people. Maybe it was just because Nine was part PR. Always something to prove, even when nobody was asking.

9-T was trying to walk out the hurt in his leg. He shot Slope a glance that was asking for approval. Slope took a deep breath and dug deep for the false compassion required of a leader of boys.

"Say, 9-T? We could sure use some sounds," Slope said. "You bring your box?"

"Chinga tu madre."

Slope sighed. "That ain't the answer to the problem." Next time he'd be the one holding the blade. He dug deeper. "Hey, 9-T? That was real good, doing him that way. Showed class."

9-T brightened and puffed up with pride. "That's 'cause I'm a genius of sneak." Recent phrases clamped to 9-T's mind, leading to repetition, Slope thought. "That's right, sure is" he told 9-T, who beamed and started walking near like a normal child.

"My box, it in the back seat. I be right back."

Slope watched 9-T swagger away, then shook his head. "More like a genius of brag."

Scrap Iron said, "Say what?"

"I got good ears," Slope told him.

Scrap Iron got up and wandered off deep in thought, the tire iron resting on one shoulder, the bridal veil on the other. Lionel took his place, lazily turning the handle of the juice squeezer. Lionel was Slope's youngest and brightest, bright enough not to need a nickname. They watched the fire billow and sputter; the firemen were beginning to get it under control.

"Tyrone's gonna owe me money," Lionel said casually. Slope figured Lionel would succeed him, when he was too old or too dead. Lionel waved a hand at the trucks.

"Like to have me one of those hoses."

"To do what with?"

"Keep out the neighbors."

Slope guffawed and slapped Lionel on the back. 9-T sauntered toward them, boom box by his ear. Reaching awkwardly up with his free hand, he was playing with the dials, rushing past stations, raising and lowering the volume; static and music zoomed, stuttered, died, unnerving the men in the wet and foam-covered yellow slickers. Slope leaned over to quietly dis 9-T, but Lionel was tracking past him. "Hey . . . ?" Lionel said.

Slope turned to where Lionel was scoping this shambling honky kid, glassy eyed and coming their way, like he didn't know which from how from where.

9-T's eyes lit up with cruelty.

"Dig it," he said gleefully to Slope. "This we gotta do something with."

Slope wasn't listening. He was busy gauging the kid's sense and the level and sincerity of his own compassion.

"Motha's fucked," 9-T said happily.

"He's something," Slope agreed. Wasn't that hard to see God hadn't given the boy a mind.

9-T had his sights set on other parts of the anatomy:

"Hey, Slope, hey man? How we gonna do him, how we gonna fuck with him?"

"I don't know."

"Break his legs?"

Slope shook his head.

"His arms?"

Slope shook his head.

"That O.K., déjamelo a mí. I figure out something."

Leaving it set to static, 9-T put down his box, spun around and, shoes sparking, hiphopped over to the white boy. Slope watched as the child's features broke apart in confusion, his eyes following 9-T as

216

he pranced around him, bobbing his head and uttering low gutter cries.

"Hard to tell which one's in worse shape," Lionel said to Slope, who nodded.

"Ain't it though."

The rest of the Nine Deuce had turned from the fire to watch 9-T and the boy with a mix of pleasure and disgust. David pulled his head back as 9-T tried to blow soft affections in his face.

"Maybe I do him like the Sad Witch," 9-T said, tugging lightly on David's belt.

"He ain't got no cart," Web called out.

"I find something." 9-T's wild eyes danced about. "Hey, Scrap? Gimme your fucking pipe."

"Fuck you, nigger. It's mine."

"C'mon man."

"Chinga tu madre," Scrap Iron said.

"Maybe his cojones."

9-T flicked at the boy's crotch with long, quick fingers. David flinched but didn't attempt to escape. 9-T grabbed and held his arm long enough to tag an insignia on David's short-sleeve shirt. The light from the fire made David and 9-T's sweat shine and hollowed out their cheeks. Several of the firemen turned to stare.

"Hey 9-T?" Slope said, as 9-T felt up the boy's ass in passing.

"Yeah man?"

"Cool it."

"I'm counting coup," 9-T said, touching David on the shoulder.

"You ain't no Indian," Slope said, knowing damned well he should've let 9-T stay a posse tagger.

9-T bopped around, throwing hooks and jabs, pulling the punches up just short of David's stomach and face.

"You sure?"

"Yeah," Slope informed him.

"Positive?"

"That's enough," Slope said.

"I ain't even hurt him none yet."

9-T darted in and slapped the boy hard in the face and then smacked a sloppy kiss on his cheek and blew loudly into his ear. David's eyes were bright with damp and like those of a small, trapped animal looking for an opening to scoot through. Slope was on his feet now with steel in his voice:

"Knock it the fuck off!"

On its way to doing serious harm, 9-T's fist froze in midair. He stared balefully at Slope, whose face told him things he didn't want to hear, then his own face twisted and he kicked at the asphalt. "Sheeit. Mannnn."

"Ain't getting no scalps tonight," Lionel chuckled.

They were all laughing at 9-T now, except for Slope, who had mayhem in his heart, and the poor honky child whose legs were looking to run, only his nerves wouldn't allow. And it stayed like that for what seemed longer than it was, the heat and hurt rising in 9-T's thin, mean face until he could stand it no more, and he broke away and so did the boy, heading in opposite directions, David stumbling, 9-T just going.

CHAPTER SIXTEEN

Through the smoke, the fires and the clouds, hints of natural light were beginning to vein the darkness. The night was what you covered yourself with when you didn't want to see, Arletha Mae thought. The day was something else. She turned back to Larry. He was rubbing the sleep out of his eyes.

"Feeling any better?"

Larry snuffled and ran a sleeve under his nose.

"A little."

Arletha Mae laid her hand on the lantern. The glass was warm against her fingers, made her tingle all over. It was wondrous amazing how long the light could last. She gazed at Jason, then touched his sleeping face, wishing the momentary heat from her fingers could comfort him through what remained of the night. She loved her flesh against his. Sometimes she felt if she didn't touch him, he would vanish before her very eyes, the way those pretty people did when she turned off the TV.

"What was you dreaming 'bout?"

"Rabbits," Larry answered.

Jason's eyes were closed and relaxed, but his fingers were slowly kneading his palms. Arletha Mae let him take her thumb and squeeze it in his slumber.

"Rabbits. That's nice."

"You couldn't guess," Larry said ruefully. His neck and face felt like they'd been savaged by teeth and his buttocks were sore from being in one place for too long. Gripping the toilet bowl's rim with one hand, he shifted his weight.

"You look pretty sleepy yourself. Maybe you should get some rest?"

Arletha Mae shook her head. "Can't. Got respons'bilities. Him. You." She rested her chin on her knees and smiled a keeping secrets smile at Larry. "I got these here thoughts."

"What kind?"

"Clean," Arletha said in a way that wasn't quite. "I been thinking we be saved soon, all our prayers answered."

"Hope you're praying for both of us, because I don't believe in it." After the homosexual had tried to pick him up at Midnight Mass, Larry had willed himself to go back to church. Church hadn't worked out.

"That's too bad," Arletha Mae said, "but it don't matter. I got 'nough faith, it cover us all."

"Glad to hear it."

Arletha Mae returned his grin. "When we saved, I come visit you in the hospital, bring you some flowers."

"Flowers?" Larry tried to stifle a twitch on the left side of his face.

"Hmm hmm. And Pastor Manley's blessings."

"Pastor . . . ?"

"Where I go to church. North Springer Baptist."

"I think we drove past it."

"Need some fixing up but that don't matter neither. It a house of the Lord." Arletha Mae briefly closed her eyes and raised a hand, her fingers spread. "I done sinned but I been brought to His glory."

"Yeah?" Larry said. She was so clean in her conviction, she made him feel dirty. Not that he could blame himself. Only angels he'd been around lately wanted to push him off a high-rise cloud.

"Pastor Manley, you oughta hear him preach the Word. When he get goin', the rafters do shake."

"I can imagine." Funny thing was, he could. He regretted the lack of something this solid in his life. His religion had always been fear and self-doubt.

"I sing in the choir," Arletha Mae told him.

"Yeah?"

"Lead."

Larry wasn't having trouble imagining this either. Maybe she really did have a voice. With the right lighting and makeup, it was possible she could make an impression.

"You never done read the good book?"

"The Bible?"

Arletha Mae nodded.

"A long time ago," Larry said. "In Sunday school." He always sat slouched in the back, in hope the teacher wouldn't call on him.

"I ain't real good at reading." Arletha Mae still had trouble with her letters. "My granny, she help me. She say it out loud real slow and I say it with her. Over and over, 'til it stay right here in my head." Arletha Mae closed her eyes again and worked at the words:

"The Lord is my light and salvation. Whom shall I fear? The Lord is the strength of my life. Of whom shall I be afraid?"

Larry was moved, more by her awkward sincerity than by the eloquence of the language. "What's that?" he asked, after the lump had left his throat. Arletha Mae's eyes opened like flowers.

"Psalm number twenty seven."

"It's nice," Larry said.

"And true," she said quietly. "Praise the Lord in His mercy and wisdom." She had been near falling asleep, but what had saved her, the sweet and powerful curings of His hand on her soul, had raised her back to waking.

"Granny, she say everybody, they got this one chance, minute in time, when baby Jesus and the Ghost shine their light down on 'em, showing the way outta the darkness. My chance was Wanda Lee."

"Wanda Lee?"

"Girl I went to Marcus G. with." Big old sister, wide and strong, heart to match. "Come visiting one day when I was down and couldn't no way get up. Got in my face and done stayed there. Got me lissening 'cause she been like me. Done bad things."

"What kind of bad things?"

"Jus' bad." Leaning on the Life, high boot strut, pussy tied to any wallet that opened. "Sat there on my bed talking night to morning, feeding me the Word 'til strength started coming back in me, 'til she gets me by the arm and leads me to Baptist." Past the cocks and the cum on my face and the blood needle in my veins and the tracks riding higher and higher on my arms, past the pain and sorrows and death breathing hard in my mouth.

"And Baptist took me in, Pastor Manley and all the brethren, giving me guidance on the straight and narrow." And not one minute of it easy, for it wasn't jus' what the Life put on the table; she had these urges, the fire below, need for a man, some loving, devil's doing, and he'd sneak on in during the night, into her sleep, get her sweating and thrashing on the sheets; she could feel his horns, his tail, his cloven feet, and she'd try and push him away, and she'd be clutching herself down there as though she could stem the flow of the juices of sin, only it'd always end up the same, with her scratching that itch that jus' would never never go away. "No, it wasn't easy," she was telling Larry now. "Sin got so many ways whispering in your ear, and I can't say I was nowhere perfect, but Lord knows I tried, got most it behind me." No more joy boy studs, no more beat you near death

222

tricks, and that razor stayed in her drawer gathering more rust. No, she wasn't perfect, but damn, she was better.

Arletha Mae gazed at Larry, knew that in the light from the lantern, her face was free of all guilt. "When you take God into your life," she said evenly, "it changes things." She smiled down at Jason. "Changes things, that's all." She remained deep in a mood that was like a soothing shadow, then she added, "Church. That's where I met Michael."

"Jason's father."

"Huh huh."

"Tell me about him," Larry said. "You said he's around. Where's around?"

She shook her head.

"Your turn. Tell me more 'bout you."

"Nothing much else to tell."

Arletha Mae smiled softly.

"Try."

Ben sipped his drink and shifted on the couch. Irene was on the phone in the kitchen, where coffee was perking. Ben tipped his head to get an angle on her. She was standing in profile, her skirt hiked high enough to reveal some thigh. Ben was on his third Scotch. A couple of more shots and she'd look like the dragon lady.

"I'll make it a thousand," Ben called out. Irene stared at him in dismay. Turning away, she spoke low into the mouthpiece briefly, then got off the phone and returned to the living room with coffee for Ben, none for herself. Keeping the liquor in his other hand, he hitched forward and carefully accepted the cup. He had a buzz on but wasn't drunk, except with pain and his constant guilt.

"I'd rather have another one of these," Ben said, holding up his glass.

Irene sat in the chair facing him. "You've already had two more than our agreement."

"So I lied. Most people do."

"Not to me."

"Lucky you."

"Drink your coffee."

Ben sipped his Scotch. "Any success?" he asked.

"They're coming right over. They should be here in ten or fifteen minutes."

They were what Irene had come up with. Ben had asked if she knew anyone who would drive him around to look for David for a price. She mentioned these two cousins, the only fools she knew who would put up with a call at this late hour. She described them as 'Crazy boys.' Ben had told her they sounded like his heart's desire.

"Hand me the drink," Irene said firmly. "I did you a favor."

"What kind of favor?"

"Please?"

Ben reluctantly gave her his Scotch without spilling too much on the carpet.

"Thank you." She set the glass down beside her chair.

"What kind?"

"I told them five hundred. You were getting carried away."

"You're right." He'd started at three hundred. The thousand was because they'd balked. He only had six eighty four and change in the bank, but the liquor had flushed rash promises out of him. She really had done him a favor.

"Think they'll take a check?"

"You'll have to ask them." Irene shook her head. "This is stupid, a mistake. I don't know what I was thinking of."

"Helping me find my son?"

Irene frowned but nodded. "Drink your coffee."

Ben drank. The coffee was strong and he winced. His left foot was falling asleep again. He leaned forward and rubbed it with idle pleasure; the anticipation of wheels and direction had at least temporarily chased his despair. He smiled at Irene, felt he should sample more of her life, let her share the grief. He picked up the photo on the coffee table. "How long were you, you know?" he said, studying Mr. Osawa.

"A few months." She had opened the curtains and was watching the street.

Ben returned the picture to the table, taking elaborate care to place it where it'd been.

"Did you know his wife?"

"She called the office sometimes."

"Is she a nice person too?"

Irene faced him, eyes flashing a cold anger. "Don't," she warned.

"I'm sorry. I didn't mean that the way it sounded." He made a demonstration of drinking from the cup. "That's good coffee."

"Don't patronize me either."

"I wasn't."

But of course he was. Silence took over the room. Ben stared at a grandfather clock in a corner. 2:48. There was an inevitability to the steady swing of the clock's pendulum, not unlike his life.

"Where's your wife?" Irene said finally.

"Cleveland."

Irene looked at him from under raised brows. "Oh?" she said with a slight smile.

"We're divorced," Ben told her.

Irene nodded thoughtfully. She casually crossed her legs. He noticed that one of her nylons was starting to run.

"She's remarried." Maggie of the flying bloomers.

Irene nodded again. Her expression was impassive.

"She left you with the boy?"

Ben found her phrasing strange, an inversion. "She couldn't handle it," he said.

"Why not?"

Ben owed her one, owed her the truth. "He's retarded." The stigma stuck in his throat. Embarrassed, he looked away, then back to find that Irene's expression had softened.

"I'm sorry," she said.

"That's what everyone says."

"I suppose there isn't much else to say."

"Saying nothing at all usually works for me. Do you mind if I have my drink? There really isn't much left."

Irene reached down and gave him back the glass. He thanked her and tasted the liquor. The clash of the Scotch with the coffee didn't sit well on his stomach.

"Are *you* handling it?" Irene asked him.

"No."

"What's his name?"

"David."

"It's a nice name. Was he named after someone?"

"Don't patronize me."

"I wasn't."

They smiled shyly at each other, an acknowledgment of some sort of uneasy rapport.

"He's named after my father." Ben handed her the Scotch. "Here. I've had enough."

She surprised him by drinking what was left. Her posture relaxed. She sat holding the empty glass in her lap. The grandfather clock chimed three.

Ben looked at the front window. "What's keeping them?"

"It hasn't been that long." Irene raised her wrist and checked the time. "I'm two minutes slow." She reset her watch. Its slim band was gold and flecked with several subtle rubies. Probably a secret gift, Ben thought.

"He said he was getting a divorce. I didn't press him. It really *wasn't* that serious. Besides, I knew he didn't mean it."

"Mine did."

226

"Obviously. How did David deal with it?"

Ben laughed ruefully. "It was hard to tell."

"Were there any good times?"

"Sure, we were good-time kids," Ben said dryly. "Fucking party animals." Maggie of the do me from behind.

"I mean with your son."

"That's also pretty hard to tell."

"Is it?"

Ben didn't like the way her eyes were judging him. He reached for a pack in his pocket before remembering he didn't have any cigarettes. "You haven't been smoking," he said.

"I don't like to at home," Irene said. "It's alright at work."

Ben looked down at the dark surface of his coffee and ran a finger over the lip of his cup.

"David likes to swing. For hours. I push him as long as I can stand it." Last week he'd tensed up and pushed so hard, David had almost lost his grip on the chains. That night Ben had dreamt that David had fallen into Schultz's yard and been destroyed by his lawn mower. "He likes to watch anything on TV. He likes to make sounds. It's gotten to where I almost understand him."

"He doesn't speak?"

Ben shook his head. The coffee looked deep enough to drown in. Irene asked what David looked like, was he tall, short, heavy, thin? Ben told her he was average. He showed her the snapshot he had left in his wallet. She said David had a beautiful face. Ben said this was fairly common for his condition. They made some more conversation that didn't amount to much, then brakes and punk rock squealed as a car pulled up out front, arriving with a heedless joy that spoke of everything that was missing in Ben's life.

CHAPTER SEVENTEEN

J.D. was walking down an avenue that was a reminder of war. The sidewalks and street were thick with articles of clothing, empty bottles, glass, guard bars, steel gates, pieces of green awning, splashes of blood, pools of brightly colored gas; whatever had been dropped, broken, torn off, lost, spilled. Shops were down to framework and piles of gray ash, cars were blackened hulks, their upholstery smoldering, warped by heat to a texture as soft as cushions. A taxi was on its side, burning. Stenches crossed and joined in the heavy air; burnt rubber, grease, smoke, oil, soot, and ghosts of manic anger. There wasn't a police presence, there wasn't any presence at all. The anger had moved on, indiscriminately prowling for other locations and ways to spend itself. Just like old times, J.D. said to himself as he knelt to tie a shoelace. He wasn't a white cowboy or revolutionary or soother of the old or emotionally maimed. He was just a grunt with a habit of looking for the rim of the world.

Down the street a single building was still intact, a barbershop with an enormous candy cane over its door. A sloppy hand-printed sign taped to the window said, FUCK ALL OF YOU. J.D. figured this gesture of hasty defiance explained why the brothers had left the establishment alone.

The door was unlocked. He went inside and flicked on a switch, lighting up the room and the candy cane, which began to lazily revolve. The shop had an old fashioned appeal, the honed scissors, bottled oils, scalp fresheners, waxes, the tufts of hair on the floor. J.D. settled into a swivel chair. The Army life. You humped then you rested. Gripping the chair's arms, he turned and faced the long mirror. His features and grooming were thoroughly fucked. Could use a shave and a trim. Not too short. Only officers went for whitewalls. The first K.I.A. he'd seen was a lieutenant whose temple had been shredded by shrapnel; another flash recollection of the war torn. Studying his own reflection, he tried to imagine what he'd look like laid out in a coffin draped by the flag. Waxed, he decided. Should have been him instead of Henry.

A phone by the cash register rang. J.D. found this curious. Pushing out of the chair, he went over and picked up the receiver. There was a pause then the line went dead. The phantom caller brought on a neglected impulse. Opening his wallet, he found momma's number in Lansing, wedged between an unredeemed pawn ticket and a one-way to Seattle. The scrap of paper was wrinkled, torn, brown with age, but neatly folded. He let the phone ring forever, but no one answered. She was either dead or moved or balling some Jack.

Breaking the connection, J.D. dialed the operator and attempted to coax her into putting him through to the Hanoi Hilton. Unable to get anything amounting to cooperation, he settled for Caesars in Vegas, where he futilely tried to book a room for Christmas. Then he tried to call the police to give them misleading tactical advice, but all the lines were busy. Hauling a directory out from under the register, he phoned a 24 hour takeout in a nearby city and ordered a BLT with mustard on the side.

"You gotta be fucking nuts," the guy on the other end said, when he heard where J.D. was.

"Somewhat," J.D. admitted as the line went dead. Having about run out of relatives and neighbors, J.D. called home.

"The Paradise," Bobby answered. He sounded straighter, almost efficient. A radio was on low in the background.

"Got a room?" J.D. asked with a deadpan delivery.

"For what night?"

"This one."

"Let me check. Wait a fucking minute, hold on . . . that you, J.D.?"

"Good guess."

"Hey, J.D., hey man . . ."

"Hey, Bobby?"

"Got you some shoes."

"Did I ask?"

"I thought. Anyway, your size, almost."

"Kinney's?"

"Payless. I'm branching out."

J.D. could hear the gravelly shadings of *Chantilly Lace* on the radio. In college he had joined a clique that made up dirty lyrics for the romantic hits of the day. Although he had lost his virginity when he was sixteen, a member of this ridiculous group, a sloe-eyed, big-breasted girl, had given him his first real kiss with the Big Bopper spinning out magic on an old, battered RCA console. When she pressed against him, he'd thought he was in love.

"So what's going on, man?" Bobby was saying.

"I'm doing sick, stupid things." Some things never changed. "What about you?"

"Me too," Bobby said.

"Where's Rokowski?"

"Rokowski? Right here. On the floor."

"Dead or alive?"

"Jeez, I don't know. Let me check."

J.D. studied himself in the mirror while he waited. He looked ancient as well as thoroughly fucked. He mulled over the ghost of his future, an embellishment on his thoughts in the rest home. If he lived to old age, say sixty, his cuffs would drag and he would wear his socks to bed and moan that his dick didn't have a drain. On the day of his death, thin to the point of extinction and thick with senility, he would cover his naked body with spray cologne and Sta'-Put glue to complete his self degradation. Then he would shuffle as far as his spindly old bones would allow—maybe a block—until his heart stopped.

He sighed and sneered at himself, at the beast in the mirror; these projections were irrelevant and absurd, of course, but then irrelevant absurdity was the right tone to assume before any conversation with Bobby.

Bobby came back on the line:

"Sorry took so long. Had trouble finding a fucking pulse. See, I wasn't specifically sure where to look."

"The big toe," J.D. suggested.

"I don't think so," Bobby said uncertainly.

"But he's . . . ?"

"Still breathing. Sucker's asleep. After you hung up, we had a helluva set-to. Even took a little nap myself."

"Sounds like you're wide awake now, like you're taking care of business."

"Yeah," Bobby said proudly. "I even checked in this couple. You wanta hear something fucking funny? They didn't even fucking blink when they seen Rokowski."

"What'd you do with the money?"

"Pocketed it. What do you think, I'm fucking crazy?! No guarantees Monday, you know. Hey, you know something else? My fucking nose is dripping blood."

"Occupational hazard?" J.D. ventured. The radio had moved on to *Why Do Fools Fall in Love?*

"Think Rokowski did it, but I can't be sure. It's kinda like this leaky faucet, but believe me, I ain't leaving no mess. I got Redis from the john to catch it, here on the fucking counter."

J.D. had heard enough. He started to say something like goodbye, but Bobby didn't give him a chance.

"You ever listen to this bell they got here to punch? It's a fucking trip."

J.D. tolerated Bobby's repeated ringing until he heard a frantic scratching noise behind him. Turning, he saw one of the puppies from the pet store, the plump white spaniel, whining and worrying at the glass entrance.

"Excuse me, Bobby. There's someone at the door."

"Like who the fuck?"

"That's what I'm gonna find out."

"Okay," Bobby said warily. "Be careful, man."

Placing the receiver down on its side, J.D. went to the door and let the puppy in. The dog, who rushed in and loved up his boots with its wet muzzle and paws, kept under his feet as he returned to the phone.

"Who was it? Your friend Henry?" Bobby was losing it. J.D. guessed he'd shot up in the neck again.

"Henry's dead, babe." The time they'd done the gallery, J.D. had made the mistake of telling Bobby about him.

"Jesus, man. I'm sorry."

"Long time ago." Just bones in a box now. *Fools* had ended. The disk jockey was seducing the airwaves with deep chamber bites. Bobby started rambling again. J.D. had this theory that Bobby didn't have any memories at all, that his past was his present. Maybe it was the drugs or his itch to be black, or maybe Bobby was just a soldier of his generation; MTV and midnight hots and a three-second attention span. More bones in a box.

"So what about it, what do you think?" Bobby asked.

Looking at himself in the mirror, J.D. pushed up the skin under his left eye; a face lift would have been a consideration in another life.

"About what?" he asked Bobby.

"What we were talking about. What were—?"

"Nothing, babe," J.D. interrupted. "We were just taking in the sounds."

The radio was playing another sentimental favorite, Little Richard's *Tutti Frutti*. J.D. watched the puppy leave a puddle on the floor, while along with the music, agitated squeaking filtered through the receiver, the probable sound of Bobby pacing while running a hand through his hair and picking at his zits. "I need a shower," he said rapidly, then to J.D., "No, man, hell, I was talking about us meeting up. You gotta be dying out there and this shit I got, it's fucking primo. Besides, I ain't cut out for this kinda work. Goddamn bell's driving me nuts! So where the fuck are you?"

J.D. gave him a rough idea.

"Shit," Bobby said, "that's a long ways."

J.D. could hear the synapses of Bobby's brain groping for connections.

"Maybe I could hitch?"

"You got a pen, pencil?" J.D. asked.

"What the fuck for?"

"So I can give you the address."

"Oh yeah, sure."

There was some loud, frantic fumbling on the other end of the line. When Bobby came back on, J.D. had to repeat the street name and number several slow times.

"Be right there," Bobby said confidently.

"Looking forward to it."

"Fucking A."

With the knowledge that Bobby would never show, J.D. hung up. The gumps and geeks of the world couldn't deliver on their promises, but then that was true of just about everyone.

J.D. was suddenly overcome with a fatigue bred by guilt and half a load. For his generation the past kept a grip. Lowering himself into a sitting position on the floor, he let his thoughts wander.

When he was thirteen, a stray, emaciated tabby had come around crying for a meal, but momma had this allergy. Couldn't feed it, couldn't keep it, so J.D. had chased the cat out into the rain. The animal objected with a pitiful howl of outrage before hobbling away on stiff, weak legs. The next day he found the cat dead in an alley. This had troubled his sleep and waking hours for a month, still did now and then.

So did other memories. The girl who'd taken his cherry, she'd missed a period. Her tears when she thought she was pregnant, her tears when she discovered she wasn't; both times had stuck, as did near everything with his momma. And there was Le spun by that bullet and Henry under a poncho that covered what was left of him, and the thought of Henry Rodriguez brought those fucked, jinxed, and miserably blessed days back.

J.D. had met Henry in Basic. He'd been a solid one sixty, ten of it baby fat, the rest muscle, a hundred plus pushup Mex. He and J.D. became boon buddies during training. Henry had a past, one that was happy. Big family. Holiday dinners, carving knives and high riding spirits; he had the color snaps to prove it. In Nam they'd shared a hooch and mind soothing substances of black-market repute. What you got was what you needed, because people got themselves killed absolute dead. The first in their platoon was Tillman. Got a leg blown clean off by a snug claymore. Just this stump under his hip dangling bloody cords. Thing was, Tillman's reflexes hadn't realized what had happened. He'd thrust forward with the stump once, before gravity put him out flat.

Others followed in short time. Gave you a tour of the insides, brains, guts, cavities, nerves, whatever could be shredded or spilled. Never witnessed one swinging dick buy it in a way you could put on a postcard. 'Ain't none of you doing this with dignity'; that was God's voice in your ear. Henry rolled with this in-your-face truth better than any man J.D. ever saw. Kept his mud through it all, the firefights, the dust-offs, the John Rebs looking to rearrange, Charlie sneak into your dreams, the bitter rains, the fevers, the waiting, the losses, the whispered and convulsive fears.

For Henry it was over in an instant. They were in the jungle on a let's-see-what-we-can-fuck-with prowl, establishing ownership rights. Henry had gone ahead on point. J.D. was next in line, slacking some space behind him. Henry could move, this itch to see what was waiting; he could open up a spread. J.D. could hear him thrashing through the vines and elephant grass, then he lost the sound. J.D. had stood there with his B.A.R. out from his hip, part of him, and the sun was a ring of God's unholy light, burning into his eyes, his skin, along with the silence which kept deepening in waves. Something had happened to Henry, he was sure, and his certainty kept tightening until all his nerve ends were in his trigger finger. And then his head jerked to something thrashing toward him, and there was this explosion of absolute mayhem so loud, so bright, brighter than the sun, he thought it must be in his head. And the next thing he knew, the next thing he remembered, he was throwing himself over Henry's rent body, there was so much blood, and he was sobbing, 'God man look what they did to you, look the fuck they did,' sobbing out the words and tearing at his own shirt. Then later, much later, the lieutenant had taken him aside and told him what had actually happened, and that's when J.D. had covered his face with his hands and sobbed some more, saying, 'Oh God fuck oh man fuck God it shoulda fucking been me.'

J.D. heard a rustling by his feet and his hand went for the .32 in his coat pocket but it was only the puppy whimpering. He looked down at the liquid brown eyes and idly stroked the soft fur. No way I'm getting any rest, any peace, he said to himself. There ain't none.

Getting to his feet, he left the shop. The puppy stayed at his heels. Outside, the lazy light from the candy cane rearranged shadows and J.D. slipped through them. In its eagerness to keep up, the puppy kept bumping into his boots. J.D. stopped walking and faced the dog.

"Go on, get the fuck away. This ain't no sweetbread Disney flick."

The puppy sat on its haunches, tipped its head, regarded J.D. the way it had the snake.

"You figure it out yet?"

The spaniel brushed its tail over the sidewalk and barked. J.D. dismissed it with a wave and resumed walking. The dog resumed following him. Spinning around he threw up his arms to frighten the puppy, which jumped back but didn't run.

"Shoo." J.D. stamped his foot. "Fuck off. I don't have nothing for you." If it had been raining, he might have reconsidered.

He was looking for a stick when he heard the rumble and creak of heavy vehicles. After a long moment a small convoy twisted around a corner and came his way, an olive colored jeep followed by three olive colored transport trucks with canvas canopies. National Guard, Lord have mercy.

When the procession neared J.D., the jeep stopped, forcing the trucks to do the same. There were three men in the jeep; the driver and an officer up front, a soldier in the back with an M-16 growing out of his leg. Light from the burning taxi polished their helmets and uniforms. The officer had the dangerous eyes of a man venturing armed into the unknown.

"Get off the street."

His voice was sharp and clear, but his thin lips barely moved, as though he were a ventriloquist nearing perfection in his act. J.D. wondered who was supposed to be the dummy.

"I lost my dog," J.D. said agreeably.

"Your what?"

"My dog."

"Is that him there?"

There was no texture to the officer's inflection, just this dead parody of inquisition and command. J.D. glanced around, spotted the mutt whizzing on a lamppost.

"Right," J.D. replied. The officer and the driver were facing him, but the soldier in the back hadn't moved; his posture was as wooden as the M16. J.D. tipped his head, looking for strings.

"Remove the animal and return home immediately."

The officer was equal to the worst of the tight asses at Howard. Color him dark and the man would fit right in. J.D. figured he could fast draw and drill him before anyone could react, but knew this was a revisionist impulse. History was on this ofay cat's side, not to mention muscle.

"On my way," J.D. said, scooping up the dog, which squirmed then went limp with contentment. J.D. went left, the convoy went straight. The trucks were packed with reservists. Short time, easy travel. No humping under the shadows of Hueys and Chinooks or through a wild and raging wilderness where you ended up on your knees. If he could run from his past, he would, but all he could do was walk. It was what he did. Ain't no rim, he thought.

Just movement.

Irene placed a tentative arm around Ben's waist, offering support on their way out to the car. He shrugged her off. The fatigue and the liquor seemed to have found a happy union in his body, lifting most of his pain. He could walk now with only a slight hitch. Drunks did worse. Staggering a few feet, he took in the vanishing night. The glow from the fires had dimmed, but the air was still thick with the odor of distant smoke.

"I shouldn't have called them," Irene said, taking him by the arm.

"I know."

"You shouldn't be doing this."

"I know," and Ben did, but he felt his options had been reduced to almost zero.

When they reached the curb, the cousin on the passenger side got out and opened the rear door for Ben while Irene made the introductions. The one standing was Kap Kim. The one behind the wheel and with the gun bulge in his jacket was John Kim. She'd described them as crazy kids, but to Ben they just looked like fading delinquents. They might have been twins. Both were pushing twenty, rounding into plump adulthood. They had slicked back midnight hair and the kind of eyes that suggested nylon masks, and they were wearing canvas shoes and chinos and matching black lowrider leather jackets. Their car was a late-model Datsun 280Z, nose to the pavement, rear raised in a way that seemed to welcome high-velocity sodomy. Their license read LUVU2.

"Cute plates," Ben lied, as he eased onto a back seat cluttered with heavy metal tapes and an amazing number of crinkled candy wrappers. Kap grinned—he had a chipped front tooth—closed Ben's door and got in up front. Irene tapped on the window next to Ben and he rolled it down.

"This is—"

"Stupid," Ben agreed.

Irene nodded.

"Thanks anyway." Ben faced front as John impatiently raced the engine.

"Ben?"

He turned to her voice. She reached in and fervently squeezed his hand. "Good luck," she said.

For an instant, Ben thought he caught something in Irene's smile, as though she saw him as a possible replacement for her dead lover. Then he nodded and she released his hand and it was metal to the floor, an engine squeal, muffler pop, and snake trails over the asphalt. Ben braced his hands against the seat until John got the steering under control. Rolling up the window Ben looked back at Irene. She waved and he waved back.

"You look like shit, man. Want some candy?"

Ben turned. Kap was grinning at him, offering a handful of molar breakers. He wondered if the boys had been drinking too. Liquor was in the air, but he couldn't tell if it came from his breath or theirs.

"I don't think so," Ben replied. He was already starting to regret a gesture that smacked of bravado, booze and injury.

"Got all kinds," Kap told him.

Ben selected one to be polite. He put it in his jacket pocket. "I'll save it for later."

Kap frowned, faced the windshield and peeled a wrapper. "Like to hear some sounds?" he asked, tossing the small, hard candy into the rank air and catching it in his mouth.

"No," Ben said. What was on the back seat promised murderous decibels.

John was taking a residential street at sixty. The shocks were great, no bounce. Ben considered mentioning this but he didn't want to offer any encouragement. Tract homes ticked by. Several were pink. None were on fire. A small measure of relief. But ain't that America, Ben thought.

"You mind slowing down?"

"Sure thing, boss."

It was the first time John had spoken. He had a trace of the same accent as Kap, barely a thread to join them to the motherland. Ben looked over John's shoulder. The needle dropped to fifty five and steadied.

"You don't even know where we're going," Ben said peevishly. Maybe if he'd offered more than once to pay Irene . . .

"Sure," John said. "We're looking for your kid."

"At this speed he'd just be a blur," Ben said. The barbs helped take his mind off what might have happened to David. He found that his edge came easily. He begrudged John and Kap their callow panache, their capacity to behave foolishly, to make mistakes, choices that had been denied his son. Ben glared at the Koreans, resented them with a passion he needed to get him through the rest of the night.

John brought his speed down to forty before leveling off. He had a queue. At least Kap wouldn't have to smile to distinguish between the two of them.

"I want to go home first," Ben said.

"Irene said you'd already checked it out," John said.

"I want to see for myself."

"O.K.," John said indifferently. "Which way?"

Ben told him. John hung a sharp right. Adjusting his rearview mirror, he looked at Ben, his eyes the eyes of a cobra.

"You don't look so good," John remarked.

"I never do." Ben believed this to be more truth than humor.

"Maybe we should take you to a hospital instead," Kap suggested.

"I've already been there."

"Maybe you should've stayed longer," Kap said.

"You a doctor?" Ben said sharply.

Kap snorted and looked away. "Shit, boss," he said.

"You got cash?" John asked abruptly.

Ben didn't understand the question.

"What?"

"Five hundred."

"At home."

"So it's good we're going there," John said.

"Isn't it," Ben replied.

They were there in five minutes. Smoke and flames rose from a billboard a few blocks away. Across the street Schultz's lights were out but his sprinklers were on. Ben laughed out loud; the prick probably thought this would discourage torching.

The Kims exchanged apprehensive looks over Ben's laughter then they followed him up to his porch. "David?" Ben called out as he went inside the house. His heart was acting up again, the old sensations of fear and hope. He switched on the living room light and familiar shapes rose out of the gloom. None happened to be David.

"Nobody here," Kap said, cracking a piece of candy with his teeth.

"Not necessarily," Ben said grimly. There were shadows everywhere.

Kap and John sauntered after Ben as he scoured the house; rooms, the linen closet, under the beds. The crazy kids found him especially amusing on all fours, made no effort to conceal their snickers. He fantasized lunging for John's gun and making them cry and beg. A fusillade through Schultz's windows was another pleasurable thought. He felt like his head was ticking. When he got back to his feet, David's bedroom was thick with his sweat.

Ben went into his own bedroom and locked the door behind him. He changed into clean clothes, then went into the bathroom and splashed some water on his face and ran his hands through his hair. In the mirror his face was gray and streaked, and something besides the aftertaste of Scotch was in his mouth. The corner of his left eye had also started to bleed. He daubed at the damage with Kleenex until there was no more blood, although what he could see of his eye was mottled and the skin under it was purple and swollen into a lump the size of a slug.

Back in his bedroom he dialed Maggie in Cleveland with the fear he was beginning to seek all kinds of depths. After five rings, her husband answered the phone. Jonathan Reynolds of the firm of Jacobs, Jacobs and Reynolds. Corporate law.

"Yes?"

Ben lowered the receiver. He'd hoped Maggie would answer. Jonathan's testiness unaccountably prevented him from hanging up.

"Who *is* this?"

Ben sat down on his bed and placed the phone beside him. "Don't worry, Jonathan. It's not an avenging client."

"Ben?"

"Sorry to bother you."

"What are you doing calling at this hour, Ben? It's five something here. That would make it three . . . thirty there." Jonathan sounded wide awake, although a little short of breath. Ben was disappointed. He would've preferred destroying Jonathan's sleep.

"Five thirty is pretty early for you, isn't it?"

"I always do an hour of tai chi before I go to work."

"It's Sunday, Jonathan. There as well as here."

"I have briefs that are desperately in need of repair. Have you been drinking?"

"Why?"

"You sound like you've been drinking."

"Not for a while. I haven't been smoking either. I need to talk to Maggie."

"She's asleep."

"It's important."

"Is something possibly the matter?"

This was the Jonathan Ben knew and hated. That tone of solicitous arrogance common to his profession. He'd gone to an ivy-draped school. He did marriage counseling on the side.

"Yes," Ben said. "Something's possibly the matter."

"I'll get her."

Ben heard Jonathan put down the receiver. He also thought he heard him mutter, "Son of a bitch."

The eye was bleeding again. Ben pressed a tissue to it while he waited for his lost love. He could hear John and Kap pillaging the kitchen.

Maggie came on the line. "Do you know what time it is?" Her voice was fuzzy but pissed.

"I already discussed that with Jonathan."

"He said you've been drinking."

"He made that up."

Maggie let out an exasperated sigh that was clearly for Ben's benefit.

"What's the problem? If you're calling to let us know about the rioting, we saw it on the news."

"It's David." Ben heard her sharp intake of breath.

"David?"

"He's, um, missing."

"Missing? What the hell is *that* supposed to mean?" The Maggie he knew. Angry. Lashing out. Jonathan's voice was sneaking in behind her, asking what the fuck was going on.

"Just what I said," Ben told her. "He wandered off." Just like you.

"How could you, Ben?" Pure, cold fury. "How could you?"

"Don't worry. I'm trying to find him."

"I can see that," Maggie said. "That's why you're on the phone."

"Listen to me, I'm trying. I got hurt. Beaten up."

"You're not making any sense." Not an ounce of sympathy or respect. He never could be a hero to her.

"You *did* call the police?"

"Many times."

"Why'd you call here?"

"I thought you should know."

"To see if you could upset me?"

"You don't sound upset. Mad, but not upset."

"Goddamn you."

"I thought you should know, in case anything happened."

"You bastard."

"As his mother, in case."

"You fucking bastard."

Ben hung up with the realization that he hadn't been seeking depths but rather closure. He examined the tissue and found the bleeding had let up again. The phone started ringing. He reached for the receiver, then thought better of it. The ringing stopped before he was out of the room.

The Kims were lounging about in the kitchen, drinking sodas.

Kap drained a Pepsi, crushed the can and winked at John. "That didn't sound like a happy conversation."

"It wasn't." Ben got matches and a pack of Winstons out of a cupboard. "You ready to go?"

"Our money," John said. He was leaning against the sink, his eyes full of mirth and eager for quick change. Ben opened a drawer and got out his checkbook and a pen.

John drummed his fingers on the counter.

"You said cash."

"No, I didn't." Ben signed his name, tore off the check and handed it to John.

"Can I see your checkbook?"

"Can I see your gun?"

"Why?"

"Same reason you want to check my balance. To see if it's real."

John and Kap traded laughs. Smiling at Ben, John unzipped his jacket and displayed the revolver, leaving no doubt as to its authenticity. Ben gave him his checkbook. John verified the balance, which he showed to Kap. Kap handed the book to Ben in exchange for the check.

"This puts you out on the streets," Kap said, pocketing what Ben gave him.

"He's my son. You ready?"

Ben left the doors unlocked and the lights on, just in case. Firing up a Winston on the way to the car, he offered the pack to the Kims, but neither smoked. Ben was glad. He didn't particularly feel like sharing. Pulling away from the curb, John didn't peel any rubber. Ben felt they'd established the right blend of mutual distrust and respect.

CHAPTER EIGHTEEN

She had him dangling, no doubt about it. I tell you about me, you tell me about you. Larry minded and he didn't; another thing there was no doubt about; talking was pushing them that much closer to daylight.

"Try," Arletha Mae repeated. "Like when you was a boy?"

"I already told you. I shagged flies and ate ice cream."

"And you got them two hits. What 'bout your folks?"

"They were just parents. I guess you'd call them nice."

From the way her smile flattened out, Larry knew she'd caught the lie. Get up you sissy, that was his father's refrain. The visual props were clenched fists and bulging veins.

"My daddy, he call from 'Bama now and again," Arletha Mae said, tracing a pattern over the concrete floor with her finger.

"That's nice." Last call from his old man, there was blood over the wire; 'why haven't you done this, why did you do that?' Larry could part six seas and fry the devil in his own juice and it still wouldn't be good enough for his father.

"You get into trouble alot?" Arletha Mae asked, looking up into the light from the lantern.

"You mean . . . ?"

"When you was little."

"Mischief, kid stuff." He searched his past for examples. "I stuck a live frog in a neighbor's mailbox on a dare." And he stole. Change off his uncle's dresser. A lunch pail at school. A tape deck from his father's car, made it look like a common break-in. After a while he'd assumed the fallacy of the successful thief, believing his moves were too smooth to stick. Then one day his father caught him with George Washington in his pocket and stretched him out over his bed; the strap marks lasted a week. The whipping scared and shamed him into a brief affair with religion which didn't last much longer than the welts. The way Larry saw it, God was playing on the other team.

"Bet that old frog like to scared the pants off him," Arletha Mae laughed.

"I don't know. I didn't stick around."

"You get 'long good with other kids?"

"Ups and downs." A black teammate had once laughed at the size of his penis while they were showering. Larry had gone home tight as a drum, muttering, 'Lousy, filthy nigger,' stretching out the slurs to cover the entire race. His mother told him that judging people by their color wasn't right but his father wasn't completely convinced.

"Larry?"

"Huh?" He wondered how many more questions she was going to ask. These weren't exactly enjoyable memories.

"You kinda shy, ain't you?"

Larry stared at her dumbfounded. Her smile was coy. What did she think they were doing, where did she think they were; flirting in a bar?

"No, I wouldn't call myself shy. More like quiet." Like his mother. She knew when to keep her mouth shut; when she was around his father. Intimidation was the mood of their household. Not that he ever saw his father strike her. Close but no cigar. Sometimes, Larry wished she'd raised her voice. The echoes might have shaken his father up, or triggered a violence that would have at least been a resolution. One of his fantasies as a teen had been just such an explosion; a savage hand, a shriek of pain, his mother staring up in terror from the floor. Then before his father could strike again, Larry would spin and drop him with a perfect punch thrown straight from the shoulder. Down on all fours, his father would cringe and Larry, hovering huge over him and quivering with a right-minded fury, would warn him to never, never do that again. A grand gesture like this could have changed Larry's life, peeled away his insecurities. He might be married to Sharon, have a home where there was no reason to remain silent or shout.

"Why're you smiling?"

Arletha Mae's voice, level and curious, woke him up. "I'm not," he said, frowning. She let it go.

"Still think you shy."

"Maybe I am." Sharon hadn't been the first girl he'd had trouble with. At the dances in high school he'd been among the boys who lined the wall, never daring to ask a girl out on the floor. One time a girl had asked him and the pressure of her magical proximity and his hormones and his pants had caused him to ejaculate. The girl hadn't been the only one to notice. Larry had been the brunt of snickered asides for longer than welts or the nearness of God.

"There, there, there." Her comfort was for the baby, who was playing dead dog, hands drooping at the wrists. "There, there, there, ain't nothing to worry 'bout." Dead to the world. Dreaming way down the line of that punch thrown straight from the shoulder.

Arletha Mae shifted her attention back to Larry.

"Why'd you become a police?"

Just when he was starting to like her. Karl's battered, bloody face mushroomed before him, two cute black bunnies dangling by their teeth from his ears.

"Good question," Larry admitted.

"You musta had some kinda reason, like maybe feeling it was a calling?"

"Sort of." Not really a lie. Protect and serve. He always was a sucker for slogans, the confusion of motives and emotions canned in a phrase. The social conscience, a helping hand, the brotherhood of man. The reality was something else. At the Academy there had been forty blacks in a class of five hundred. The instructors used neutral language around them, but out of their hearing, they made jokes that began with lines like, 'How many niggers does it take to screw a spic?' Despite his mother's better instincts, Larry often joined in the laughter; at least no one was laughing at him. He worked hard to fit in and finished in the middle of his class, not a bad place to be. His father seemed surprised he'd passed at all.

The precinct he was assigned to wasn't a desirable choice, inner city, as Karl described it, a war zone. The percentage of minorities at the station house was higher than at the Academy, but the attitudes were the same; jokes, incidents of harassment: A watermelon left on top of a black cop's locker, a swastika painted on the windshield of a Jewish officer's car. The responses were different: The black challenged the perpetrators, whoever they might be, to fight, the Jew bought a can of paint remover. For the most part trouble was avoided and the factions, by age and color, went their own ways. Black cops hung out in the neighborhood, whites went home to the suburbs. Karl, who was responsible for the watermelon, was an elder in his church. He kept a Bible and copies of *The American Spectator* on his nightstand, rifles behind glass, and airbrushed animal heads on the walls. At the time of his death he was two months behind in his child support and spending fifty a week on hard liquor. "Why, don't I seem like a cop?" Larry found himself asking now.

"Police is police." Arletha Mae had had some experience. Been busted a dozen times for prost. Revolving door. The three *b*'s. Booked and bailed and bused. Given a one-way to welfare.

Larry asked himself what he was seeing. It wasn't that hard getting into her head, her thoughts were on her face. She was turning inward, away from him.

Just where he wanted her to be.

J.D. had been going in circles, been down this road before. Story of his life. Somebody was pulling his strings.

East 92nd looked the same as when he'd been here hours ago; steam from a grate and long shadows. Lord knows he'd tried to get rid of the puppy, but the mutt stayed at his heels, whimpering for attention or food. "Ain't got neither," J.D. informed him brusquely. They went past edgy shadows and pools of gold streetlamp light, and the building that served as lounging quarters for Slope's joy boys. J.D. glanced at a high window. No light. Nevertheless he took care as he went past the alley, where the kid called 9-T had materialized, and where the darkness and dark brick took on the aspect of the macabre. There were no surprises this time.

J.D. kept walking until he reached DeJaynes street. The only commercial light on the block was the neon of Fat Jack's, made pale by the gradual illumination of the sky. Having this need for something that was bad for him, he headed for the bar. A recent sign under the neon read PROTECTED BY 8-TREY in no-nonsense letters; the possibility of another unpredictable encounter held a perverse appeal. Going through the club's door, J.D. left the puppy outside to find its own circles.

The juke was silent and the clientele had thinned to the sexy lady in the primed-to-the-skin green dress. She was sitting well down in a chair, legs splayed, testing the tolerance of her skirt, and she had a glass of amber colored booze flat on a table and barely touched by her hands. She failed to take note of J.D.'s arrival.

The young bartender didn't take in much more; just an indifferent once-over as J.D. ambled to the aquarium at the back of the room

251

and watched him feed the fish, which came in a variety of sizes and glitter colors, blues, greens, yellows, fantail reds. They glided sinuously through the coral and flora, their scales casting off the tank's interior lights. With a large hand whose knuckles were pronounced, the bartender delicately scattered grains of food over the surface of the water. Ignoring the flakes, one of the fish lurked in a cave open at both ends, its round eyes regarding J.D. balefully.

"That one's got a dog's face," J.D. remarked.

"So people say."

The bartender, having taken off the pressed white shirt he had been wearing earlier, was down to a designer teeshirt. An anchor tattooed on his large left biceps dipped as he scattered more food.

"You don't feed them regular, they change colors," he said. "Angers up their blood."

"That one there looks like a shark."

"That's correct."

"In its infancy, but still . . ."

"You feed them regular," the bartender said, "their instincts stay dormant."

"That's a nice tattoo."

"Thank you."

"Professional looking. Get it in the Navy?"

The bartender gestured with a loose wrist to the woman.

"She does them. Twenty bucks basic design, more if you're of a mind to be showing off. You feel like something on your arm?"

"I already got something."

The bartender yawned to show he didn't give fuck all.

"A few tracks," J.D. said. "Not like there's been a squad of mosquitoes there."

"I'm twenty nine years old and I already done seen it all." The bartender shook out the remnants of the flakes from a cellophane bag into the water. "Is this a paying visit?"

J.D. decided on something that wouldn't kill him just yet.

"Draft."

The bartender strolled toward the bar. The beer was certain to fill J.D.'s bladder. Deciding to give the hops room, he walked toward the head. The checkerboard was folded at the table where Harold of the inscrutable shades had reigned.

"Mess in there," the bartender let J.D. know. "I ain't got around to cleaning up."

"That's alright."

"In the morning." The bartender reached up and straightened the TV over the bar.

"Was she hurt bad?"

"Most the blood's the trick's."

"What I figured."

J.D. went down the short, dark hallway and through the door. Blood speckled the mirror over the sink, spots of blood were on the porcelain and on the floor's gray tiles. A bloody tooth and one of the whore's high heels were side by side. Part of her wig, nearly as red as the blood, was under the closed door of the empty stall.

J.D. relieved himself at the urinal. His piss was tinged with his own blood; it'd been a long night. He shook off and zipped up and washed his hands. The taste of his vices was in his mouth and he hawked up phlegm, slowing the flow of the water to wash it down the drain. The whore had left her pink lipstick on the sink. In flowing calligraphy, J.D. wrote God Plus Man Equals Watever on the mirror; in the glass his face was the color of delirium. Turning off the faucets, he left the john with an improved sense of how fucked up he really was.

Out in the main room the lady in green was still deep in her mood. The bartender had the ceiling TV on; National Guardsmen probed ghostly streets in full combat gear, following the treadmarks of Armored Personnel Carriers. A newscaster cut in to update the body count. Sixty three people were dead. Five policemen, three soldiers, two firemen, eight alleged innocents, the rest rioters. Four people were missing. A police helicopter had been wounded.

J.D.'s beer was waiting on the counter. He took it over to the juke, whose interior light had a celestial glow. The selections were new and old and in-between, a range. He fed a quarter into the machine and *Chantilly Lace* slipped into the minds and hearts of all ghosts present.

The woman took a moment to turn, a casual shift of smooth dark hair and smoother thigh. Up close he could see she was at least forty, lines sketched by small concerns under her eyes. The eyes themselves were unusual, with a brightness beyond drugs or booze. She was wearing obelisk earrings and a perfume that stated its purpose.

"You want to dance?" Pressed against him. Almost like thinking you're in love.

"No," she answered nonchalantly.

"You did earlier."

"Waiting on my second wind."

"Okay if I sit?"

"Suit yourself," the woman said, adjusting an earring.

Setting his mug on the table, J.D. pulled up a chair and sat facing her. Putting his hands in his pockets, he leaned back and stretched out his legs in an attempt to present an image of debonair funk, king of each and every lonely back road.

"Where's your hat?" the woman asked.

"Gave it to the needy," J.D. told her. "This place your religion?"

The woman leaned forward and touched the middle of her chest. "My religion's here." She took in the room. "This is something else."

A sax burped clashing flats and sharps from the juke, a solo with a direction.

"You know what a saxophone always reminds me of?" J.D. said. "A snake starting to uncoil."

"Reminds me of a cock."

J.D. smiled, knew he could talk to this woman. She had a straight-on style of instant dispatch. "Well . . . ," he said.

"In a friendly manner of speaking."

"Now that we got this understanding—"

"No more trouble tonight," the bartender urged from behind the counter. "I'm begging you please."

There was a scratching at the front door. The bartender was polishing glasses as he watched TV. "Sound like some animal trying to get in," he said.

"Usually is." The woman's eyes, the bright deep brown pupils, were level on J.D. He broke the eye contact and knocked back his beer, then got up and walked to the door. The boot sole he'd glued was coming loose, another image of debonair funk. Humming a song only he could hear, he let in the puppy, which grinned and loved up his ankles. The woman asked if the dog was J.D.'s. The bartender asked if he was housebroken.

"Well . . ." J.D. said.

"What's his name?" the woman wanted to know.

"Whatever you call him, he's bound to answer," J.D. told her as he attempted to shake the puppy off his leg.

"Precocious," the bartender remarked.

"No kidding," J.D. replied.

The bartender filled a saucer with Amaretto and set it down on the floor. "Got milk, right?" The puppy lapped up the amber liqueur eagerly.

"Dogs get drunk," the bartender said, watching.

"I heard that too," J.D. nodded.

"I done more than heard," the bartender said. "I've seen them so happy they lick up the world, then next day it's chin dragging on the floor."

"He should have a name," the woman said. "Ain't right."

"Working on it," J.D. told her.

"Got balls to breed a neighborhood," the woman noticed.

The bartender chuckled. "Look at him lap it up."

"You want him?" J.D. asked the bartender.

"Fuck no. Ain't got no use."

When the saucer was scraped clean, the bartender picked up the puppy and carried him over to the tank, where he introduced him to the fish, which had names. The glow from the juke was beckoning J.D. again and he went over and started the Big Bopper spinning a second time, then returned to the woman's table and sat down.

"I'm a creature of repetition," J.D. admitted.

"Ain't we all," the lady said. There was liquor left in her glass. She could make a drink last a damned long spell.

"He was killed in a plane crash, you know," J.D. said, resting his elbows on the table, which creaked and shifted with his weight. The woman steadied the table with one hand, her glass with the other.

"Who's that?" she asked.

"The Big Bopper," J.D. told her. "Him and Buddy Holly and Ritchie Valens. Took off in a fucking blizzard."

"Served 'em right." The woman knocked back what remained in her glass. "Going somewheres when you can't see."

"Yeah, well." J.D. nodded. They laughed over the clear lines of bad judgment. The woman added a reminder by telling him that his beer was getting warm. J.D. said he liked it that way as his gaze swept the room: The puppy was pressing its forepaws against the aquarium and the bartender was saying, "That's Sam and Toke and Ralph," and the Big Bopper was curving bass licks with no idea of his near future, and on the TV dimensions of the present were being reduced to one.

J.D. lifted his mug and toasted the scene. He drank deeply, savoring the dense, bitter taste. The woman sat out the absence of conversation with her arms easy on the table, her legs tucked under her chair, her eyes inhabiting that secret mood he found such a sweet fascination. When their eyes eventually met, he gestured to the bartender, who was now feeding the puppy pretzels, and said to the woman, "I admire your work."

"In precisely what area are you talking?"

"The tattoo."

"Anything in particular you'd like?"

"What in particular would you recommend?"

The woman looked at him carefully.

"You don't look like you much for hearts, 'less maybe there's a dagger deep through it. Snakes, however, seem to bring you some pleasure."

J.D. grinned. Ten minutes and she knew him so well. "Trouble is," he admitted, "I don't have twenty dollars."

"You got ten?"

"Why?"

"Needles are just my second line of work," she said.

"Mine too. What's your first?"

"Reading palms. Lines of life."

"Why not."

J.D. felt warm all over, expansive, generous, even chivalrous, a knight in this woman's presence, however tarnished. He gave her a crumpled, soiled five, and five ones equally damaged. Turning his hand over she lowered her face close to his palm and traced the patterns there with a manicured nail painted a shy opaque shade.

"You got more heart than I done realized," she said, after what seemed a long time.

"Fuck the heart. I got a future?" He already knew the answer but thought he'd ask anyway. "A long life?" She took her time again, giving him value. When she looked up, her eyes seemed to have lost some of their luster.

"Up to you. No guarantees."

J.D. smiled. He was glad she hadn't lied. Without exchanging names they talked some more, making the sort of conversation guaranteed to go nowhere, not to bed, not even to coffee. Almost without realizing what he was doing, J.D. began to unburden himself. His words shaped what was in his head, the images, the sensations, the sounds, the alien landscape, the burning sun, Henry thrashing invisibly up ahead, the sensation of his own sweat gathering in all his camouflaged places, and then that vast reverberation of his gun, lingering, enduring, cause of all the dumb, sick things that had become his life since he learned he'd shot his best friend. And after a while this woman, this stranger, took his hands in hers, her eyes welling up, but he was the one weeping. Then he broke away, hurried outside and kept on walking, no direction known, kept on stalking his shadow like his past, all the sneak into your dreams, the bitter rains, the fevers, the losses, the whispered and convulsive fears.

CHAPTER NINETEEN

Ben tapped an ash from his Winston into the Datsun's ashtray, put the cigarette shakily to his lips and took a drag. They were still in his neighborhood, just under way, thirty smooth miles per hour. In the distance most of the fires were out, yet as far as the eye could see, smoke blinded the sky.

"Where we going, boss?"

There was more nonchalance than mockery in John's tone. Ben guessed this was an indication of something or other, although he couldn't discern exactly what. He didn't drink well. Alcohol of any proof confused his sensibilities. So did beatings. At least that was something he could discern.

"Try that street, over there."

John followed the direction of Ben's hand in the rearview mirror and swung a left. The school was in the middle of the block. New Vistas. A more appropriate name would have been Oh Well. That was the attitude of the staff. You couldn't exactly blame them. The facility housed forty children of limited capabilities. David fell into the bottom third, which wasn't that bad. The worst had motors that never stopped revving and tried to hump anyone or anything they ran across. Rumor had it the teachers took hopeless bets among themselves as to who would be the first to burn out. I'm a sane, rational man, Ben said unconvincingly to himself, then out loud, "Park there, in the lot."

John parked. The Koreans trawled after Ben as he walked to the playground at the rear of the school. Trash lay on the lawn, but there wasn't any trash written on the walls.

"Your kid, he goes here?" Kap asked.

"Yes."

"Be funny, right, if he's here," Kap said.

"Funny," Ben said, without a trace of humor. The morning that was still night worked his nerves and his vision; for a moment he thought he saw the dark shape of a child in a sandbox, but the shape was only a mound, a construct of a student's compulsion. Ben's gaze went to the bank of swings. Their stillness seemed unnatural, a lost function of the laws of motion.

"Not here," Kap said. "You ready to go?"

"In a minute." Ben longed for the sympathetic clichés of the custodian. The school was dark but he tried all the doors anyway, a weak hope, a bow to despair. "That's that," he said, firing up another cigarette.

John Kim was at his elbow like a conspirator in some careless backyard game.

"Where to now, boss?"

"Somewhere."

They returned to the Datsun and got in, Ben in the back. Kap broke out the hard candy. Ben declined. "Downtown," he said at last. He wondered if this could conceivably be a gesture of love rather than guilt. The possibility momentarily unsettled him.

"Where the trouble is?" Kap asked nervously.

Ben nodded. "I think that's where he is." Drawn by the illusionary promises of the images on TV.

"He could be other places," John ventured.

"Many other places," Kap added.

Ben said, "I've tried them."

The brothers exchanged unhappy looks. "I don't know, boss," John said, shaking his head and dropping his speed.

"I didn't pay you to drive me around my block. I thought we might get lucky, that's all."

"O.K." John increased his speed. "We go downtown." He patted the bulge next to his heart. "But first we get more than what's in my coat."

"Like what?" Ben asked. Ancient Oriental devices winked in his head.

Kap's boyish grin appeared over the seat, his chipped tooth adding a comic touch. "Like bang, bang, bang, bang." Kap fired an imaginary burst into Ben's face. Ben took it stoically.

"Automatic weapons, Uzis, what?" He pulled up the nomenclature easily, signals of distress from the news, which was always trying to take flight but was always grounded. David's dilemma. The world's.

"Scare off the jungle bunnies," Kap answered, his head bobbing.

Ben didn't let what remained of his liberal sensibilities intrude upon Kap's enthusiasm. "I'm surprised you didn't bring them in the first place."

"Hell, man, not ours," John said disdainfully. "We know some guys, but not us."

"Shit, we're just college students," Kap swore, but by then Ben had already figured that out.

The horror of it was, he had gone to the same school. During the ride to wherever they were going, Irene's cousins shared memories that Ben had at best an uneasy nostalgia for. Remember this, remember that; Ben remembered all too well. His junior year he'd exhausted his student loan and been forced to sell phone subscriptions to magazines no one wanted to buy. He considered calling his father for help, but didn't want to admit he couldn't make it on his own. The night-mare ended when he collapsed from malnutrition in Psych 3 and was rushed to County General. His experience then hadn't been any better than his recent hospital visit. He'd been left on a gurney with vague, sullen promises of care. After an hour of neglect he'd gotten up, found a pay phone and placed a collect call to his father, who sent a money order and a perfunctory note expressing his admiration for Ben's pride; his old man was a few miles short of being perfect. Maybe more than a few: After David was diagnosed as autistic, Ben's father had told him that love wasn't conditional, yet he himself had avoided proximity; aphorisms required no effort.

"Almost there."

Kap's voice brought Ben back. They were down by the docks on the west side of the city. He checked the dash clock. 3:47. Twenty minutes since they'd left New Vistas, but it seemed like they'd trav-eled coast to coast.

"Long time, right?" John said.

"To get here?" Ben replied.

"Since you were in college."

Ben took out another cigarette.

"Not so long."

John parked in front of some sort of two storey industrial build-ing, a single small window on the first floor, on the second, nothing but large windows, dark except for one low light burning through a pane of clouded glass.

"Is this a joke?" Ben's heart was suddenly missing beats; this could be something else. Fear coiled around him until he had trouble breathing. Kap rested an arm on the seat and grinned at him.

"Don't worry. They live here."

"These guys?" Ben asked hoarsely.

Kap's grin widened. "Right."

"Jesus, where?"

"Inside," Kap answered.

Ben turned to John, fixated on his right arm. John's hand came up.

"Don't worry," Kap said.

John adjusted the rearview mirror so he could see Ben.

"They're there," Kap said.

"Shit, boss," John chuckled. "Your eyes got awful big." John's own eyes widened in the mirror.

"I'm fine," Ben said curtly. "Just don't waste any more time."

"Just a fucking building and a bunch of fucking boats," Kap said.

"Who are they?" Ben asked.

"Friends of the family," John said.

Facing Ben, Kap twisted his mouth into a Cagney sneer. "They're gangsters," he said, getting the voice almost right. "Deal in stolen goods."

"Shit," John muttered with irritation to his brother, then to Ben, "Wait here."

John and Kap got out of the car. Ben watched them walk quickly to the building, where John pounded on a delivery entryway with the side of his hand. A light went on, then the delivery door slid slightly open to reveal a short, bald Asian, his features shadowed by the gray light of early morning. John gestured to the car. The man peered over John Kim's shoulder. Words were exchanged then the man opened the door just enough to let the Kims through. The door closed and Ben waited. Another light went on in the second storey window and silhouettes appeared in the room; John, Kap, the bald man and a man taller and broader than the others. Their gestures were emphatic.

Ben got around to lighting his cigarette. There was a serenity, a balance of natural and dormant functions to the harbor: Small craft and large, private and commercial, bobbing lightly or deadweight at anchor. The pious shriek of a gull, a buoy's bell ringing cautiously, a foghorn's lament, the silence of riggings, derricks and dreams ghosting out of a migratory mist. Ben stared through the atmosphere, tried to inhabit David's world, but his imagination was as elusive as the uneasy air.

The windows where the silhouettes had been went black. Ben waited some more then the delivery door eased open just enough to let John and Kap out. The door closed as Kap and John walked in tandem toward the Datsun, unwieldy blankets in their hands. The gull landed on a piling and watched with Ben. The light in the first-floor window went out, the buoy's bell rang softly, the foghorn lamented, the mist twisted with the whims of the breeze. When Kap and John got into the car, they brought the chill of the harbor with them.

John turned on the ignition. The engine stuttered then steadied. The gull flew off lazily toward the fading moon. As John drove away from the docks, the building went completely dark. The mist lifted from the car like a scarf.

Ben had a feeling they might be followed. He glanced back through the rear window, but the harbor was dead. He heard a sudden grating noise and faced front; John had turned on the wipers to clear the windshield of moisture. The blades snicked with slow menace as they smeared and erased the drops. Briefly, Ben was held by the rhythm; he could almost feel the blades' rubbery glide changing the texture of his changed skin. He touched the distension of his lower lip, the spongy, unreal mass. John's blanket was on the front seat, Kap's was across his legs. Ben watched Kap remove the blankets, watched him with a sense of awe, as though he were about to reveal a liberating truth, but then John turned off the wipers and all Kap uncovered were guns, an AK-47 and an Uzi.

The Datsun glided along the concrete shoreline, paced by its own reflection in the water. They drove past the corroded side of a freighter that had the size of old wars. John and Kap tried to engage Ben in an exchange of insults, but he no longer had any desire to participate. His eye had started to bleed again. He drew Kleenex out of a pocket and stopped the trickle. Kap lit up a joint and the two boys began to converse softly in Korean as they left the harbor behind. They drove by a lopsided warehouse and a dump yard thick with examples of contemporary misuse. Ben's mouth was bleeding. It seemed like too much effort to wipe off the blood.

Everything they passed—stores, buildings, streets, the occasional fire—seemed without design, randomly dropped here or there to no purpose. The miles edged by, yet Ben was back where he'd begun, bargaining with despair, dealing in stolen goods of the heart. He thought of David's first birthday, before the smiles and hands of adults withdrew with knowledge. David at six at the zoo, his eyes amazed over the array of life. David, in his world. The way his hand knew the shape of things when he took up pad and pencil. His fascination with the motion of color and lights. The lost music that rose in his throat over everything new. Wiping the blood from his mouth, Ben entered David's skin, felt what his son must be experiencing. He would see the fires as pretty but know if you touched the flames it would hurt and change your flesh. He would know that other things hurt too. His mother's absence, his father's eyes. On some remote level he might question the value of his life. The answer would take the shape of pain as lasting as faith.

Ben felt the pain coursing through him and the knowledge of his failure to accept his son brought tears to his eyes. Indifferent to his anguish, the Kims were sharing the joint. As they drove deeper into the battered city, gray and still and pocketed by smoke, Ben realized that what he was feeling was also America, the desire to abandon or replace whatever was damaged or flawed. And with that realization some, not all, of the guilt lifted from him, for Maggie had walked but he had stuck. And knowing that was worth something, he smiled, and his smile became one of confidence that he would find David.

They went down more streets, Ben scanning alleys, doorways, anywhere a frightened child might hide. Then John carelessly took a corner and Ben saw the Guard, the checkpoint barricade, the other guns, the whole stationary scene rushing phantasmagorically toward the windshield through stray smoke, and someone was shouting, STOP, FUCKING STOP! But John was locked in his stoned fear, eyes, arms, legs, foot frozen on the wrong pedal, and the lowered Datsun built for abuse and LUV shimmied and bucked straight on into the bullets and through the hasty white wood, and glass was suddenly everywhere, on the seats, in the eyes, and Ben was yelling, JESUS GOD NO NOT NOW and Kap was screaming and John wasn't saying anything at all; he was slumping gently into the wheel and the car struck the curb then spun and thudded and came to rest.

"You ain't Henry and I ain't giving you no name, you might just as well forget that sorry hope."

J.D.'s eyes were on his own shadow on the sidewalk, but he was talking to the dog. The puppy had followed him out of Fat Jack's and was keeping at his heels.

"And I ain't your momma. No milk in these tits, babe. And don't wag your fucking tail. Cute's never worked real well with me, except maybe when I was young and going to movies. Go on back there, go on. They got pretzels and high sugar booze, good things in life. Shit, man, I ain't got squat for you, how many times I got to say it, do it with slide trombone, old soft shoe?"

Deciding he was either slipping into sentiment or losing his fucking mind, J.D. stopped growling at the dog, even though one-way bullshit beat giving in to his scarred and neglected heart.

He moved onto another vacated boulevard of ripped up asphalt, shell casings by the curb, blood on the pavement. Le's blood had stretched the width of the sidewalk to the street, running down into the gutter. The boy had tossed a grin over his shoulder as he sped away on his bike, leaving his satisfaction fixed in the stunned air. The bystanders had looked long and hard at J.D., as though he were the one who'd pulled the trigger. Another Hallmark memory.

J.D. tripped over a place where the sidewalk buckled. So damned tired, stracked, weary of it all, he stopped to rest, leaning against a sagging dry-wall that just took his weight. The puppy lay down next to his boots and shivered. It was fucking cold. He shuffled his feet and rubbed his hands together. His fingers and toes were stiff, his hands and feet chunks of ice. He blew into his palms, watched his breath form and vanish in the air. Like to have me some of those cutoff gloves, he told himself, one of the great downchild inventions of man. He looked around. Jesus, but it was quiet, a ghost town. A week before Henry was killed, they'd gone into a village sent all to hell by short-range 155's. Same fearsome silence, total except for flies scouting the blood of dismembered bodies and the hammer strokes you could hear in your chest.

The puppy whimpered. J.D. looked down at him with compassion. "You just don't know, you just don't know." A faraway siren climbed and fell. An ache separated itself from the rest of his pain, took a moment to locate; the tip of his penis was throbbing. The next time he urinated, he'd wince and curse and his piss would come out slow and thick and bright red. He reached inside his pants and loosened the pressure of his underwear. A hole for your dick, he thought, there's one for a patent. "Where the fuck am I?" he said out loud.

He got his bearings. A few hundred yards away he could see the cluster of warehouses he'd passed earlier, the buildings flat and hazy in the confusion of darkness and light, the railroad tracks just beyond. He listened for the whistle of a distant train, but all he could hear were echoes of the long night. He reached into the right pocket of his coat and felt the inviting steel of the .32, reached into his left pocket and felt his works. He could make that choice here or wait, draw it out until he reached the tracks. "Better place to die," he said, better place to take that journey, not much farther to go.

Gathering up what was left of himself, J.D. pushed off from the wall and spoke to the dog as they walked. "Keep on, you ain't going to like what you see, but maybe it's time you learn, and when it happens, just scout the blood and move on," and he said this in cadence, the lift of the words carrying his heavy feet until the distance seemed no greater than the limits of his heart.

CHAPTER TWENTY

Ben was experiencing a range of textures and surfaces. Scrunched down on the back seat, belly, legs, the right side of his face pressed against the vinyl, he was looking for a place to burrow, all the juices in his body jumping to the beat of fear. "Don't hurt him," he repeated, then with a little defiant authority, "Get the fuck away!" Hands were prying his fingers loose from the edge of the upholstery one by one. His eye that was open wildly observed the incremental loss of his traction, the straightening of each finger, as though being measured for a ring. Then his hands were helpless fists, his wrists in the vise of the other hands, fingernails digging into his skin and someone was dragging him by the ankles across the seat, his clothes scritching with an electric rending as blown-out glass smeared past his vision.

Clear of the car, he took the jolt of the short fall with his forearms, kept his palms on the asphalt to support his weight while he twisted from the hips, struggling to break loose. Arms and legs bent, at crazy angles, he was screaming and having a helluva time catching his breath and so was Kap, who was just a contained blur of spinning colors in the middle of the street. "Let the fuck go!" Ben was yelling and Kap was yelling about the same thing, only louder and more intense, so his voice was a ribbon that kept getting snipped.

"Put a muzzle on that Chink!" someone yelled and a soldier chopped at Kap's head with the butt of his rifle; the blow glanced off, nearly twisting the rifle out of the soldier's grip, angering him, so that he planted his feet, took aim and chopped harder, dropping Kap to his knees. The soldiers holding the boy hovered over him, then they released his arms and he fell slowly onto his face and lay still.

Ben felt the tension leaving his body, resistance replaced by compliance. He glanced at the two soldiers who had his arms pinned to his sides. They had peach fuzz on their pink cheeks. "I don't have luck in cars," Ben found himself saying, and then, "I was afraid for my son." The soldiers looked at him as though he were a few miles short of any kind of sense.

Avoiding their eyes, Ben tried to grasp the scene. Six or seven national guardsmen were standing around dumbfounded. Others were collecting the ruined roadblock, examining the crushed and splintered wood as though each piece were a prize worthy of their mantel. Some had come out of a flat gray stucco building down the street. An officer ordered them to go back inside. They did so reluctantly, looking back over their shoulders at the wreckage. A few soldiers had grouped around the Datsun, which was up against a concrete wall. The fender was smashed at the point of impact and glass was on the ground, sparkling in a pool of spreading crankshaft oil.

Ben could see John slumped against the driver's door. A soldier was tugging on the handle, which refused to give. The soldier swore then used both hands and the door sprung open, throwing the soldier off balance and depositing John onto the sidewalk. His head struck first, tossing his queue and a spurt of blood. A chubby soldier put a hand to his mouth, pivoted and threw up. Another soldier squatted and picked up John's wrist and felt for a pulse.

"Jesus H. Christ!"

The soldier looked up and watched the approach of what had to be the officer in charge.

"Is he dead, Tucker?" the officer asked.

Tucker put down John's arm.

"No sir. I think he just fainted."

"Jesus," the officer swore, shaking his head.

Ben suddenly felt a tightness in his chest. "I'm having a little trouble breathing."

"Captain?" one of his captors called. "This one's having a problem."

The officer turned. "A problem? My God, what now?" He walked toward Ben, who repeated he was having trouble breathing. The captain stopped in front of him and took in his face.

"You look alright, everything considered."

"Just a little trouble."

The captain sighed in exasperation.

"Sit him down."

Lowering himself to the street with the help of the two soldiers, Ben sat with his chin on his heaving chest until his breathing leveled off. Bored with John Kim, several soldiers wandered over to watch him. Ben gazed sheepishly at the soldiers, embarrassed over calling attention to what was only an excursion of his nerves.

"I'm alright." Ben started to push up to his feet. A soldier reached down to help him. He waved the man off.

"I'm alright."

"Glad someone is." The captain sniffed close to Ben. "You've been drinking."

"A little."

The captain pulled a face that wasn't unfriendly.

"Yeah. A little. Seems to be your style."

"I have to find my son."

The captain looked at Ben curiously, the way others had. "We'll get to that later." He clapped Ben on the shoulder. "C'mon. Let's get some coffee first." His hand stayed on Ben's shoulder as he walked him down the street.

"Coffee?" Ben said.

The captain pointed to the flat gray building where light shone past an open door.

"Over there."

They reached Kap first. His eyes were closed and he was motionless, except for the slight lift and fall of his chest. The soldier who had struck him was wiping off his rifle butt with an old newspaper from the street. Blood seeped through the compress a medic was holding tight to Kap's skull. The captain removed his hand from Ben's shoulder and gazed down at Kap with disapproval.

"How's he doing?" the captain asked.

"He's alive," the medic answered.

The captain grunted and glanced back at John Kim, who was sitting up now. His head seemed loose on his neck as he tried to focus. The captain grunted again then led Ben to the gray building. The logo over the entrance read COMIENDO FACIL; Easy Eats. They went inside. The place was a cafeteria, food under glass and depressing lighting. Soldiers were busy unloading field rations, weapons and bulletproof vests. A soldier with his belly hanging over his pants was provoking the controls of a walkie-talkie. A soldier with granny glasses and the thin face of a French aesthete was filling Styrofoam cups from the cafeteria's coffee machine.

"Have a seat." The captain drew back a chair.

Ben sat, knew if he didn't stay compliant, they would lock him up and he would never find David. The captain asked if he liked his coffee black or mixed? Ben told him it didn't matter. The captain went and got two Styrofoam cups, placed one in front of Ben and suggested he try it.

Ben left the coffee untouched while the captain went around the table and sat opposite him. The captain tasted his coffee, winced, and asked Ben his name. Ben told him. The name stenciled on the captain's shirt pocket was Koehler. Ben hadn't noticed until now.

"Gene," the captain said. "With a G." Ben watched Gene Koehler's drab green eyes searching for the lies in his silence.

"I have to find him, you have to help me," Ben said finally.

"Your son."

Ben nodded.

"Where did you lose him?"

Ben shook his head helplessly. Koehler sighed, took off his helmet and ran a hand over his crewcut.

"What were you drinking?"

"Scotch."

"I'd be drinking too if I could," Koehler said pleasantly. "Night like this. You really should try the coffee. It kills the taste of the liquor, which in my experience, gets pretty ugly after a while."

Ben indifferently took a sip. The coffee was foul and he grimaced. Koehler shrugged.

A large cop came through the door and Koehler excused himself. The cop showed Koehler something; Koehler's back was to Ben, so he couldn't see what. After a few seconds Koehler put whatever it was into his shirt pocket. The cop glanced at Ben with a wary hunger before going outside. Koehler returned to the table and sat down.

"What did he want?" Ben asked.

"You."

"And?"

Koehler gave Ben part of a smile. "I told him we were doing just fine. Your mouth's bleeding, you know." Koehler pulled a napkin from a chrome holder. Ben waved him off.

"That's okay. I've got my own." Ben got a Kleenex out of his pants pocket with some difficulty and dabbed the blood from the corner of his mouth.

"Will you help me find my son?"

"First tell me what happened, Ben, then we'll talk."

Patience, Ben told himself.

"Starting when?"

"Those Chinks you were with. Who are they?"

Ben gave him their names. "They're college students."

"Right," Koehler said. "With an Uzi, an AK-47 and a .45."

"There was a reason for that."

"I'm sure."

"Did your soldiers have to shoot?"

Ben was the recipient of that look again; a few miles short. "You've got to be kidding," Koehler said.

"Not really," Ben replied.

"A car comes at you, you think you're going to stand still for it?"

"If you knew me better, you might say maybe."

Koehler found this amusing, sort of. His green eyes came to life and his mouth, the chapped lips, twisted into something resembling a grin.

"You're a pretty strange fella," he said.

"I've had one of those nights."

"Yeah." Koehler sighed.

Taking out his mangled pack and matches, Ben lit up. "You're being very reasonable about this," he said sincerely. "Will you help me find him?"

"You should try the police."

"They don't have the time."

Koehler coughed and brushed the smoke away from his face.

"Jesus, I don't know, that's not what I'm here for. How old is he?"

"Ten."

"I've got a boy who's twelve." Koehler looked away. "We saw a guy knocked out of his shoes," he said quietly.

"Oh?" Ben was beginning to wonder who was strange.

"That's right." Koehler idly turned his helmet on the table. "He was crossing the street. Drunk ran the light and hit him at, I don't know, eighty, ninety miles an hour. Didn't stop."

Circumstances were strange, Ben supposed, not people. Slippage of the norm.

"It was a couple years ago. Out for a Sunday drive with the family." Koehler picked at the lip of his cup. His voice softened. "I wish my kids hadn't seen that. They still have nightmares."

Ben nodded. He understood. Not so much slippage as the norm amplified. The mundane trying to take flight. The cigarette tasted bitter in his mouth. He put it out on a napkin. The burn mark it left was as precise as pain.

Koehler rested his elbows on the table and stared solemnly into Ben's eyes.

"Your face. That's not from the crash. You've been beaten up. Am I correct?"

Ben nodded. Koehler looked satisfied. He removed the check Ben had written from his shirt pocket and gestured to the door.

"The officer found this on the one who was driving. My guess is, and the officer was of the same opinion, they took advantage of what was going on, grabbed you, worked you over and forced you to sign."

"That's pretty logical," Ben admitted, "but it isn't what happened."

"No?" Koehler looked disappointed.

"No."

Koehler sighed again and drained his cup. He set it down and absently broke off pieces of Styrofoam while Ben explained the beating, Irene, the docks, all of it. Without hesitation or shame he told Gene Koehler that David was retarded. Koehler kept picking at the Styrofoam, occasionally pausing to glance at him. By the time Ben was finished, there wasn't much left of the cup.

Koehler got up and found a phone. Ben watched him call the precinct where Ben had filed the missing person's report. After he hung up, Koehler returned to the table and said, "What am I going to do with you now?"

"Help me," Ben said, then without equivocation, "Damn, but I want him back." The words grabbed at him.

Koehler suggested some air. He walked Ben outside, where the scene had lost all sense of drama. John was passive in the back of the cruiser, absently fingering his queue. Kap was sitting dazed in the street. Tucker and the soldier who had thrown up were drinking coffee.

Ben took in the bracing breath of early morning. The rim of the horizon was a soft red, but the sky was darkening with a promise of rain. A bright sheen of dew was on the sidewalk, offering the possibility of slippage.

Koehler went and talked to the big cop once more, their voices low. The cop shook his head twice then frowned and nodded. Koehler clapped the officer on the shoulder then rejoined Ben.

"And?"

"They're still going to want you."

The large cop's eyes grazed Ben.

"You can't let them," Ben said anxiously.

"We agreed it could wait until later," Koehler replied.

"Then you'll help me?"

Koehler didn't answer. Instead, he watched as the two officers got Kap to his feet, cuffed him, and took him groggy but combative toward the squad car. Kap twisted and swore before he suddenly went limp with either exhaustion or obstinance. The cops half carried, half dragged him to the cruiser and muscled him onto the back seat next to his brother. Unfocused hate burned in Kap's eyes, then gave way to tears as he put his manacled hands to his face.

After the cruiser drove off, Ben asked again about David. Koehler shrugged and angled his wrist to check the time. Ben fired up a Winston, watched the plumes drift. Koehler watched with him, then said, "Wait here," and went back into the cafeteria.

Ignored, Ben paced. Things drifted around him—the low conversations of the soldiers, the murmur of distant traffic, the squawk of a walkie-talkie—but he stayed removed, on the edge of his emotions. He was experiencing some guilt over the Kims, but not much; the brothers had behaved stupidly, brought their grief upon themselves. David was all that mattered now. Thinking of his son he felt a spasm of fear. Patience, he reminded himself. Stay calm, stay steady for your boy. Still, he couldn't help but wonder what was taking Koehler so long? Looking cautiously through the door, he saw the captain talking to a beefy soldier. The soldier looked away and shook his head. Ben sighed and stared at the sky. He couldn't see any fires, but their heat remained in the air. Rain would be nice, he thought idly.

Koehler came outside with the thin soldier who wore granny glasses. The name on his shirt was Henderson.

"Paul," Koehler said.

Ben and Paul Henderson shook hands.

"Paul volunteered to help you find your boy."

Ben was confused. "On foot?"

"We can spare a vehicle," Koehler said.

Ben thanked him. Koehler was modest about his charity, a little embarrassed, looking off at the sky. Ben dropped his cigarette on the sidewalk and stubbed it out with his shoe, then Henderson led him past a splash of Kap Kim's blood to a jeep with high tires and high seats.

Henderson got behind the wheel, resting his rifle within easy reach against the back seat. Ben got in beside him. Henderson engaged the engine and asked Ben his son's name. Told Ben he had a three year old himself. Henderson's voice was prairie common, serious and careful. When he asked which way, Ben pointed east in the direction of the moon, which seemed an offshoot of the sun.

. . .

J.D. was trying to decide on a direction. East felt right. The sky was deeper there, red and gray, blood and weight, colors to feed the mood of roaming desires, and he crossed a street populated only by amputated cars. He'd come full circle, back to the block of industrial sprawl behind chain-link. He dragged the barrel of the .32 along the fence as he walked. The rattle drew the puppy's attention. The dog barked up at the gun, as though it were a bone of burying potential. "The difference between man and animal," J.D. told him, "is the ability to tell who and what goes under."

J.D. stuck the revolver back in his coat pocket. Up ahead there was a short span of chain-link that had been torn asunder by an anonymous gesture. J.D. decided this looked to be a shortcut to paradise or some such delusion. He patted his coat pockets, felt his choices, then parted the wire and went on through to the other side, the puppy right there with him.

Blacktop and tarps and forklifts and heavy equipment and scrap lumber lay before them. J.D. led the puppy toward the warehouses, maintaining a pretty brisk pace for a weary grunt and a mutt not long removed from the nipple. "I am here to inform you," he said to the creature, "here to let you know, son, that by belonging to a species of limited knowledge, you are cursed and blessed, both for the same reason; your needs are all in the present, without the lift of the future or the drag of the fucking past." He said this solemnly, punctuated by epithets over the itch on his chin, the aches in his back, his neck, his dick, his knee, the hitch in his stride and his life. The puppy waited until J.D. was finished riling the air, then pissed on the first building they reached.

"Well . . ." J.D. remarked, then, "Pretend I'm on point and the sun is out." The puppy wagged its tail, scampered through the puddle of its own making and fell in behind him. The warehouses they walked between had high, dirty windows and smelled of sulfur, grease and the sweat of low wage labor.

Before they were clear of the buildings, J.D. could see a thin column of smoke melding with the gray air. When he reached open ground, he saw the source. A black family—man, woman, two small kids—was warming by the fire from an oil drum. Wearing bulky cast-offs, they resembled a tableau and a forgotten lesson, people who would persevere no matter what. Carefree, the puppy ran ahead to the children, who were young enough—the boy around three, his sister maybe a couple of years older—to regard it apprehensively. The girl reached out tentatively, enough encouragement for the puppy to let itself be picked up and comforted by the girl's embrace.

"What's his name?" the man asked.

"I don't know," J.D. said. "He's just kinda hanging around."

"Sorta like everyone I know," the woman said.

The couple made room for J.D. by the fire, which sparked and wove with the motion of the air. J.D. warmed his hands and watched the man study the distance. Smoke showed that a few heavier fires were still burning.

"Winding down, looks like." The man's voice was as raw as curettage.

"Been some night," J.D. said.

"Sure has," said the man.

The woman said, "It'll pass."

J.D. took in her face; still in the flush of youth, the weather of a hard life only beginning to take off the bloom. Her man was older, double her age, solid through the calves and shoulders, scar tissue over the eyes, a thin scar on one cheek. A gym bag, red Everlast gloves laced to the strap, was near the man's feet.

"You a fighter?" J.D. tried.

The man looked at his hands, the distinct veins, the scar tissue on the flat knuckles.

"When I can," he said, putting his hands in the pockets of his sweatpants. "Ten and fourteen, three draws. It's a living, though not of late. Ain't had a fight in eight months. I stay in shape best I'm able.

Things will pick up." He watched his children frolic with the dog. Catch me if you can.

"We had an apartment on East Forty-third," the woman said. "Jus' had to give it up." She pointed to a dilapidated warehouse. "We been living in there, 'cept sometimes it's colder in than out."

"We're gonna be heating up some coffee," the man told J.D., "you wanta stick round."

"Thanks, but I need to be going."

"Sure," the man smiled. "That's the way I useta be."

"Some people change," the woman said with satisfaction.

J.D. nodded and started on his way. The puppy hesitated, looked at the kids, then ran after J.D. The girl began to bawl. J.D. stopped, scooped up the puppy and carried him to her.

"Be better off with you folks than with me."

"Can't feed him," the woman said.

The man said, "We'll manage."

The girl gazed shyly up at J.D. He held the puppy out to her.

"Here. Take him."

The girl's smile came slowly then she opened her arms and hugged the puppy to her. J.D. patted the animal on the head, experienced more of a sense of loss than he expected. He turned away quickly and walked.

"Take care," the man called after him.

"You too," J.D. said, and he waved goodbye without turning, just like in the movies. He kept on walking, toward the tracks, where the weeds flourished.

Except for what looters had broken or abandoned, the streets were empty. Occasionally, a checkpoint glided by, the faces of the soldiers heavy with ennui and the hour. Ben found it impossible to share their mood. He looked for distractions. The weather. Dark clouds were moving in from the north. After the weather, Paul Henderson. Ben drew him out about his family. He was married to an older woman, by ten years. Her pregnancy had been difficult. The Cesarean had been five weeks early, but their daughter was fine. Normal. They were from Oklahoma. They had come here because there wasn't much there.

Ben realized that he had let the ease of the conversation lull him, but now his anxiety returned; if they found David, the circumstances and his condition might be appalling. A scene of climactic proportion unfolded in Ben's head: They would be driving slowly down yet another block. Suddenly, they would hear the roil of a mob from around a corner. Henderson would hit the gas and take the corner in a wild weave, and rushing toward them through the windshield, Ben would see the brutal beating in the middle of the street, backlit by the requisite atmosphere of a streetlamp. David's hand would lift through the frenzy then fall. Henderson would brake and fire a warning round in the air and the mob would fly apart except for two; fixed in their savagery, the thugs would continue to smash down at David with their fists and Ben would bolt from the jeep and fling them far aside and he would pick up David's rent flesh—the damage to his body equal to the damage to his mind—and carry him to a station of healing and comfort.

When they found David, it was without drama or flair. He was crouched in an alley, peering out from behind a dumpster, hiding like a frightened animal or, more simply, a frightened child. Ben put a gentle hand on Henderson's arm and the man pulled over to the curb and Ben climbed out. In the gray, softening light of morning, Ben's injuries were clear and David shrank from his face. Then David was in his arms. Ben hugged him carefully, as though his son's bones might break.

CHAPTER TWENTY-ONE

"**W**ish I was home," Arletha Mae said within the space her most earnest thoughts and desires inhabited. "Jason and me."

"You will be, soon," Larry assured her.

"You too."

Larry nodded. With the arrival of dawn he was really beginning to think it might be true.

Arletha Mae hummed and rocked Jason, holding him close. "Snug and warm," she said, and briefly she stayed in the dream of her other life.

"In the morning, granny she scold me for being out so late, Girl, you be the death, she say, the death. Then she smile, let me know it be alright. She be sleeping jus' now, sitting where she always do, fronta that ol' TV, curtain open, waiting on the sun. That be most her days. Says ol' folks, they sleep jus' like dogs on in the years. Sleep and church, that's most her time." In the glow of the lantern Arletha Mae's smile seemed restrained by a sad affection.

"Church was where I met Michael."

"You were going to tell me about him."

Arletha Mae gazed at the wonder of her child.

"He done some wrong. Come to Baptist to let Jesus make him right."

"What kind of wrong?"

Arletha Mae's attention stayed on Jason as she continued to rock him.

"The kind there be round here. Nine Deuce Crips. They say he kill three men, but he swore to me, hand on the Book, it ain't true. All he want was off the streets. No more walkin' down that sinning path." Journey she knew so good herself. He was a hard man, come in hard like her. God offered His love and Michael kept on turning, turning on away 'til she took him by the hand and showed him the grace of the light. He was the first and onliest man she let inside her, and she loved him 'cause he didn't make her do nothing 'cept what she wanted to do, and what she wanted was everything she had to give.

"Gave so much." Jason growing inside her, the promise of a life free of temptation and doubt. Michael's anger when he learned, she knew that was jus' the child in any man trying to stay inside.

"He's in prison. Serving hard time."

"For what?"

"Got drunk and beat a man near to death." So damn hard, getting the child out.

"How long?"

"Little over a year. Got half a year to go." So damn long. "He write me these letters."

Larry watched her put Jason down and open up her purse. She dug around inside, took out two envelopes, held them to the light, returned one to her purse. She got up and handed the other to Larry. The envelope was sliced open at the top, end to end. Larry looked up questioningly at Arletha Mae.

"Go on," she said, "read it. What I give it to you for."

By the time he had gotten the letter out, Arletha Mae had re-

284

turned to sit with Jason. He read the awkward penmanship as best he could:

Derest Arletha Mae,

I loves you my derest loves you with all my hart. It so hard and mean and crul being in here out you to toch. Aint nobody know what it like being in here. It worser than the streets. Least there you got frends. Here it jus peoples desiring you no damn good. Some got guns. Some got knifs. Aint no difrence they gards or cons. I seen things seen them every damn day. Seen a man walk up fas to nother stick him so hard ten times aint nobody lift no hand to stop it. Seen gards throw a buket of piss thru bars on a man onliest cause they done thinks it funy. Seen a man with his dick up a sissy knif cutting into his throat blood driping on down shower water washing it way. Seen a man got to where he don talk nobody but hisself. Heard a man scream and scream til they take him screaming way gards and men watching so quiet noone hating noone that whole short time. Seen a life traded for a pack. Seen and heard so many things jus gets me to wondring why God do and make us these ways? Aint no answer. Jus way it is when things aint the way you wants them to be. Guess that bout all. Gard coming down lites going on out. Mine to.

Goodnight my derest.
Yore sweet loving man Michael.

Larry put the letter back in the envelope. He noticed that the postmark was over three months old. He looked up at Arletha Mae. She was searching his eyes for what he might have to say about what he'd just read, but an opinion was beyond his scope.

"Was that another letter from him, what you put back in your purse?"

Arletha Mae looked at Larry for a long time. He could see conflicted emotions in her face, then she opened her purse and took out the other envelope. She carried it to him without comment, then went back to Jason. The letter was from Arletha Mae's sweet loving man, but addressed to Wanda Lee Haines. The postmark was a week old.

"Wanda Lee," Larry said. "Isn't she . . . ?"

"One showed me the path. Read it."

He took out the letter. It began, *Derest Wanda Lee, I loves you my derest, loves you with all my hart.* Larry felt the color leave his face.

"She give it to me yesterday. Said she wanted me to have it 'cause she was my friend. I opened it, left it sitting. Wanted to know but I couldn't. Jus' couldn't."

Larry skimmed the rest of the letter, which mostly said the same things as the letter to Arletha Mae, except for the end where Michael had written, *Hope you don want no babys.*

Larry slowly refolded the creases and slipped the letter back into the envelope. It took even longer before he could look at Arletha Mae. When he did, her eyes were steady with the certainty of loss.

"I don't think he's coming back to you," Larry said carefully.

Arletha Mae nodded. "I don't neither. Knowed it in my heart for a long time. Jus' never wanted to believe it." She sighed in a way that seemed to take in her whole body and gazed outside at the gathering clouds.

"Wish it'd rain," she said softly. "Put out all the fires."

"Look," Larry said, although he didn't know at what.

She faced him. "I'm looking." She was keeping herself together.

"You've got other things." A courage he wished he could share. "A career, your faith."

Arletha Mae smiled tolerantly at him, child in the man, faced what she hadn't, what he wouldn't.

"No, I jus' an ugly ol' thing God don't care nowhere, nohow 'bout. What I got is Jason. But that's 'nough."

Her eyes, their honesty, wouldn't leave Larry alone. "Time we be going," she said. "Got this feeling you can walk."

"I can't."

"Got this feeling, can if you try."

Larry shook his head fiercely, felt his eyes welling up, mirrors of his weakness.

"I can't."

"I'll help you."

"I just can't. I'm not strong enough." The words came out choked and broken and he could barely keep back the tears, but the compulsion to confess overwhelmed his embarrassment. "I've never, never in my life done anything, not one damn thing that was strong. Not one thing I can be proud of."

"I'll help you."

"Not one."

"I'll help."

He realized her hand was on his shoulder. He opened his eyes. She was kneeling in front of him, her gaze level with his. He looked straight into her eyes, the strength there.

"Try," she said.

His nod was slight. She smiled and touched his face the way a lover might, then she took him under the shoulders. He let her strength lift him to his knees, to his feet. The blood, the knowledge of his weakness, rushed to his head and he felt dizzy. He wobbled but her hands steadied him.

"You be alright."

"I can't."

"Try."

"I—"

"Ain't so hard."

She placed an arm around his waist, placed an arm over his shoulder. He took a cautious step with his bad leg and the pain shot all the way up his side. When he put his foot down, he couldn't quite stifle an expression of what the effort cost him.

"Think of something else," Arletha Mae said.

He tried, but all he could think of was the next step. He took another, then another. He tightened his nerves, tried to ignore the knives that shredded his insides. When he realized he could accept the pain, he smiled.

"That's it," Arletha Mae said, and she kept him moving. They reached the door. The first bloom of morning was on the ground and she could feel God's glory in the climbing sun. As she paused to take in its warmth, she thought she heard, for just a moment, that ol' high cymbal, and she laughed out loud over the wonder of it and Larry laughed with her.

9-T heard the laughter and spun, certain someone was laughing at him. He had been striding through the project, kicking at the dirt and swearing over his most recent humiliation, and now his eyes went to the sound; through a doorway, fair distance yet clear in the sunlight, he saw Arletha Mae and the white cop and he raised his gun, the weapon coming up fast as instinct, sweat and hate in his eyes. "Chinga la puta," he said, and he squeezed the trigger then walked away thinking, It ain't no thing.

Arletha Mae dropped hard to her knees. His support gone, Larry stumbled and dropped with her. Her hands were pressed to her belly. Redness was spreading from between her fingers.

"I am paying," Arletha Mae said, so softly, Larry could barely hear. The words didn't register, only his disbelief.

The baby was crying.

Her hands slipped from her stomach. Larry reached out but he was too far away to break her fall. She landed hard on one cheek. Her arms were at her sides, her palms up, her fingers curled and slack.

The baby was crying.

Larry pulled himself over and turned her onto her back. There was so much blood, so damned much. He beat the ground with a fist and stripped off his shirt and pressed it against her belly, but the blood kept coming. Her face glistened in the sun and her hair was dampening with sweat and she sucked in air and her chest heaved convulsively, once, twice, and he beat the ground again then placed a hand on her forehead, could feel the heat there turning cold. The blood was seeping through his shirt and he pressed down harder on her belly.

"I'll get help."

Her eyes focused on him dully. She smiled faintly and nodded.

"Take Jason with you."

"You're not going to die."

The baby was crying.

"Take him."

Larry was crying.

"You're not going to die."

"Please."

Larry screamed for help. No one answered. He replaced his hands on his shirt with Arletha Mae's.

"Press down."

The night was what you covered yourself with when you didn't want to see.

Her hands slipped away from his shirt. He put them back.

The day was something else.

"Press."

The day was

"Please?"

Her hands stayed in place. Her eyes were empty. Her heart was still.

Larry squeezed his eyes shut and sobbed and ground his knuckles into the dirt. Then he went to Jason, got the baby in his arms, got somehow to his feet. He took steps. Each one cost him pain past belief but he kept going. His bad knee buckled and he almost fell. He managed to keep his balance and the baby in his arms.

He would carry this child as far as he had to go.

J.D. lowered himself to one knee by the tracks; his legs ached too much to crouch. He went deep into his pockets and laid his works and the .32 on the gravel and dirt surrounding him. Choices. Right or left. Fast or slow.

He gazed about at things he would never experience again. The sky, the earth, the city (not much fucking loss there), the range and limits of colors and sights. His eyes, his mind, followed the rails, the iron music, the familiar anticipation. Dawn was the best time for hopping a boxcar, when the morning was just starting to wake. He checked the horizon, tried to guess the time by the height of the sun. Had to be after six. If they were awake or alive, Bobby and Rokowski would be making up: "Fuck you, man, look at my fucking head, fuck you, look at my fucking nose, but hey look man, I'm sorry, fuck you but hey, I'm fucking sorry too." J.D. smiled. The gumps and the geeks of the world. He wished them well.

This wasn't the right mood. He should be offering a final penance. He lowered his head, saw himself at Henry's gravesite. There would be lilies of the field by the stone and an epitaph of suitably bitter drollness and he would mouth the proper and inadequate apologies; sorry, man, sorry I left you without a life. I've said some useless prayers, beat myself up bloody until I can't recognize who or what I am, don't know what more I can do.

This wasn't the right tone. He looked down at his works; penance was what was at his feet. He didn't have enough left to knock him kicking, but if he went in deep, it would be over in minutes. Not enough time to run through all his sins, although he could cover a fair amount of the ground. He would mouth more sorrys, the words coming slower and slower until they were simply letters, then a blank page.

No. Blank was the wrong color, ODing too redolent of the young. Down to one choice, he picked up the .32 and opened out the cylinder, touched the single bullet left in a chamber. He lined up the shell with the firing pin, snapped the cylinder shut and placed the gun's muzzle to his head. There would be a flash of light and then darkness. His body would lie by the tracks. A dog would sniff his hand and leave. Flies would gather. Scavengers would partake of his flesh. The rain would make him a stew of foul odors.

Wrinkling up his nose, he lowered the revolver: Maybe this shit could wait a while, a week, a month, a year. There were still a few places to see, that rim to stumble across, and if God didn't love man, then maybe man, at least this particular one, could try loving himself a little. And maybe it was also time to shed the old guilts, Henry, Le, all the things he could do nothing about. Getting creakily to his feet, he cracked his neck and rubbed his legs. The weather was getting into his joints, another sad old story. He started to walk, leaving his works and the .32 on the ground; time as well to shed his vices.

Halfway through the tall grass he halted and returned to the tracks. Stooping, he picked up his works and the gun, .32 in the right pocket, syringe and powder and bottle cap in the left. What the fuck, he thought. A man needs what he needs.

J.D. went through the grass to the nearest street, stepped down the sidewalk humming an old blues standard, *Open Road.* "I'm leaving because I hate to go," the lyric ran, a vagabond's refrain. He tromped along, listening to his feet. His sole was flapping again. Damn near time to get some new boots.

A car approached from behind and he put out his thumb. The car went by and he kept walking, past a fucked-over church. The message out front was GOD IS WATCHING YOU. J.D. gave the sky that promised either rain or wet heat a slit-eyed glance. "This is kinda what I figured," he said and kept on, thinking I ain't never going to be what anyone wants me to be.

Time passed, then another car went by without slowing. That was alright. He knew he'd get a ride. There was always a rig driven by some no fucking color cowboy willing to travel as far as J.D. Lawson's imagination would allow.

Maybe he'd go back on home. See if momma was still alive.

Ben woke to the sound of rain. His bedroom window was blind with water and the rain beat against the roof and the air crackled with summer lightning. In the confusion of the weather and his senses, he imagined he heard David cry out and he went to the boy's room, but David's sleep was untroubled and secure. Ben sat on the bed and watched him breathe. After a while David woke. Ben took his hand and wished his son could understand the things he wanted to say. In the dark morning light an awareness seemed to flicker in David's eyes, something like understanding, faithless, lasting, a precious cheapness.

EPILOGUE

With the rain beating against the stained glass windows, the woman gazed down at her niece lying in sweet repose by the altar, then she found a seat among the mourners, the brothers and sisters and the only white face, everyone dressed in black. Lowering her head, she thought of how many years had passed since she had been here, and then Pastor Manley began the eulogy, asking the Lord to hand Arletha Mae the key to that path where there was no fear or dying or hate, and as he spoke, something of the tarnished innocence of the girl seemed to enter the church. And then without a word or a gesture, the choir took over, lifting hands and hymn in the old high way, building the feeling until you could almost hear the one missing voice singing out against the darkness.

Singing out.

ABOUT THE AUTHOR

Frank Norwood is a social worker in Los Angeles. He lives with his wife in North Hills, California.